PRAISE FOR

LEGEND OF A SUICIDE

"The reportorial relentlessness of Vann's imagination often makes his fiction seem less written than chiseled. A small, lovely book has been written out of his large and evident pain. 'A father, after all,' Vann writes, 'is a lot for a thing to be.' A son is also a lot for a thing to be; so is an artist. With *Legend of a Suicide*, David Vann proves himself a fine example of both."

—Tom Bissell, *New York Times Book Review*

"As the title suggests, the stories in *Legend of a Suicide* approach a private mythos, revisiting, reinvestigating, and reinventing one family's broken past. They also transport us to wild, uncharted places on the Alaskan coast and in the American soul. Throughout, David Vann is a generous, sure-handed guide in some very dangerous territory."

—Stewart O'Nan, author of *Songs for the Missing*

"Headlong narrative pacing, a memorable train-wreck father who gives Richard Russo's characters a run for their money, and a sure, sharp, inviting voice. So hard to put down that I am thinking of suing David Vann for several hours of lost sleep."   —Lionel Shriver, author of *So Much for That*

"His legend is at once the truest memoir and the purest fiction. . . . Nothing quite like this book has been written before."
—Alexander Linklater, *Observer* (London)

"Brilliant. . . . Vann's prose follows the sinews of Cormac McCarthy and Hemingway, yet has its own nimble flex."
—*The Times* (London)

"Vengeful yet sorrowing and empathetic, plausible yet dreamlike, and completely absorbing."
—Christopher Tayler, *The Guardian* (London)

"As primal and unforgiving as the Alaskan wilds where it's set."
—Bret Anthony Johnston, *Men's Journal*

"David Vann's extraordinary and inventive set of fictional variations on his father's death will surely become an American classic." —*The Times Literary Supplement* (London)

"A reckoning. . . . A very difficult book for the very best reasons: it is written with great honesty and journeys unflinchingly into darkness. . . . A message of profound sympathy and sadness, anger and regret, *Legend of a Suicide* is the melting away of one man's past and the reshaping of tragedy into art."
—Greg Schutz, *Fiction Writers Review*

"A powerful new voice has emerged in fiction."
—*The Sunday Times* (London)

"A truly great writer."

"For the imagery alone and for the sentences, the book would be a treasure."

"Extraordinary. . . . Reminiscent of Tobias Wolff, Vann's prose is as pure as a gulp of water from an Alaskan stream."

LEGEND OF A SUICIDE

HARPER  PERENNIAL

NEW YORK • LONDON • TORONTO • SYDNEY • NEW DELHI • AUCKLAND

DAVID VANN

LEGEND OF A SUICIDE

STORIES

HARPER ● PERENNIAL

This book is the winner of the 2007 Grace Paley Prize for Short Fiction.

The Association of Writers & Writing Programs, which sponsors the award, is a national nonprofit organization dedicated to serving American letters, writers, and programs of writing. Its headquarters are at George Mason University, Fairfax, Virginia, and its website is www.awpwriter.org.

"Ichthyology" appeared in *The Atlantic* and was reprinted in the *Anchorage Daily News* and the *New York Times* online.

"Rhoda" won first prize in the River City Writing Awards in Fiction (judged by Susan Minot) and appeared in *River City*.

"A Legend of Good Men" won first prize in the *Fish Stories: Collective I* Best Fiction Contest and appeared in the premier issue.

"The Higher Blue" appeared in *Fourteen Hills*.

"Ketchikan" appeared in *StoryQuarterly 2006*.

"Ichthyology," "Rhoda," and "A Legend of Good Men" collectively received a Henfield/ *Transatlantic Review* Award.

An earlier version of this collection received second place in the Pirate's Alley Faulkner Society Prize for the novel.

A hardcover edition of this book was published in 2008 by the University of Massachusetts Press.

HarperCollins books may be purchased for educational, business, or sales promotional use. For information please write: Special Markets Department, HarperCollins Publishers, 10 East 53rd Street, New York, NY 10022.

FIRST HARPER PERENNIAL EDITION PUBLISHED 2010.

Library of Congress Cataloging-in-Publication Data is available upon request.

ISBN 978-0-06-187584-7

10 11 12 13 14   ID/RRD   10 9 8 7 6 5 4 3 2 1

For my father,

JAMES EDWIN VANN,
1940–1980

CONTENTS

LEGEND OF A SUICIDE

ICHTHYOLOGY

MY MOTHER GAVE birth on Adak Island, a small hunk of rock and snow far out on the Aleutian chain, at the edge of the Bering Sea. My father was serving two years as a dentist in the Navy; he had wanted Alaska because he liked hunting and fishing, but he obviously had not known about Adak at the time of his request. Had my mother known, she would have scratched out the request herself. Given enough information, my mother has never made the wrong choice.

So it was that she refused to have her sweltering, jaundiced baby yanked out of Adak's underground naval hospital and thrown into the jet that sat waiting on the runway for more than six hours. Because my temperature was 105 degrees and still climbing, the doctors and my father recommended I be flown to the mainland, to a real hospital (no one on Adak survived even a mild heart attack while we were there—no one), but my mother refused. She was certain, with what my father always described as an animal, instinctive fear, that the moment I was borne aloft,

I would perish. She placed me in an ordinary white bathtub filled with cold water, and there I survived. Flourished, even. My orange, blotchy skin gradually calmed to a healthy baby pink, my limbs unlocked, and I flailed my legs in the waters until she lifted me out and we both slept.

When my father had finished his sentence with the Navy, we moved to Ketchikan, an island in southeastern Alaska, where he bought a dental practice and, three years later, a fishing boat. The boat was a new twenty-three-foot Uniflite fiberglass cabin cruiser. Still wearing his dental smock beneath his jacket, he launched the boat late on a Friday afternoon as we cheered from shore. He slipped it into its stall in the docks, and the next morning he stood on the edge of those docks looking down thirty feet through clear, icy Alaskan water to where the *Snow Goose* sat like a white mirage on the rounded gray stones. My father had named it the *Snow Goose* because he had been filled with dreams of its white hull flying over the waves, but he had forgotten to put in the drain plugs the afternoon of the launching. Unlike my mother, he had neither eyes nor ears for matters below the surface.

That summer, as we flew back over the waves from a day of fishing (my father had had the *Snow Goose* raised and cleaned, proof that persistence sometimes can make up for a lack of vision), I would be on the open but high-sided back deck with the day's catch of halibut, flopping into the air with them each time my father sailed over one wave and smashed into the next. The halibut themselves lay flat, like gray-green dogs on the white deck of the boat, their large brown eyes looking up at me hopefully until I whacked them with a hammer. My job was to keep them from flopping out of the boat. They had terrific strength in those wide, flat bodies, and with a good splat of their tails they could send themselves two or three feet into the air, their white undersides flashing. Between us a kind of understanding developed: if they didn't flop, I didn't smash their heads with the hammer. But sometimes, when the ride was especially wild and we were all thrown again and again into the air and their blood and slime were all over me, I gave out a few extra whacks, an inclination of which I am ashamed. And the other halibut, with their round brown eyes and long, judicious mouths, did see.

When we docked after those trips, my mother would check everything over, drain plugs included, while my father stood by. I played on my knees on the weathered boards of the dock, and once saw a terrifying creature crawl from a rusty tin can that had been knocked on its side. Repulsed by those barbarous legs, I howled and went over backward into the water. I was fished out soon enough, and thrown in a hot shower, but I didn't forget what I had seen. No one had told me about lizards—I honestly never had dreamed of reptiles—but on first sight I knew they were a step in the wrong direction.

Shortly after this, when I was nearing five years old, my father began to believe that he, too, had made steps in the wrong direction, and he set out in search of the kinds of experiences he felt he had been denied. My mother was only the second woman he had ever dated, but to this list he now added the dental hygienist who worked for him. The nights at our house were soon filled with a general keening of previously unimaginable variation and endurance.

I abandoned ship one night when my father was crying alone in the living room and my mother was breaking things in their bedroom. She didn't utter any human sounds, but I could chart her progress around their room by imagining the sources of wood snapping, glass shattering, and plaster crumbling. I slipped out into the soft, watery world of Alaskan rain-forest night, sound-less except for the rain, and wandered in my pajamas down the other side of the street, peering in dark, low living room win-dows and listening at doors, until at one door I heard a hum-ming sound that was unfamiliar to me.

I went around to the side of the house, opened the screen door, and pressed my ear to cold wood. The sound seemed lower now, almost a moan, barely audible.

The door was locked, but I lifted up the rubber corner of the welcome mat and, just as at our house, the key was there. So I went in.

I discovered that the buzzing sound was the air-pump filter on a fish tank. Something about wandering alone through someone else's house was awful, and I moved solemnly across the linoleum to take a seat high on a kitchen stool. I watched the orange-and-black-striped fish suck at pebbles and spit them out. The tank contained larger rocks, also: lava rocks with dark caves and cran-nies out of which peered many tiny round fish eyes, shiny as foil. Some had bright red-and-blue bodies, others had bright orange bodies.

I thought perhaps the fish were hungry. I went to the refrig-erator and saw sweet pickles, opened the jar, and brought it back for the fish to see. I found slots on top of the tank, toward the back, and dropped the pickles in, one or two at first, then the whole jar, slice by slice, and finally poured the juice in, too, so that the tank water swelled up and ran in beads over the side.

I stared at the pickle slices floating brightly with the fish, some of them sinking and twirling. They bounced slowly over the bright pink and blue rocks below. The orange-striped fish had all flashed about the tank as I had been pouring, but they, too, now moved slowly. They leaned a little to one side as they swam, and several rested on the rocks. Others stretched their long, see-through cartilage mouths at the surface every few moments and sucked for air. Their side fins rippled as delicately as fine lace.

When the pickle slices had settled more, they rocked like sleeping fish just above the pink and blue gravel, and the real fish rocked silently beside them, as if in gentle groves of eelgrass and sunken lily pads. The image was beautiful, and in that moment of beauty I strained forward.

I pressed my hands and face close to the glass and gazed into the mute black core of one of those silvery eyes. I felt as if I, too, were floating, gently rocking, oddly out of place, and in that flicker of a moment I caught myself feeling the rocking and, per-ceiving myself perceiving, realized that I was I. This distracted me; then I forgot what had distracted me, lost interest in the fish, and, after slapping my feet across the linoleum of the kitchen floor, passed again into the soft, dark rain.

Three years later, after my mother and I had moved down to Cal-ifornia, I was given a fish tank of my own and decided to become an ichthyologist. My parents had separated, of course, startled nearly as much by what I had done as by what they themselves had been doing all along. Any connection between my vandalism and their nighttime exchanges was completely mysterious to them.

My first aquarium was only a clear plastic tray of the kind most often used to hold nuts and bolts. In it were two goldfish I had won at the county fair and some gravel my mother had bought at Sal's Fishworld on our way home.

I watched over those thin, pale goldfish, but the tray had no cover, and after our cat, Smokey, snagged them with his paw and ate them on our countertop as I watched, unable to move, my mother took me down to Sal's and bought a proper ten-gallon tank with a bubble filter, more gravel, a wide-leaved plastic plant, a piece of volcanic rock with a hole in it, a few goldfish, and even one of those orange-and-black-striped fish I knew from Ketchikan, which I now discovered were called clown loaches.

We watched those fish every evening, cleaned their tank every weekend, and also survived the occasional ich plague: a sudden, mysterious proliferation of white spots on fins and tails that threatened to kill them all.

We buried the first of the deceased in elaborate ceremonies, during which my mother would sit beside me on her knees in the dirt and I would wear an old white bedsheet. The fish themselves were always wrapped in many layers of toilet paper, placed in small boxes, and buried six inches under, where the cat wouldn't dig them up.

Soon we just flushed the fish down the toilet and replaced them, but even then they were all I thought about. I wrote reports on them at school in lieu of book reports. My elementary school teachers never seemed to catch on, but apparently believed I had read books titled *The Clown Loach, The Silver Dol-*

lars, The Iridescent Shark, and *The Plecostemus, or Bottom-Sucker.*
Everything in human life was to be found in that tank. Yellow-
and-black angelfish floated delicately by, all glamour and glitz,
while behind them trailed their waste in streamers. Suckers at
the bottom of the tank ate this waste, spat it out in disgust, and
roved on, still hungry. And within five minutes of placing two
new silver dollars in the tank, I saw real brutality. These silver
dollars were large, thin fish, nearly identical in shape and shine
to the coins after which they had been named, and once out of
their plastic bag from Sal's, they swam up on either side of my
one lazy, boggle-eyed iridescent shark. This iridescent shark had
been badly misnamed; he was in actuality no more than a long,
thin goldfish with a shiny body and two large, bulbous eyes. The
silver dollars were slick and merciless and knew how to work as a
team. In one quick flash each went for an eye and sucked it out.
They didn't even swallow, but let the round, billiard-ball eyes
float dreamily down to the rocks, where they were ingested by
the sucker fish.

My mother was swift in her retribution. The silver dollars
were netted and flushed within minutes, and we spent that evening together watching the iridescent shark bump blindly into
the sides of the tank, waiting for him to die.

As we spent these years in California leading steadily more cir-
cumscribed lives, my father ranged farther and farther up in
Alaska, and everything he did seemed to lack sense. He had
never enjoyed dentistry, and felt now that perhaps fishing was
more what he wanted to do. In this I believe he was right, and
he was certainly earnest, but he didn't think ahead very well. He

sold his practice, ordered a beautiful, expensive, sixty-three-foot aluminum commercial fishing boat, to be completed before the halibut season, and persuaded my uncle to be the crew. They had fished together for sport all their lives, but neither of them had any experience on a commercial fishing boat, and they were to be the only two on board. My father's lone-explorer image of himself would have been undercut if he had worked first on another boat or had hired a captain.

He named this boat the *Osprey*. Whereas the *Snow Goose* had been a bird to fly its white wings over the waves on short one- and two-day sport-fishing jaunts, the *Osprey* was a more wide-ranging creature. With wingspans of up to six feet, ospreys are known to soar far out over the waters in vast arcs and circles, and they often soar alone.

The *Osprey* was not finished on time, so my father and my uncle entered the season a month and a half late. In their hurry they fouled up one of the halibut lines they had set, thus jamming for more than a week the huge hydraulic wheel that pulled the fish in, and of course they caught almost nothing. The loss of above $100,000 that year on fishing alone left my father undaunted, however, because he had already entered the last beautiful, desperate, far-ranging circlings of his life.

My uncle tells of one night on the bridge of the boat when my father, having lost for the seventeenth consecutive time at gin rummy, instead of looking glum and muttering an insincere congratulation, curved his back suddenly and spread wide his arms. Standing up on his captain's chair amid the blue-white glow of radar and sonar, he stretched out his chin, tilted what my uncle remembers to this day as a distinctly curved beak, and squawked out, "Three degrees starboard!" My uncle adjusted the automatic pilot accordingly, and in the morning they set what was to be one of only three or four successful lines that trip.

This correlation between my father's predictions and actual success was rare. The hardware store he had also invested in that year collapsed, as did the price of gold, the IRS's patience with his tax dodges in South American countries (he was angry at having to pay Social Security, which, ironically enough, supported us after his death), and his relationship with his receptionist-turned-fiancée. In short, the year was not a good one. I spent all of four days with him, in mid-January.

Each night during that vacation, as I lay in a sleeping bag on the hotel-room floor at the foot of his bed, I heard his tossings and turnings until very late and sensed, with the assurance children sometimes have, that he would not be my father for much longer. His movements came in cycles that were closing in steadily around him. He kicked wildly at the sheets, groaning in frustration, anger, and despair, until they billowed and ruffled like an offshore wind, then sank face first, utterly resigned and collapsed, into his pillow to weep. Then he began the cycle again. I assumed all along that he thought I was no longer awake, since he had never to my knowledge let himself weep in front of anyone. But one night he spoke to me.

"I just don't know," he said aloud. "Roy, are you awake?"

"Yes."

"God, I just don't know."

That was our last communication. I didn't know, either, and I wanted only to shrink farther down into my sleeping bag. He had a terrific pain in his head that painkillers couldn't reach, an airiness in his voice that was only becoming more hollow, and other mysteries of despair I didn't want to see or hear. I knew where he was headed, as we all did, but I didn't know why. And I didn't want to know.

My father ranged farther and farther that next year in the *Osprey*, changing gear for albacore off Mexico, then again for king crab in the Bering Sea. He began to sport-fish off the wide, high stern, and one day caught several large salmon, which he gutted on the spot. With the return to port and sale of the failed *Osprey* imminent (after two years of severe losses he could no longer even get a loan), with the IRS closing in, and with no further flights imagined, he took his .44 Magnum handgun from the cabin and walked back to stand alone on the bright silver stern under a heavy, gray-white sky and the cries of gulls, his boots slathered with the dark blood of freshly caught salmon. He may have paused for a moment to reflect, but I doubt it. His momentum was made up only of air, without the distraction of ground. He spattered himself amid the entrails of salmon, his remains picked at by gulls for several hours before my uncle came up from the engine room and found him.

My mother and I survived. Not having taken off to any heights, we had nowhere to fall. We drank clear bouillon soup with a few peas in it after my uncle called and told us the news, and in the evening, as the light in the sky faded to blue and then black, we sat in our living room, in the fluorescent glow of the fish tank, watching. The iridescent shark had learned to find his way around by now and bumped less frequently into the glass. The empty sockets, their rawness originally laced with thin tracks of blood, had been soothed and covered over by an opaque white film. The tiger-striped archer fish, who was half jaw, half tail, who swam always at a forty-five-degree angle to the surface of the water, and who could spit sizable water pellets, was skimming his strong lower lip along the surface, waiting, and at some point—I have no idea when, since time stands still after a death, with no sensation of passing—I rose to bring him the jar of flies. I let one into the air space between hood and water, covered the hole again with tape, and sat down beside my mother to watch this ritual of the familiar, a relic from what our lives had been, but I knew that I had lost interest. The archer fish tensed up, danced in a fluttering circle with his hooked lip at the surface the fulcrum, followed the mad flight of the fly with quiet deliberation, and spat his pellet of water with such celerity and yet so little movement that it seemed not to have happened at all, and yet there was the fly, mired in the water, sending off his million tiny ripples of panic.

RHODA

WHEN I FIRST saw my stepmother, I thought she was winking at me. I winked back. But she only frowned, and her right eyelid never lifted. She was wearing a yellow wedding dress, with no veil or train, and had turned to see me just as I was passing the front row of pews, carrying the wedding rings on a small velvet pillow. I don't believe I so much as glanced at my father. I saw only this new woman whom my father had hidden away until now from everyone, who had dark, dark hair, pale skin, and a dropped eyelid that, on closer view, made her terribly beautiful.

My new stepmother, Rhoda, untied the ring for my father with thin white fingers. I looked up again at that blank eye, drawn to it—it was open slightly—and realized too late that she was watching me. Her other eye was brown and shiny. She laughed out loud, right there in the middle of the service in front of everyone, at the same moment that she was slipping my father's ring onto his finger. Her laughter startled all of us, but especially my father, who looked around as though it had come from somewhere else in the church. His mouth opened slightly as he looked up, and for the first time in my life, I saw him frightened.

At the reception, Rhoda ate carefully, cutting her food into tiny squares. She knew she was being watched. Our tables were set on my father's lawn, along the edge of which ran a small walnut orchard with a creek and two mountainsides of brush in the background; there was plenty to view, but everyone looked only at Rhoda. And the moment she excused herself and walked into the house—to use the bathroom, we assumed—my grandmother opened fire.

"It's too bad your mother can't be here today," she said to me, wedged as I was between her and my father, with no hope of escape. Though Rhoda's parents hadn't come to the reception or even the wedding, her older sister was sitting directly across from us. "I don't know why he couldn't have stayed with your mother," my grandmother went on. "Did you know this Rhoda's only twenty-four years old?"

"Margaret, this is not the place," my grandfather broke in.

"Oh, I'm not saying anything. It's just that we've always liked his mother so."

"Margaret?" His voice rose on this, and he put his hand over hers on the table.

"Can I get you more of anything, Mom?" my father asked. He wasn't looking at Rhoda's sister.

"She's essentially one-eyed," my grandmother whispered to my grandfather, loud enough so we all could hear.

"Jesus," my father said.

"That's okay," Rhoda's sister said. "We know it's meant well. It's just the situation that's awkward, is all."

"That's right," my grandmother chimed in. "That's what I was trying to say."

"She's coming," I whispered.

Rhoda gave us all a careful looking-over as she sat down. "You've been talking about me, haven't you?"

"Well, of course," my grandmother said, smiling. "You're the bride."

My father and Rhoda didn't have a honeymoon. They had me for the weekend instead, and they gave me presents. This was a form of bribery, perhaps.

I was on the porch, watching the sun go down between two mountains, the air warm and dry. I could hear the sucking noises of quail in the bushes. The guests had all left, and the only sign that remained of the wedding was the smoldering hibachi.

"Happy Wedding!" my father and Rhoda both sang out as they stepped onto the porch.

Rhoda gave me a Walkman. I must have looked a little stunned, because she frowned again. I wasn't used to expensive presents. Then my father handed me my first gun, a .30-.30 carbine for deer.

"Try it out," he said. "There's a gray squirrel up there." He pointed to the large oak in front of us.

I had seen the squirrel, too—about twenty feet up. I could have hit it with a Wiffle ball.

"It isn't loaded," I said.

"There's a shell in the chamber. Just pull back the hammer."

I pulled back the hammer and aimed at that squirrel. He was eating something, turning it over and over in his hands, with spindly black fingers, his gray cheeks pink now in the light and rippling as he munched, one eye looking right at me. I pulled the trigger and saw a chunk of meat fly from him like a small red bird. He seemed to explode. There was the sound of rain through the trees as bits of him fell back to earth.

"You got him," Rhoda said.

That evening, we drove into town, to Rhoda's parents' house, and I met Rhoda's mother. She sat on a barstool chain-smoking and drinking the whole time we were there. She had a dog about the same length as a squirrel, but shaved and fattened, with a smashed face and angry little eyes; the thing hid under her stool growling so loudly it was hard for us to hear each other. Every now and then, Rhoda's mother would yell, "Shut up, Prune!" and stretch her leg down to kick it. The dog would run across the kitchen, toenails clicking and slipping on the linoleum, then run back, spitting a little as it breathed.

Rhoda's mother told me, in a smoker's rasp, "You're a good kid, aren't you."

Rhoda's father had invited my father back to his gun room, where he had a fair collection, he had said, of shotguns and pistols.

"How are you, Mom?" Rhoda asked at some point far into the conversation. It sounded as if she hadn't talked with her mother for a while.

"Your bastard father wants to leave me."

There was a long and ugly pause before Rhoda spoke. "You know that's not true, Mom. That's never been true."

"Okay. Things were never better, then." She took another swallow from her drink. "But you just got married again. Off to good times, right?" Rhoda's mother poured herself another drink and looked at me. "So what do you like to do."

She breathed smoke out her mouth into her nose. Her slacks were pink, and she had hooked her slippers under the bottom rung of the barstool. Her little dog was staring at my shins.

"I don't," I said.

She laughed, then coughed, then looked at me suspiciously. I had meant to say, "I don't know," but had lost the final word somewhere.

"He's only twelve, Mom," Rhoda was saying.

"He's a good kid." Her mother winked at me, then ground out her cigarette in an ashtray. "Hey, Billy!" she yelled down the hallway. "What's so damn interesting about those guns? Come and meet the kid."

She poured herself another.

"Dad loves you," Rhoda said.

"Open your eyes, Rhoda." Her mother stared at her. "Ha," she said and laughed, then began coughing again. "You always have been much too pretty, Rhoda. It's not good to show up your mother." She looked at me and winked. "Don't think I don't know what I'm about."

Rhoda's father came in walking slowly, looking short and wide-chested beside my father. "I think you've probably had enough," he said to his wife.

She winked at me again and downed her glass.

Rhoda's father didn't look so much angry as embarrassed and unsure. He rubbed his hand lightly over his balding head.

"What did you think of Dad's collection?" Rhoda asked my father. She was standing closer to me now, away from her mother. I could see the fine, soft hair along her neck.

"It's really something. Not every day you see a collection like that."

"Please, Sharlene. Not in front of his son," Rhoda's father said.

"It's okay, Daddy," Rhoda said, stepping toward him now. "We're not staying long anyway."

"Are you talking to me about shame?" Rhoda's mother asked with her back to all of us. "Is the man who won't be seen with his own wife in public talking to me about shame?" Prune started growling. He knew something was up, and he was crazy with it. "The man who will slink around with twats half his age?"

Rhoda's mother swiveled on her stool and pointed at her husband. "Get out of my way, Rhoda," she said, because now Rhoda was between them.

Rhoda's father put up his hands in apology, then walked back alone down the hallway.

"Coward!" she yelled.

Later that night, as I listened to Rhoda weeping and my father comforting her, I wondered whether tears came out of her blank eye. The wall separating our rooms was thin, and I could hear everything: their sharp breaths, her weeping again, and Rhoda telling my father she loved him. The strangeness of it is what I remember.

The next day, Rhoda asked me to join her at the piano. I told her

I didn't know how to play, and she said it didn't matter. So I sat beside her.

"Close your eyes," she said.

"Are yours closed?"

"Yes," she said. "Though my right eye never closes all the way."

"Can you see through it?"

"Yes. Always."

I closed my eyes.

"Put your hands up to the keys," she said. "Just listen carefully and let your fingers play."

We sat for a few minutes in silence. The space between us thickened and rolled in and out.

Her first note echoed down low. She played more notes, and they took up places in the air.

"This is great," I said.

"Listen," she whispered.

I listened until her notes all around me could have been my own, and soon a few of them were. They didn't sound half bad: a disjointed song that all fit together because her breath was so close to my own.

I don't know how long our playing went on, but I do know that I wanted it never to end and yet it ended somehow and my father clapped from somewhere behind us, a sound disagreeably sharp and loud.

"What's she like, this Rhoda?" my mother wanted to know. She was cutting the fat off chicken breasts.

"She's nice," I said.

"What else?"

I poked at the strings of lumpy yellow fat set to one side of the cutting board. "She's funny," I said.

"Oh?"

"Yeah. And I don't think she's afraid of anyone. Except her mother, of course."

My mother laughed. Then she ruffled my hair.

"Oops," she said. "Sorry about that." And she grabbed a dish towel to wipe away the chicken fat. "Is she pretty?" My mother's voice quieted on this.

"No, she's deformed," I said, and my mother laughed again.

That entire week, I looked forward to when I would play piano again with Rhoda, but the moment I arrived at my father's place Friday night, I was hustled into his car and he and Rhoda and I were rushing to her parents' house. Her mother had called.

"What does she mean?" Rhoda kept asking. She had her coat on and both hands clenched between her knees.

"It's okay," my father said over and over, after each thing she said. "I'm sure it's going to be okay."

But when we got to her parents' house, neither Rhoda nor my father could open the door. They knocked and knocked and there was no answer, only the sound of Prune growling, but neither of them would just turn the handle and open it.

So I did, finally. I let it swing wide.

"Come on in," Rhoda's mother yelled. "Billy, why don't you answer the door?"

"Daddy?" Rhoda asked.

Rhoda's father came padding down the hallway in sheepskin slippers. "Is something wrong, Rhoda?"

Rhoda turned back to my father. "I'm sorry," she said. "Take me home, okay?"

"Well that was dumb," my father said as we got back into the car. Rhoda didn't say anything. She just drew her coat around her and stared at the road. I fiddled with the ashtray on the armrest of my door. I pulled all the gum wrappers out, then stuffed them back in. I swung the metal cover open and shut a million times.

"Cut the crap, Roy," my father finally said. He gunned the motor to let me know this threat was real.

When we turned onto the gravel driveway and saw blackberry bushes lining both sides, the red bridge ahead in the lights, he asked, "What exactly did she say?"

"I'm not making things up, Jim."

"So what did she say?"

Rhoda twisted around and readjusted her seat belt. "She said, 'I love you, Rhoda. Everything is perfect here. Why don't you bring the Happy Campers over for a drink.'"

"There's no call for that, Rhoda."

"Don't be an idiot, Jim," she said very quietly.

My father looked in the rearview to see if I had heard that. I had no idea what to do, so I gave him the thumbs-up.

"She's going to kill him," Rhoda said matter-of-factly at breakfast. She looked calmly into my father's annoyance, his anger and fear. "Are you ready for that, Jim?"

An hour later, I failed my after-breakfast oral-hygiene exam.

"Numbers six and eleven still need work," said my father the dentist. "And your gums are bleeding again. You know what that means."

"Where's Rhoda?" I asked.

"I don't know," he said. He looked over his shoulder as if he expected her to be right behind him. When he called her name, there was no answer. When he looked through each room, there was no one.

Rhoda in the walnut orchard that afternoon piecing together her thousand-piece puzzle, wearing one of her great-grandmother's long, pale-blue dresses, a sun hat, and dainty lace-up boots, never looked back to where my father sat utterly lost on the porch steps. He didn't understand her. He had no idea how to comfort her.

"Nothing has even gone wrong yet," he said to me.

Rhoda had walked far into the orchard, almost to the creek, before setting up her card table and folding chair. She was facing the valley, her left side to us. Wild mustard and baby's breath grew all around her. Spider threads floating in the air above her head caught the sun, then disappeared.

"She's just going to stay out there," my father said. "No water, no word to me, not even a glance. As if any of whatever it is is any of my fault."

How still Rhoda was made her unreal. Only the occasional slight movement of her hand fitting a piece into place.

"She wasn't like this before," my father said. "This isn't the woman I married."

I looked at him then.

"I didn't mean that," he said.

I sat beside my father on the porch until the sun fell lower and my being there with him didn't seem to mean anything anymore. Then I walked through the orchard to Rhoda.

The air was still hot. There were small, clear drops of perspiration where Rhoda's dark hair had been pulled back from her forehead, moisture also along the top of her upper lip and along the curving lines of her neck.

"You're watching me, Roy."

If I had touched her neck, what would she have done? Pushed my hand away, laughed at me, smiled? That afternoon, I knew Rhoda could do anything. She could vanish. Just walk down toward the creek in her long dress, follow it, and not return, her history known to us then only in postcards or in dreams. Nothing was holding her.

"Is your father also watching me?" she asked.

"Yes."

"Is he on the porch steps, with his hands hanging off his knees?"

"Yes," I said. "Are you going to leave us?"

Rhoda looked up at me then and smiled. She looked young, much younger than my father. "Of course not," she said. "Don't think that."

All Sunday morning, Rhoda followed at a distance. She was wearing jeans, a T-shirt, and a baseball cap, but I imagined she was still wearing her great-grandmother's dress, her face hidden by her sun hat as she climbed the narrow ribbon of fire road along each ridge.

My father walked beside me carrying his .22 for quail. I could hear the shells in his pocket. Uneasy, he kept looking back at Rhoda, a quarter of a mile behind us, and soon began muttering.

"I don't know about all this," he said to himself over and over in his many ways as we rose past the calls of gray squirrels and flickers. There had been a light rain overnight. I remember how strong the dove grass smelled, bitter in my nostrils and throat. I looked up suddenly from the bright ground and everything pulled together, all the strands of cloud and blue air, as if there were a huge drain in the center of the sky that sucked it all up.

"About what?" I finally asked.

"Everything," he said, shaking his head.

"She's not going to leave," I said.

My father squinted, looking out over the brush on either side distrustfully. "I wish I could believe that."

"You can," I said. "She told me she wouldn't."

My father stopped hiking and looked at me then as if I were someone entirely new to him. "She told you?"

"Yes."

"But why?"

"I asked her."

My father gazed back at Rhoda. She was holding the front of her dress to keep it from the ground, clutching her book in one hand, floating gradually up toward us.

"Rhoda," my father said. He was reminding himself, perhaps.

After the next rise, the brush thinned out and we entered the valleys at the top, where the mountains joined. Pin-striped white

oak and clearings of pearly, blue-green dove grass. We could hear
the feathers of kestrels as they slanted past on the wind.

"Have you ever seen one of those up close?" my father asked.

"No," I said.

He stared into the sky for a long time, then took aim with the
.22 at one that was hovering a few hundred feet away. When he
fired, the slim wings seemed to falter a moment, but I could have
simply imagined it, because there was no fall.

Rhoda coming toward us, clear of the brush, had taken off her
sun hat and with her one clear eye was staring up at the bird.

My father put another shell in the chamber and waited for the
kestrel to slide by at closer range. Rhoda walked up behind him
and put her white fingers on the back of his neck. When the bird
did come, its head to the side, beak open and feathers ruffling,
I saw Rhoda close her one eye that would. I saw her neck arch
back, whipping through the air, and wings rise from her. I heard
the shot and screamed.

My father jumped sideways from me and swung the barrel
around until it pointed at my chest. This was only instinct, he
would explain later. I had startled him.

But Rhoda came toward me, held my face in her hands and
pulled it close to her own, wanting to know. "What's going on in
there?" she asked. She pulled me so close I saw into her shuttered
eye, the light-brown edge curving and perfect against the white,
its landscape bottomless, its center blocked from view.

A LEGEND OF GOOD MEN

I ONCE STOOD in a grove of trees along one end of a lake and heard a hundred tiny pellets tap through the leaves around me like rain, so gently I could have caught one on my tongue. Then the boom over the water, John's cry, my mother's cry, and their arms waving. I spread my hands and waited for another. The air had so thinned out there seemed to be no distance, as if all things—the leaves, a waterline, red flannel, fields, and horizon—could be plucked by my own two fingers. The whine and squeak of mallards' wings grew stronger, then fainter. Though I wasn't hit, I stumbled backward in a half circle, made sure I was in full view of my running mother, and toppled into the mud. This was the first time I knew gunshot from the other end.

John Laine had not meant to shoot me. He was dating my mother and was trying to win my favor. He had posted me farther to the side, behind some tules, but I had crawled over on my hands and knees, through mud and the stubble of wheat, then risen up when I heard the muffled explosion of duck wings against water. John could not have seen me until his finger was already easing back on the trigger.

From where I lay, the yells and splashing seemed to come from every direction. Then the mud oozed in around my ears. I stared vacantly into a gray sky. I'll remember this, I thought. Today is Saturday, November eighth. I'm thirteen. Even my ankles are sinking.

My mother's hands ripping me out of the mud made me smile, and that gave me away. I landed with a wet smacking sound.

"You little shit," my mother said. Then she laughed. Then John laughed, relieved that he hadn't killed me. He was a police officer, so it wouldn't have looked good.

My mother grabbed a handful of mud and threw it at him; it spread across the front of his red flannel shirt like a wound. She launched herself backward into the mud beside me and began to cry. That was the beginning of the end for John. He didn't know it as he stood there smiling nervously, unsure whether my mother was really crying or not, but he was on his way out. I squinted at him with one eye and could almost see him vanishing.

Although my mother had dated one man steadily for several years after the divorce, she didn't keep any man around for long after my father killed himself. The men she dated then were a lot like the circuses that passed through our town. They'd move in quickly and unpack everything they owned, as if they had come to stay. They'd tempt us with brightly colored objects—flowers, balloons, remote-controlled race cars—perform tricks with their beards and hands, call us funny names like *snip, my little squash plant, ding-dong,* and *apple pie,* and yell their stories at us day and night. Then they'd vanish, and we'd find no sign left, no mention even, as if we'd simply imagined them.

John was only one in a series. Angel was the most important of the ones who came before. When my mother told me Angel's name, I thought she was saying "on hell." I thought that was a wonderful idea, that one could be on hell without being in it, like "Just Visiting" on the Monopoly board. With Angel we went skiing in the Sierras, dozed in front of fireplaces, "experienced" the opera, and generally dressed more nicely. Beneath all the glitz, however, my mother was still the same. She dumped Angel in under two and a half months, with no advance warning that I could detect, late on a Tuesday afternoon. She did it over the phone. The difference was that this time she cried. I did, too, though not because I missed Angel.

Leonard was the next in the series. He occurred during the summer months. What an ugly-looking man, I thought when I first met Leonard. He was an astrologer who explained to me that my Jupiter in Venus meant I should expect big things from love. I could find no pattern at all to the men my mother picked: Angel and Leonard were as unalike as two people can be.

"Men," my mother said, "are full of surprises. They're never who you think they are." I began to imagine that all men were in costume, that somewhere down each of their backs was a zipper. Then it occurred to me that someday I would be a man, also, and I wondered about the zipper thing.

My mother and I each had our routines. She taught high school, took long hikes in the state parks near our house, read mystery novels, and sometimes disappeared with explanations as thin as, "I just need a few days," or "I'm going to visit a friend."

"Which friend?" I would ask.

"That's right," she would say.

I ate ice cream in front of the TV, did my homework well enough, and sneaked out at night with my father's rifle to shoot streetlights. Within half a year, I had blacked out whole neighborhoods and begun blacking them out again after they had been repaired.

Nothing was more beautiful to me than the blue-white explosion of a streetlight seen through crosshairs. The sound of it—the pop that was almost a roar, then silence, then glass rain—came only after each fragment and shard had sailed off or twisted glittering in the air like mist.

John Laine was exceptional in that he was the first man to last over three months. Even that day at the lake didn't faze him. There was no telling how long he'd stay.

Though I was only thirteen, John taught me to drive his pickup—the Silver Bullet, he called it—and let me speed through the back roads all over Sonoma County. If we passed another cop, we just waved. I remember vineyards in late September at a hundred miles per hour, the way their matted purple, red, and green whirled by like patches of seaweed on an overgrown ocean. John, whose voice was always calm, even as the tires were slipping beneath us like bars of soap, said I was a natural. He said I might even make a good officer one day.

John had dark sideburns he could wiggle up and down. He had descended from a tree, he told us when we asked where he was from. And before that? I asked. He pinched my nose with his rough fingers and told me to go to bed. I was sitting on the couch with him and my mother. She grinned at me and jerked her thumb toward my bedroom.

When my mother finally broke up with John, on that same couch as I hovered in the kitchen, peeking through the louvered doors, John said, "Okay," and kept holding her hand. Without a fight, my mother wasn't sure what to do. My father had wronged her in concrete ways that could be yelled about. With my father, there had been the possibility of righteousness. But with John, for both of us, there was only the ache of knowing how much we had wanted him to stay.

After John came Emmet. This was during January, when my mother was dreaming of Legoland and personal fame. With Emmet's help, she dragged our dining table into the living room, added its extra leaves until it was at full length, and commanded us to be quiet. She had written to *Motorland Magazine,* asking whether they might be interested in an article on the trip we had taken to Denmark's Legoland, and against all expectation, they had responded positively. Every evening she sat before her notes and 35-mm slides while Emmet and I sat obediently on the living room couch, Emmet reading Louis L'Amour Westerns and I doing my homework.

Emmet was a man who kept telling us who he was. And who he was kept changing. One week he had grown up in Sandpoint, Idaho; the next week it was Red Bluff, California. Shrugging his shoulders, he'd claim his memory was improving, that was all. And if you caught him in his sleep, as I once did, his claims were even wilder.

"Mittenwald," he sighed, pushing his head farther into the corner. I had found him in the back of our hallway closet at 4:30

a.m., curled around the vacuum cleaner, our old drapes under his head. "I have to; I'm from Mittenwald. Small town just north of here. Lots of fires." He had mistaken the closet for my mother's bedroom, I was sure. I could sympathize. Years before, I had mistaken that same closet for the bathroom and peed in the corner where he lay now, then pulled down two of my mother's old skirts in an attempt to flush the toilet.

"The impossible has become real," my mother told us one of those first Legoland evenings. Wearing her purple velour robe, she actually raised her hands into the air.

Emmet and I smiled at each other. He was a man who could appreciate exaggeration.

My mother's slides were of me and some Danish girl she had corralled that August along with the girl's single father. The move had been pure calculation: my mother knew that a potential magazine article would have to include two children and both parents. This girl had a blond ponytail and very large eyes. Her forehead, also, was uncommonly wide. My mother called her Helga, because neither of us could remember her name.

Helga and I drove Lego cars, held up our Lego driver's licenses, sailed in Lego boats past Lego Mount Rushmore, and shot each other with Wild West Lego revolvers. My mother's favorite slide was of twenty or thirty Lego horses and Lego men all piled up on the porch of a Lego palace while the very large and human gardener came by with a lawn mower. Helga and I were peering over from either wing of the palace. Something about that picture just delighted my mother. Quaint little Europe was a part of it, perhaps, but all those men dumped unceremoniously, along

with their horses, had its appeal, too. Plenty of hints were available, if only Emmet had cared to take note.

Toward the end of my mother's Emmet period, I traveled farther into the hills, began firing from thick patches of brush, and
nailed my first stoplight from a distance of over four hundred
yards. From *Survivalist Magazine,* I had mail-ordered a converter
kit that allowed me to shoot .32-caliber pistol shells from my
father's .300 Magnum. The pistol shells were perfect for neighborhood streetlights because they were much quieter and could
be mistaken, even, for firecrackers. With the stoplight, however,
I began using full-sized shells. The shock they gave out echoed
clear off the other side of the valley, miles away.

I ricocheted three bullets off the pavement before I finally hit
the red light. At the gas station, people ran for cover, hid behind
poles and cars, but some hid with their backs open to me. No
one could tell which direction the shots were coming from. I was
firing from too far away.

The entire stoplight bounced on its line into the air, its red
gone silver. I smelled sulfur and heard dogs yowling and sirens
from across the valley. Through the crosshairs, I watched a patrol
car screech up and wondered whether John was inside.

Pat was the man who was always laughing. Followed by
a cloud of Amway aftershave, he laughed himself in one door
and out the next. As far as I could tell, even the breakup seemed
funny to Pat.

Merril lived next door. He came over with some vegetables
from his yard a few months after his wife had left him and
didn't return home for more than three days. His back slid-

ing glass door was unlocked that entire time, so I went in.
I cataloged everything; I even opened his cheapo safe and
wrote down how much cash he had. I found copies of *Playboy*
and *The Joy of Sex* under his bed. From his medicine cabinet,
I discovered that he suffered from hemorrhoids and cold sores,
from a bad elbow and gingivitis. I saw pictures of all his kids—
grown up by then and moved out—and found even the cause of
his divorce. His wife, Carolyn Somers, maiden name Alexander,
had spelled out everything very carefully in a letter from half a
year earlier. Merril had videotaped himself having sex with one
of his daughter's girlfriends, then left the tape lying around for
years. Alise, his daughter's friend, had been only fifteen at the
time. I even watched the videotape myself. Merril still hadn't
gotten rid of it.

My mother got rid of Merril when he refused to go home one
night. It was late. She actually hit him, with a ceramic frog my
aunt had brought from New Zealand. Then she called the police,
filed the next day for a restraining order, and he left us alone.

A few weekend afternoons that summer, when Merril was sun-
ning on his lounger in his backyard, I sighted in on him with the
.300 Magnum from my mother's bathroom window. Through
the crosshairs, I could trace the flabby outlines of his gut and
even the thin blue veins in his arms. What would it have looked
like if I had pulled the trigger? One day in John's pickup, when
I had run over a pigeon at ninety and glanced in the rearview, I
had actually seen a puff of feathers.

My mother was disheartened by the whole thing with Merril.
He had been talking to her about family and commitment and
how she made him feel like he was in high school again, and she

had started to believe. I didn't mention Alise. My mother cried with me on the living room couch and told me she still missed Angel and John.

"And your father, too," she added. So then we were both crying. After a while, however, even that seemed funny.

"What a stupid, stupid man," my mother said, laughing.

"You're never going to marry anyone else," I said.

She stared out the sliding glass door. "I mean, come on," she said. "After all that?"

In early fall, post-Merril, when my mother wasn't dating anyone, when it was just the two of us, I broke into our own house. I had left the key hanging in my locker at school. We didn't have a spare hidden under the welcome mat anymore, and my mother rarely made it home before 6 or 7. So I checked all our windows and doors, and when I could find nothing that was open, I picked up a flat gray rock from our yard and smashed it through her bathroom window. I unscrewed the lock, slid the pane aside, and crawled in.

I checked the master bedroom first. I found sixteen paper bags in the closet, filled with everything from school papers to clothing to spare batteries. The inevitable rings were hidden in shoes, wrapped up in nylons. The only safe was a toy one for a child, with the combination printed plainly on the bottom. Bras and panties were hanging from clothespins, but there were no ties, so clearly this room was without men.

In the bathroom, a single purple toothbrush hung from the wall. The fact of a diaphragm in the cupboard by the sink had not been noticed before. This woman's teeth were brittle or else

she ground them together at night, because in that same cupboard she had both Sensodyne toothpaste and a plastic mouth-
piece for sleeping.

This woman kept no pictures of anyone on display, so it was
hard to tell whether she had a family. In the only other bedroom,
the wallpaper was a print of bamboo thatching that covered even
the ceiling. In the corner was a fish tank with the light turned off
and a poster listing 250 species of shark. The shark poster and the
small pairs of white Fruit of the Loom underwear strewn about the
floor suggested that a boy or several boys lived in this room. The
single pair of hiking boots in the closet, as well as the single pair
of soccer cleats, narrowed it to one boy. The guns in his closet—
a Browning .22-caliber rifle, a .30-.30 Winchester carbine, a
.300 Winchester Magnum with scope, a Winchester Model 25
.12-gauge pump shotgun, a Sheridan "Blue-Streak" pellet rifle,
and a Ruger .44 Magnum handgun—were difficult to explain.
Where had he gotten them all?

The buildup of carbon in the chamber of the .300 Magnum
indicated that the gun had been used frequently, perhaps even recently. The block of wood under his bed, shot full of holes that
didn't go all the way through, suggested that he not only had fired
the .22 but may even have fired it inside the house. The box full of
Playboys, Penthouses, Hustlers, and trash novels with "Adults Only"
on the cover suggested that this boy was some kind of pervert, and
why he kept so many pictures of his father in this same box but
not on his desk or on his walls didn't make much sense.

Right around that time, after looking through that box, I
loaded my father's .12-gauge and blew out most of our windows
and doors. It was a fairly extreme thing to do, I realized after-

ward. I went through two and a half boxes of shells before I was
done; the front doors, especially, took a lot of rounds—one for
each hinge, plus two more to knock them over. The sliding glass
door in our family room was by far the most beautiful. I blew
one small hole through its middle, about the size of a half dol-
lar. Everything was absolutely still for a moment, then the glass
began to tremble. It rippled and shook its entire length, the glass
bending in waves, then it shattered into a billion fibers.

John Laine was the only man to reappear in our lives. As I sat on
our front porch and waited for the patrol cars to arrive, I hoped
he might be in one of them, and he was. He and his partner arrived in the fourth car. They screeched up onto our sidewalk,
threw open their doors, and pointed their pistols at me, just as
the others had done. I was unarmed and willing to cooperate,
but I wasn't sure what to do. No one told me anything at first. I
was expecting a bullhorn, but they only stared at me.

I waved my hand in the air. "John," I said. Here he was, delivered practically to my doorstep.

SUKKWAN ISLAND

I HAD A Morris Mini with your mom. It was a tiny car, like an amusement-park car, and one of the windshield wipers was busted, so I always had my arm out the window working the wipers. Your mom was wild about mustard fields then, always wanted to drive past them on sunny days, all around Davis. There were more fields then, less people. That was true everywhere in the world. And here we begin home schooling. The world was originally a great field, and the earth flat. And every beast roamed upon the field and had no name, and every bigger thing ate every smaller thing, and no one felt bad about it. Then man came, and he hunched up around the edges of the world hairy and stupid and weak, and he multiplied and grew so numerous and twisted and murderous with waiting that the edges of the world began to warp. The edges bent and curved down slowly, man and woman and child all scrambling over each other to stay on the world and clawing the fur off each other's backs with the climbing until finally all of man was bare and naked and cold and murderous and clinging to the edge of the world.

His father paused, and Roy said, Then what.

Over time, the edges finally hit. They curled down and all came together and formed the globe, and the weight of this happening set the world spinning and man and beast stopped falling off. Then man looked at man, and since we were all so ugly with no fur and our babies looking like potato bugs, man scattered and went slaughtering and wearing the more decent hides of beasts.

Ha, Roy said. But then what.

Everything after that gets too complicated to tell. Somewhere in there was guilt, and divorce, and money, and the IRS, and it all went to hell.

You think it all went to hell when you married Mom?

His father looked at him in a way that made it clear Roy had gone too far. No, it went to hell sometime before that, I think. But it's hard to say when.

They were new to the place and to the way of living and to each other. Roy was thirteen, the summer after seventh grade, and had come from his mother in Santa Rosa, California, where he'd had trombone lessons and soccer and movies and gone to school downtown. His father had been a dentist in Fairbanks. The place they were moving into was a small cedar A-frame, steeply pitched. It was tucked inside a fjord, a small finger inlet in southeastern Alaska off Tlevak Strait, northwest of the South Prince of Wales Wilderness and about fifty miles from Ketchikan. The only access was from the water, by seaplane or boat. There were no neighbors. A two-thousand-foot mountain rose directly behind them in a great mound and was connected by low saddles to others at the mouth of the inlet and beyond. The island they were on, Sukkwan Island, stretched several miles behind them, but they were miles of thick rain forest and no road or trail, a rich growth of fern, hemlock, spruce, cedar, fungus, and wildflower, moss and rotting wood, home of bear, moose, deer, Dall sheep, mountain goat, and wolverine. A place like Ketchikan, where Roy had lived until age five, but wilder, and fearsome now that he was unaccustomed.

As they flew in, Roy watched the yellow plane's reflection darting across larger reflections of green-black mountain and blue sky. He saw the trees coming closer on either side, and then they hit and the spray flew up. Roy's father stuck his head out the side window, grinning, excited. Roy felt for a moment as if he were coming into an enchanted land, a place that couldn't be real.

And then the work began. They had as much gear as the plane could carry. His father inflated the Zodiac with the foot pump down on one pontoon, and Roy helped the pilot lower the Johnson six-horse outboard over the transom, where it dangled, waiting, until the boat was fully inflated. Then they attached it, lowered the gas can and the extra jerry cans, and that was the first trip. His father went in alone, Roy waiting anxiously inside the plane while the pilot couldn't stop talking.

Up near Haines, that was where I tried.

I haven't been there, Roy said.

Well, like I was saying, you got your salmon and your fresh bear and a lot of things other people will never have, but then that's all you got, including no other people.

Roy didn't answer.

It's peculiar, is all. Most don't bring their kids with them. And most bring some food.

They had brought food, at least for the first week or two, and then the staples they wouldn't want to do without: flour and beans, salt and sugar, brown sugar for smoking. Some canned fruit. But mostly they were going to eat off the land. That was the plan. They would have fresh salmon, Dolly Varden, clams, crab, and whatever they hunted: deer, bear, sheep, goat, moose. They had brought two rifles and a shotgun and a pistol.

You'll be all right, the pilot said.

Yeah, Roy said.

And I'll come and check on you now and again.

When Roy's father returned, he was grinning and trying not to grin, not looking directly at Roy as they loaded the radio equipment in a watertight box, then the guns in waterproof cases and the fishing gear and tools, the first of the canned goods in cases. Then it was listening to the pilot again as his father curved away, leaving a small wake behind him that was white just behind the transom but smoothed out into dark ridges, as if they could disrupt only this small part and at the edge this place would swallow itself again in moments. The water was very clear but deep enough even just this far out that Roy couldn't see bottom. In close along shore, though, at the edges of reflection, he could make out the glassy shapes beneath of wood and rock.

His father wore a red flannel hunting shirt and gray pants. He wasn't wearing a hat, though the air was cooler than Roy had imagined. The sun was bright on his father's head, shining in his thin hair even from a distance. His father squinted against the morning glare, but still one side of his mouth was turned up in his grin. Roy wanted to join him, to get to land and their new home, but there were two more trips before he could go. They had packs filled with clothing in garbage bags and rain gear and boots, blankets, two lamps, more food, and books. Roy had a box of books just for school. It would be a year of home schooling: math, English, geography, social studies, history, grammar, and eighth grade science, which he didn't know how they'd do since it had experiments and they didn't have any of the equipment. His mother had asked his father about this, and his father had not given a clear answer. Roy missed his mother and sister suddenly and his eyes teared up, but then he saw his father pushing off the gravel beach and returning again and he made himself stop.

When he finally crawled into the boat and let go of the pontoon, the starkness hit him. It was nothing they had now, and as he watched the plane behind them taxi in a tight circle, then grind up loud and take off spraying over the water, he felt how long time might be, as if it could be made of air and could press in and stop itself.

Welcome to your new home, his father said, and put his hand on top of Roy's head, then his shoulder.

By the time the plane was out of earshot, they had bumped the dark, rocky beach and Roy's father was out in his hip boots pulling at the bow. Roy got out and reached back for a box.

Leave that for now, his father said. Let's just tie off and take a look around.

Nothing will get into the boxes?

No. Come here.

They walked through shin-high grass, bright green in the sun, and up a path through a small stand of cedars to the cabin. It was weathered and gray but not very old. Its roof was steeply peaked to keep off the snow and the entire cabin and its front porch were raised six feet off the ground. It had only a narrow door and two small windows. Roy looked at the stovepipe jutting out and hoped that it was a fireplace, too.

His father didn't take him into the cabin but skirted it on a small trail that continued farther up the hill.

The outhouse, his father said.

It was the size of a closet and raised up, with steps. It was less than a hundred feet from the cabin, but they would be using it in the cold, in winter snow. His father continued on.

There's a nice view up here, he said.

They came to a rise through nettles and berry, the earth breaking beneath their feet, grown over since it had last been traveled. His father had come here four months earlier to see it once before buying it. Then he'd convinced Roy and Roy's mother and the school. He'd sold his practice and his house, made his plans, and bought their gear.

The top of the hillock was overgrown to the point that Roy wasn't tall enough for a clear view on all sides, but he could see the inlet like a shiny tooth sprung out of the rougher water outside and the extension beyond to another distant island or shore and the horizon, the air very clear and bright and the distances impossible to know. He could see the top of their roof close below him, and around the inlet the grass and lowland extending no more than a hundred feet at any point, the steepness of the mountain behind them disappearing at its very top in cloud.

No one else for miles around, his father said. Our closest neighbor as far as I know is about twenty miles from here, a small group of three cabins on a similar inlet. But they're on a different island, and I can't remember right now which one it is.

Roy didn't know what to say so he didn't say anything. He didn't know how anything would be.

They hiked back down to the cabin then, through a sweet and bitter smell coming from one of the plants, a smell that reminded Roy of his childhood in Ketchikan. In California he had thought all the time of Ketchikan and rain forest and had formed an image in his imaginings and in his boastings to his friends of a wild and mysterious place. But put back into it, the air was colder and the plants were lush but still only plants and he wondered how they would pass the time. Everything was sharply itself and nothing else.

They clunked up onto the porch in their boots. His father opened the lock on the door, swung it wide for Roy to step in first. Roy when he went in smelled cedar and wetness and dirt and smoke and it took a few minutes for his eyes to adjust properly to see more than the windows and begin to see the beams above and how high the ceiling went and the rough look of the planks for the walls and floor with their sawed-through knotholes but the smooth feel of them nonetheless.

It all seems new, Roy said.

It's a well-built cabin, his father said. The wind won't come through these walls. We'll be comfortable enough as long as we keep wood for the stove. We have all summer to prepare things like that. We'll put away dried and smoked salmon, too, and make some jam and salt deer. You're not going to believe all the things we're going to do.

They started that day by cleaning the cabin. They swept and dusted, then his father took Roy down a path with a bucket to where a small stream fed into the inlet. It ran deep through the short meadow, making three or four S-cuts in the grass before feeding out through the gravel and dumping a small fan of lighter stuff, sand and dirt and debris, into the saltwater. There were waterbugs on its surface, and mosquitoes.

Time for the bug dope, his father said.

They're all over the place, Roy said.

All the fresh water we could ever want, his father said proudly, as if he had put the stream there himself. We'll be drinking well.

They put repellent on their faces, wrists, and the backs of their necks, then set to wiping down everything in the cabin with bleach and water to kill all the mildew. Then they dried it with rags and began bringing in their gear.

The cabin had a front room with the windows and the stove, and it had a back or really side room with no windows and a large closet.

We'll be sleeping out here, his father said, in the main room by the fire. We'll put our stuff back there.

So they carried in the equipment and put it in the closet, the stuff that was most precious and most needed to stay dry. They packed in the supplies, the canned goods along the wall, the dry goods in plastic in the middle, their clothes and bedding near the door. Then they went to gather wood.

We need dead stuff, Roy's father said. And none of it will be dry, so maybe actually we should just gather a little to take inside and then we should start building something off the back wall of the cabin.

They had brought tools, but it sounded to Roy as if his father were discovering some of this as he went along. The idea that dry wood was not something his father had thought of ahead of time frightened Roy.

They brought in a twisted pile of odd branches, stacked it near the stove, then went around back and discovered a piece of the wall that jutted out into a kind of box and was in fact for firewood.

Well, Roy's father said, I didn't know about that. But that's good. We'll need more, though. This is just for a little summer trip or a weekend of hunting. We'll need something all along this wall. And Roy wondered then about boards, about lumber, about nails. He hadn't seen any lumber.

We'll need shingles, his father said. They stood side by side, both with their arms folded, and stared at the wall. Mosquitoes buzzed around them. It was cold here in the shade even though the sun was high. They might have been having a discussion about some kind of trouble Roy was in, they were so removed from what they were looking at.

We can use poles or saplings or something for the supports, his father said. But we need some kind of roof, and it has to come out a ways for when the rain or snow is blowing sideways.

It seemed impossible. All of it seemed impossible to Roy, and they seemed terribly unprepared. Any old boards lying around? he asked.

I don't know, his father said. Why don't you take a look up around the outhouse and I'll poke around here.

Roy felt there was a kind of leveling. Neither knew what to do and both would have to learn. He hiked the short distance to the outhouse and could see the plants already ground down by their passing. They would wear paths in everything, everywhere they went. He circled the outhouse and stepped on one small board that had been overgrown. He pulled it out, scraped the dirt and grass and bugs off it and saw that it was rotten. He tore it apart in his hands. Inside the outhouse was a roll of toilet paper with water stains at the edges and a seat nailed onto the wooden bench and a smell different than a portable toilet because it didn't smell like chemicals or hot plastic. It smelled like old shit and old wood and mildew and old urine and smoke. It was grimy and damp and there were cobwebs in the corners. He saw two pieces of board about two or three feet long, stacked behind the toilet, but he didn't want to pick them up because he couldn't see well in the shadows and he didn't know what they had been used for or whether they had black widows on them. One of the daughters of his father's neighbors in Fairbanks had been bitten by a whole family of black widows when she'd put her foot into an old shoe in the attic. They had all bitten her, six or seven of them, but she hadn't died. She'd been sick for over a month. Or maybe this was just a story. But Roy had to leave suddenly. He jumped back fast, let the door on its spring slam itself shut, and wiped his hands on the thighs of his jeans as he backed away.

Find anything up there? his father called.

No, he shouted, turning back down toward the cabin. Just two small boards maybe, but I'm not sure what they're being used for.

How's the outhouse? His father was grinning when Roy got to him. Is it going to be something to look forward to? The big event?

No way. It gives me the creeps in there.

Wait till you have your butt hanging out over the void.

God, Roy said.

I found a few boards under the cabin, his father said. Not in great shape, but usable. It still looks like we're going to have to make a few boards. Ever made boards before?

No.

I've heard it can be done.

Great. He could see his father grinning.

The first bit of home schooling, his father said. Board-Making 101.

So they cut up what they had and looked out in the forest for support poles and a log or tree big enough and fresh enough for boards. The forest was dimly lit and very quiet except for dripping and the sounds of their own boots and breath. Some wind in the leaves above, but not steady. Moss grew thickly at the bases of the trees and over their roots, and strange flowers that Roy remembered now from Ketchikan appeared suddenly in odd places, behind trees and under ferns and then right in the middle of a small game path, red and deep purple in stalks thick as roots, waxy-looking. And fallen wood everywhere but all of it rotten, coming apart in dark reds and browns as they touched it. He remembered nettles in time not to touch the hair that looked like silk and he remembered what they had called conks on the trees, though that word seemed strange now. He remembered knocking them off with rocks and taking them home to engrave on their smooth white faces. What he remembered most was the constant sense of being watched.

He stayed close by his father on this initial trip. He was alarmed that neither of them was carrying a gun. He was looking for bear sign, half hoping for it. He had to remind himself constantly that he was supposed to be looking for wood.

We're going to have to cut fresh, his father said. Nothing here will be new enough. The wood rot sets in too fast. Is any of this coming back to you? Are you remembering Ketchikan?

Yeah.

It's not like Fairbanks here. Everything has a different feel. I think maybe I've been in the wrong place for too long. I'd forgotten how much I like being by the water, and how much I like the mountains coming right up like this and the smell of the forest. Fairbanks is all dry, and the mountains are only hills and every tree is the same as every other tree. It's all paper birch and spruce, pretty much, endless. I used to look out my window and wish I could see some other kind of tree. I don't know what it is, but I haven't felt at home for years, haven't felt a part of any place I've been. Something's been missing, but I have a feeling that being here, with you, is going to fix all that. Do you know what I mean?

His father looked at him and Roy didn't know how to talk with his father like this. Yeah, he said, but he didn't. He didn't know at all what his father was really saying or why he was going on like that. And what if things didn't work out the way his father was saying they were going to work out? What then?

Are you all right? his father asked, and he put his arm around his boy's shoulders. We'll be all right here. Okay? I'm just talking. Okay?

Roy nodded and stepped out of his father's grasp to continue looking for wood.

They brought what little they had found back to the cabin, and it was clearly not much of anything, so his father took out the ax, but then looked up at the sky and changed his mind. You know, it's getting a little late in the afternoon here, and we need food and we need to set up our bunks and stuff, so maybe this should wait.

So they got at the dry wood that was in the small box behind the cabin, which they found had an access door from the inside, and they used some of this wood to get a fire going in the stove.

It will be our heat, too, his father said. It'll keep us toasty, and we can get it to slow-burn all night if we close off the vents.

We'll need that, Roy said. Though he knew it wouldn't be like Fairbanks here. Single digits and below zero would be rare. His father had promised everyone that. He had sat in their living room with his elbows on his knees and stressed how safe and easy it all would be. Roy's mother had pointed out that his father's predictions had rarely come true. When he had protested, she'd brought up commercial fishing, the hardware store investment, and several of his dental practices. She hadn't mentioned either marriage, but that had been clear, also. His father had ignored all this and told them that mostly it would be above freezing.

Once they had the fire going, Roy went for cans of chili in the other room and his father asked for bread, too, to toast on top. It was dim in the cabin, even though it was still afternoon outside and the real darkness wouldn't come until very late. He did remember this, all the evenings as a little kid he'd had to go to bed while it was still light. He wasn't sure what the rules were now, but it seemed like all the normal ones about homework and bedtime were off. He'd never be busy and never have to get up for school. And he'd never see anyone else other than his father.

They ate their chili out on the porch, their booted feet dangling. There was no railing around the porch. They watched the calm inlet and an occasional Dolly Varden leaping. There were no salmon leaping yet, but that would come later in the summer.

When's salmon season again?

July and August mostly, depending on the type. We might get the first run of pinks in June.

They stayed on the porch after they were done and didn't say anything more. The sun didn't set but sat low on the horizon for a long time. A few small birds came in and out of the bushes around them, then a bald eagle came down from behind, the sun golden on its white head, its feathers a chalky brown. It flew to the end of the point and landed in the top of a spruce tree.

You don't see that everywhere, his father said.

No.

Finally the sun started dipping down and they went inside to arrange their sleeping bags on backpacking pads on the floor of the main room. Roy could see red in the sky outside their narrow window as he and his father undressed in darkness. Then they lay in their bags, neither one of them sleeping. The ceiling vaulted out from Roy and the floor hardened beneath him and his mind wallowed until finally he drifted off, then came back because he realized he was hearing his father weeping quietly, the sounds sucked in and hidden. The room so small and Roy didn't know if he could pretend not to be hearing, but he pretended anyway and lay there awake another hour it seemed and his father still hadn't stopped but finally Roy was too tired. He stopped hearing his father and slept.

In the morning his father was grilling pancakes and singing softly, "King of the Road." He heard Roy wake, looked down at him grinning. He lifted his eyebrows up and down. Hotcakes and cream-of-mushroom? he asked.

Yeah, Roy said. That sounds great. It was like they were just camping.

His father handed down a big plate of hotcakes with cream-of-mushroom soup on top and a fork and Roy set it aside for a moment, pulled on his jeans, boots, and jacket, and they went out onto the porch together to eat.

It was late morning, a breeze already coming up the inlet and forming small ripples in the water. The surface was opaque.

Did you sleep well? his father asked.

Roy didn't look at him. It seemed his father was asking whether he'd heard him weeping, but his father had asked as if it were a regular question. And Roy had pretended just to be sleeping, so he answered, Yeah, I slept all right.

First night in our new home, his father said.

Yeah.

Do you miss your mother and Tracy?

Yeah.

Well, you will for a while probably, until we get settled in here.

Roy didn't believe he could get settled to the point of not missing his mother and sister. And they were going to get away periodically. That had been another of his father's promises. They would come out every two or three months or so for a visit, two weeks at Christmas. And there was the ham radio. They could pass along messages with that if they needed to, and messages could be passed to them.

They ate in silence for a while. The pancakes were a little burned and one of them doughy inside from being too thick, but the cream-of-mushroom on them was good. The air was cool but the sun was getting stronger. This was like *Little House on the Prairie* or something, sitting out on a porch with no railing and their boots dangling and no one else around for miles. Or maybe not like that, maybe like gold miners. It could be a different century.

I like this, Roy said. I'd like it to stay sunny and warm like this all year.

His father grinned. Two or three months anyway. But you're right. This is the life.

Are we gonna start fishing?

I was just thinking about that. We should start this evening, after we work on the lean-to for the wood. And we'll build a little smoker back there, too.

They put the dishes in the small sink, and then Roy went to the outhouse. He held the door open with one foot and inspected all around the seat as best as he could, but finally he just had to use it and trust that nothing was going to take a bite out of him.

When he returned, his father grabbed the ax and saw and they went looking for board trees. As they walked through the forest, they looked at trunks, but mostly it was just hemlock in here, no thicker than four or five inches. Farther up the draw the trees shrank even more, so they turned around and went down along the shore to the point, where a larger stand of spruce grew. His father began chopping at the base of one that was farther in and partway around the point.

Don't want to wreck our own view, he said. It occurred to Roy that maybe chopping down trees here wasn't even legal, because it was some kind of National Forest, but he didn't say anything. His father had been known on occasion to ignore the law when it came to hunting, fishing, and camping. He had taken Roy hunting once in suburban Santa Rosa, California, for instance. They had only the pellet gun and were going for dove or quail on some land they found beside a road that was fairly out of the way. When the owner walked down, he didn't say anything but just watched them as they got back into the car and drove away.

Roy took over with the ax, feeling the thud each time through his arms and studying how white the chips of wood were that flung out loosely around the base.

Careful how it falls, his father said. Think about where the balance is.

Roy stopped and studied the tree, then moved halfway around it and gave the last two blows and it fell away from them, ripping down through branches and leaves, other trunks quivering under the shock and looking like a crowd of bystanders at some horrific scene, all of them trembling and thrown and an odd silence afterward.

Well, his father said, that should be good for a few boards at least.

They stripped the branches and put them in a pile to go through later for kindling and, Roy thought to himself, a possible bow and arrows. They got at each end then to carry it back to the cabin, but it was much heavier than either of them had expected, so they sawed it into sections then and there, most at about two feet but two longer sections for longer boards, for the sides of the smoker especially. Then they carried the pieces to the back of the cabin and stood around afterward looking at them.

We don't have the right tools.

No, Roy said. We'll have to just use the ax or saw or something. What do you usually use to make boards?

I don't know. Some kind of tool we don't have. I think we can stand them up on end and saw, though.

So they tried a piece like that, stood it on end and placed the saw across at about an inch from the edge and worked it through slowly, trying to keep straight.

The pieces are all going to be different sizes, Roy said.

Yep.

It turned out that it took a long time and didn't work well and was more of a one-person job since they had only one saw, so Roy went in for the fishing gear and put their poles together on the porch. He tied a Pixie on each line, with a swivel about three feet above it, then walked around back. His father was still working on the first board.

His father didn't look up but kept at his work. His breath

was puffing out in the cold and his face looked gaunt like a bird's—small sunken eyes, thin lips, a nose that looked almost hooked right now, and a light fringe of hair that seemed no more than a ruffle.

I have the poles ready, Roy said.

Catch us a big one, his father said and looked up for a moment. And then get your sawing hand ready. I see now this job is going to take us about the next four months.

Roy smiled. All right. I'll be back.

The point was windier. Roy stood at the edge where the wind waves were up to two or three feet slapping into the shore and he could see whitecaps out there. He hadn't realized how sheltered their little cove was. He walked up and down the shoreline for a few minutes, gazing at the white polished rocks and into the tree line behind that was up on a ruff of grass and dirt and root that skirted the beach everywhere and everywhere was exposed. He didn't know how the dirt stayed there, but when he studied it up close, he saw that it was mostly moss and root. He thought of bears and looked around and saw no sign but walked back to the point, within view of the cabin, and threw his lure out across the mouth of their cove to catch the salmon tumbling in or slipping out.

He couldn't see his lure or any fish at all, but he remembered times in the coves around Ketchikan of standing on the bow of his father's boat and seeing the fish everywhere beneath him. They would have that here in later months, but still he hoped today he might catch an early one.

When something did hit, it was a small Dolly Varden, a white flash and tug. He pulled it up easily onto the smooth rocks, where it gasped and bled and he removed the hook and smashed its head and it died. It had been a little while since he'd caught a fish, almost a year. He bent down to look at it and watch its colors fade.

You were spawned on rocks like these, and to these rocks dost thou return, he spoke and grinned. Thou hast becometh lunch.

He built up some rocks around it to keep the eagle away, and he thought of his last English class and the plays they had done and how he wouldn't have any of that this year. He didn't have his friends, either, and there were no girls here.

As he trundled his lure back across the mouth again and again, he was thinking of girls in school and then of a particular girl and kissing her on the way home. He got an erection thinking about it and looked toward the cabin, then pulled in his line and went back into the trees, where he leaned against one tree with his pants open and masturbated and imagined kissing her and came. He had figured out how to masturbate less than a year before and he did it usually three or four times a day, but he hadn't been able to since he'd arrived because his father was always there.

He sat down by another tree and felt lonely and thought of all his missed opportunity.

Then, bored, he fished again, caught another the same size, and returned to his father. The afternoon was getting later by now, the light richer and the view of the mountain as he walked back very beautiful.

His father was still sawing when he came up.

There you are, his father said. Hey, looks like dinner. Dolly Varden, both of them?

Yeah.

Great. And he started singing what sounded like a sea chantey. Oh, the Dolly Varden came swimming, and up he grabbed his rod. And caught two or three and brought them back, and ate them with his grog.

His father smiled, pleased with himself. Better than radio?

Definitely, Roy said. This was an odd father he was seeing out here. I can cook them while you finish up. How's it going?

His father pointed at his pile. Looks like ten or fifteen of the finest shingles anywhere, I'd say. And all very uniform. We know about quality control here on the ranch.

The ranch, Roy said. Looks like a pretty small spread.

The herds are farther back on the island.

Yeah, Roy said. I'll fix some dinner. He cleaned the fish out front at the water's edge and watched the guts just under the water, caught on the rocks and streaming back and forth with the small waves that came in. They looked like aliens. One had what looked like eyes.

He started the fire in the stove, then put the fish in a pan with butter and pepper and went back out to the porch feeling like a pioneer, feeling so good he walked around back to his father and watched him and talked until he figured the fire was hot enough and he went back in and rearranged the coals and fried up the fish.

They had the Varden out on the porch with sourdough bread and some lettuce and dressing.

Enjoy the lettuce, his father said. It won't last more than a week, and then we're down to canned veggies only.

Are we gonna grow anything?

We could, his father said. We'd need seeds, though. I didn't think of that. We can have Tom bring some next time he flies in.

You'll order by radio?

His father nodded. We should try it out, anyway. The evening's the best time, so maybe we can set it up after dinner.

They watched the sun getting lower. It was so slow they couldn't see it dropping, but they could see the light changing on the water and on the trees, the shadow behind every leaf and ripple in the sideways light making the world three-dimensional, as if they were seeing trees through a viewfinder.

They put their plates in the sink and brought the radio gear into the main room, in the far corner. His father plugged it into two large batteries and then remembered the antenna.

We need to put this on the roof, he said. So they went out and looked and decided it was too big a project and decided to wait for the next day.

That night, late, his father wept again. He talked to himself in small whispers that sounded like whining as he cried and Roy couldn't make out what he said or fathom what his father's pain was or where it came from. The things his father said to himself only made him weep harder, as if he were driving himself on. He would grow quiet and then tell himself another thing and whine and sob again. Roy didn't want to hear it. It frightened and disabled him and he had no way of acknowledging it, now or during the day. He couldn't sleep until after his father had ceased and fallen away himself.

In the morning, Roy remembered the crying, and it seemed to him that this was exactly what he was not supposed to do. By some agreement he had never been witness to, he was supposed to hear it at night and then by day not only forget but somehow make it not have happened. He began to dread their nights together, though they had had only two.

His father was cheery again in the morning and cooking eggs and hash browns and bacon. Roy pretended to be sleepier than he was and having a harder time awakening because he wanted to think and he wasn't ready yet to join in on the cheer and the forgetting.

The smell of the food cooking, though, got him up finally, and he asked, So are we doing the radio today?

Sure, and the wood shed and smoker and why don't we build a little summer cottage?

Roy laughed. It's true there are a lot of things.

More than eggs in a salmon.

They ate on the porch again, Roy thinking it would be a lot harder in bad weather, when they'd have to sit cramped in that little room inside. This morning was overcast as it was, though it was still warm enough for only a sweatshirt. He remembered it had been gray like this or drizzling most of the time in Ketchikan. He liked how it looked on the water, how the water became a molten gray, the sea heavier than anything and impossible to see into, and how the salmon and halibut rose up out of this.

After breakfast, they set about installing the antenna but could not find a way onto the roof. They didn't have a ladder, and there was no lip at the edge, nothing to hold on to, no high rails or other walls to brace against. His father stepped away from the cabin and walked around it several times.

Well, he said, without a ladder, I guess we're not going up there. And even then, I'm not sure how high a ladder is going to get us.

So they strung the antenna along the edge of the roof. It turned out that the antenna was only a long cord on a spool anyway, so the solution seemed fine. But when his father set up the radio and tried the reception, they couldn't hear anything clearly. It was only static and ticking and odd warped sounds that reminded Roy of old science fiction, of black-and-white TV, Ultraman and Flash Gordon. And this was supposed to be their only contact with anyone else.

Are we going to be able to talk with anyone? Roy asked.

I'm working on it, his father said, impatient. Hold it down for a sec.

It doesn't seem like it's changing at all, Roy added after another few minutes of warping.

His father turned and looked at him tight-lipped. Go do something else for a little while, okay? You can work on sawing the shingles.

Roy went around back and looked at the shingles and started in on one, but he didn't feel in the mood, so he found an elbow in one of the larger branches that came out at forty-five degrees. He sawed about eight inches from either end of the elbow and started carving the piece down with his pocketknife to make a throwing stick. He wondered if there were any rabbits or squirrels up here. He couldn't remember. He'd make a fish spear, too, and a bow and arrows and a rock hatchet.

He worked on the throwing stick, flattening the sides and

rounding the ends, until his father came out, saying, I can't get the damn thing to work, and then saw what Roy was doing and stopped. What's that?

I'm making a throwing stick.

A throwing stick? His father turned away and then turned back. Okay. That's fine. Never mind. You know, I'm losing it here already, and the whole point was to relax and find a different way of living, so fine. Let's quit this project and just take a break.

He looked at Roy, who was wondering whether his father was really speaking to him.

Why don't we go for a hike? he said. Get out your rifle and shells. We're gonna take a look around today.

Roy didn't say anything, because the whole arrangement felt too shaky. He wasn't sure they wouldn't have a different plan in a few more minutes. But his father went inside, and when Roy followed him, his father was in there taking his own rifle out of its case, so Roy went for his, too, and stuffed some shells in his pocket and grabbed his hat and jacket.

Better bring your canteen, too, his father said.

When they set off, it was still before noon. They entered the hemlock forest and followed a game trail up and down small hills until they came to spruce and cedar at the base of the mountain. The game trail they were on petered out and they were hiking then on blueberry and other low growth, trying to keep their footing in the scrub. The earth beneath was uneven, spongy and full of holes. They passed hemlocks again and rested to look out over the inlet. They were both winded, already at least five hundred feet above their cabin and the mountain above them so steep they couldn't see its top but only the curve of its flank. The cabin below looked very small and difficult to believe.

The other islands, his father said. You can see them much better from here.

Where's the mainland?

A long ways behind us, past all of Prince of Wales Island and some other islands, too, I think. In the east. That's one thing we won't see much of, is the sunrise. We're in shadow until mid-morning.

They stayed there a while longer looking out and then grabbed their rifles and started climbing again. Small wildflowers crumpling beneath their boots and hands, moss and the blueberry that wasn't yet in season and odd grasses. There were no animals around that Roy could see, and then he saw a chipmunk on a rock.

Hold on, Dad, he said, and his father turned. Roy reached back and flung his stick. It went wide of the chipmunk about ten feet, bounced several times, and stopped about fifty feet down the mountain.

Oh, man, he said, and he left his rifle, retrieved the stick, and returned.

I guess we won't count on that getting dinner for a while, his father said.

As they rose higher, they started hearing more wind and a few small birds flitted past. They still weren't on any kind of trail.

Where are we going? Roy asked.

His father kept hiking for a while and finally said, I guess we're just going up to the top and have a look around.

Farther up, though, they hit the cloud line. They stopped

and looked down. It was overcast everywhere, and no bright light, but the low areas were clear of fog and cloud, at least, and warmer. Here on the edge great fans of cloud reached down and then were blown past. Above only a few faint outlines and then everything was opaque. The wind through here was stronger and the air damp and much colder.

Well, his father said.

I don't know, Roy said.

But they continued on higher into the clouds and cold and still there was no trail. Roy as they passed tried to make from the dim shapes around them bear and wolf and wolverine. The cloud enclosed him and his father in their own sound so that he could hear his own breath and the blood in his temples as if it were outside of him and this too increased his sense of being watched, even hunted. His father's footsteps just ahead of him sounded enormous. The fear spread through him until he was holding his breath in tight gasps and couldn't ask to go back.

His father kept hiking on and never turned. They climbed past the tree line and past the thick low growth to thinner moss and very short hard grasses and occasional small wildflowers showing pale beneath. They hiked over small outbreaks of rock and finally mostly rock and they climbed up steeper cairns holding the ground above with one hand, their rifles in the other, until his father stopped and they were standing at what seemed to be the very top and they could see nothing beyond the pale shapes below them disappearing after twenty feet, as if the world ended in cliff all around and nothing more could be found above. They stood there for a long time, long enough for Roy's breath to calm and the heat to go out from him so that he felt the cold on his back and in his legs and long enough for the blood to stop in his ears so that he could hear the wind now passing over the mountaintop. It was cold, but there was a kind of comfort to this place in the way it enclosed. The gray was everywhere and they were a part of it.

Not much of a view, his father said, and he turned and they descended the way they had come and they did not speak again until they were out of the clouds.

His father looked across the low saddle extending to the next ridge and then at what they could see behind this saddle, more mountains beyond and uncertain in the gray. Maybe we should just head back down, he said. It's not very warm or clear, and there don't seem to be many trails.

Roy nodded and they continued down through the low growth to the small forests at the mountain's base and along the game trail to their cabin.

When they got there, it didn't look right. The front door was hanging slantwise on one hinge and there was trash on the porch.

What the hell, his father said, and they both jogged over and then slowed when they got up to the cabin.

Looks like bears, his father said. That's our food on the porch.

Roy could see ripped garbage bags of dry goods and the canned goods spilling out the door over the porch and onto the grass below.

They might still be in there, his father said. Put a shell in the chamber and take the safety off, but don't get jumpy on me, and keep the barrel down. Okay?

Okay.

So they levered in shells and walked slowly toward the cabin until his father went up and banged on the wall and yelled and then waited and nothing moved or made a sound.

Doesn't seem like they're here, he said, but you never know. He went up on the porch then and pushed the broken door aside with his barrel and tried to peek in. It's dark in there, he said. And bears are dark. I hate this. But he finally just stepped in and stepped back out again quickly and then slowly stepped in again. Roy couldn't hear a thing, his blood was going so crazy. He imagined his father thrown out the front door with the bear after him, his gun knocked away, and Roy would shoot the bear in the eye and then in the open mouth, perfect shots the way his father had told him he would have to aim to kill a bear with a .30-.30.

His father came out again, though, unharmed, and said the bear was gone. He tore up everything, he said.

Roy looked inside and it took a few minutes for his eyes to adjust but then he saw their bedding all torn up and food everywhere and the radio in pieces and parts of the stove taken apart. Everything wrecked. He didn't see anything that was still whole, and it did not escape him that this was all they had to live on for a very long time. They had no way of calling anyone else now, either, and they had no place to sleep.

I'm going after him, his father said.

What?

There's no sense in putting everything back together if he's still out there and can just do this again. And it might not be safe for us, either. He might come back again at night looking for more food.

But it's late and he could be anywhere, and we have to eat and figure out what to sleep in and . . . Roy didn't know how to continue. His father wasn't making any sense.

You can stay here and put things together, his father said. And I'll be back after I kill the bear.

I have to stay here by myself?

You'll be all right. You have your rifle and I'm going to be following the bear, anyway.

I don't like this, Roy said.

Neither do I. And his father took off. Roy stood on the porch watching him disappear up the path and couldn't believe what was happening. He felt afraid and started talking out loud: How could you just leave me here? I don't have anything to eat and I don't know when you're coming back.

He was terrified. He walked around the cabin like this and wanted his mother and sister and his friends and everything he had left behind, until finally he was getting cold and hungry enough that he stopped, went in, and started inspecting the sleeping bags to see if anything was usable.

His father's bag was still almost in one piece. It had only a few small tears in it. But his own bag had been used as some kind of toy. The upper half of it had been shredded and the stuffing strewn all over the room. He could use the bottom half still, he thought, but there would be no way to repair the rest.

The food was almost all wrecked. Some of the bags of flour and white sugar and salt were still intact, but only some of them, and the brown sugar for smoking had been eaten completely. There were still some cans of food that had only been dented, but most had been punctured.

Roy put the pieces of the stove back on that had been knocked off. He started a fire in there, put the only two cans of unopened chili in a pot that wasn't too badly dinged up, heated the chili, and sat out on the porch waiting for his father.

When it got dark and still his father wasn't back, Roy reheated and ate the chili, both cans because he couldn't stop. I ate your chili, he apologized out loud, as if his father could hear.

Roy stayed up that night, in his father's sleeping bag on the porch with his rifle across his knees, and still his father didn't return. When morning came he hadn't slept and he was hungry and felt sick and very cold from being out on the porch, so he went inside.

The radio wasn't hurt too badly. It had just been sat on or something, it looked like. But still it might not work anymore. Roy couldn't tell. He wanted to be able to do something, something useful, but he just didn't know anything about the radio. So he went back outside in his boots and his warm jacket and hat and gloves, all of which were still okay, and he started sawing shingles. He kept his rifle near him with a shell already in the chamber and the safety off and he sawed and thought about shooting his gun into the air a few times. His father would come then, but he'd also be angry, because the shots would be about nothing. He wanted his father just to return. He didn't like this at all. He had no idea what to do.

When it was afternoon, he had made only a few shingles and had a blister on his thumb. The shingles were impossibly difficult. Something wasn't right about how they were doing it. His father hadn't come back and he hadn't heard any gunshot, so he got up to write a note saying, I've gone looking for you. I'll be back in a couple hours. I'm leaving in the afternoon.

He set off the way his father had gone, but he realized quickly that he had no idea which way to go. He looked at the ground and could see faintly the signs that they had walked here yesterday. Occasionally a bootprint but mostly just torn-up dirt and flattened grass. He followed this trail, though, to where the mountain started and there was no way of seeing any track in that spongy stuff and he hadn't seen any trail heading off the main one, so he sat down against the mountain and tried to think.

His father hadn't left him anything to go on. He hadn't said where he'd be going or for how long. So Roy just sat there and cried, then walked back down to the cabin. He tore up the note and sat on the porch looking out at the water, and he ate some bread and peanut butter and scooped up a little of the jam from where the jar had been smashed on the rocks below the porch. Ants and other bugs had gotten to most of it, but he saved almost a spoonful of stuff that looked okay. He got back on the porch, ate it, looked out toward the setting sun, and waited.

His father returned just after dark. Roy could hear him coming down the path and he yelled out, Dad?

Yeah, his father answered quietly and came up to the porch and stamped his boots and looked down at Roy with the rifle across his knees.

I got him, he said.

What?

I got the bear, up in a draw about two mountains over. Got him this morning. Did you hear the shots?

No.

Well, it was a ways.

Where is he? Roy asked.

Still over there. I couldn't carry him back. And I didn't have my knife. Just the gun. I'm sure hungry now, though. Do we have any food left? Did you catch any fish?

Roy hadn't thought about fishing. There's a little bit left, he said. I'll heat something up for you.

That'd be great.

Roy went to work then on heating up a can of cream-of-chicken soup, their last can of it, with a can of corn and a can of string beans. His father had his flashlight out and was working on their lamp. He must have smelled the paraffin and given it a bat, he said.

By the time the food was warm, the lamp was operational again and they could see inside the cabin.

What did it look like? Roy asked as he set their food down on the floor.

What?

What did it look like, the bear?

Just a black bear, not very big, a small male. I saw him down below me late this morning, rooting around the bushes. I hit him in the back with the first shot, and it knocked him down but then he was thrashing around a lot and screaming. My second shot hit him high in the neck, and that killed him.

Jesus, Roy said.

It was something, his father said. Next time, we'll have to skin one and salt and dry the meat. Any salt left, by the way?

Yeah, we have a bag of it still.

Good. We can also just leave some saltwater out in a pan and let it evaporate on a sunny day, which should come about twice every million years.

Ha, Roy said, but his father didn't look up from his food. He seemed very tired. Roy was, too. That night he fell asleep almost immediately.

He dreamed he was chopping up bits of fish and every piece had a small pair of eyes and as he chopped, there was a moaning sound that was getting louder. It wasn't coming from the pieces of fish or their eyes exactly, but they were watching him and waiting to see what he would do.

Roy woke to his father moving stuff around their cabin, cleaning up and sorting things out. He yawned and stretched and put his boots on.

That bear cleaned us out pretty good, his father said.

I'll have to fix my sleeping bag, Roy said. He had slept in the bottom half of it with all his clothes on, including his jacket and hat and a small blanket his father had thrown over him.

Yeah, that and the radio and the door and my rain gear and most of our food. We'll have to fix it right up.

Roy didn't answer.

I'm sorry, his father said. I'm just a bit discouraged by this. He spoiled a lot of our food, and some of it could have been saved yesterday but now the bugs are all in it, so we're going to have to just throw it out. We have freezer bags, you know, that you could have put some of this stuff into.

Sorry.

That's all right. Just help me sort through it now.

They continued sorting, and what they had to throw out, they carried in a garbage bag a hundred yards away and buried in a pit.

If another bear comes along, maybe it will smell this first and come over here and dig and we'll be able to shoot it before it gets over to the cabin.

Roy wasn't real excited about shooting more bears. The last one already seemed like a waste. Do you think that bear you got was the bear that did this? he asked.

His father stopped shoveling for a moment. Yeah. I tracked it. But it could have been a different bear possibly. I lost the trail a few times and had to pick it up again, and it is pretty odd that that bear was so far from home. So we should keep a lookout just in case.

Roy decided he wasn't going to shoot unless the bear was attacking one of them, especially if they weren't going to skin it and eat it. How much did it scream when you shot it?

That's not the kind of question you ask.

When they had finished burying the wrecked food, his father walked back to the cabin and put the shovel inside. They stood on the porch then and looked out at the water, which was still and gray.

We need to get our food situation together, he said. You can start fishing and I'll work on the smoker. We need the wood shelter, too, and we need to cut some wood, but I can't do everything at once, and first we need to eat. If you catch anything, gut it for eggs and put out another couple of lines on the bottom with the eggs. Just tie the lines off to something and we'll leave them there around the clock.

So Roy went to the point again and cast across the mouth. It was a long time of catching nothing. He started by staring at the water as he fished, feeling like a fish would be there any moment, as if he could wish one onto the end of his line, but then he started looking off across the channel at the islands. There were a few whitecaps farther out, and in the distance, at the edge of the horizon, a fishing boat passed. It was far away, but Roy could see how it was humped up in front and he imagined even that he could see the spreaders, but that was just imagination. And then he was daydreaming about how he'd have to shoot their flares off this beach and try to get the boat's attention because his father had been gored by a bear and half eaten, and then a fish finally hit and he pulled it in, surfing it fast across the water, its head wagging, because it was only a small Dolly. He got it on the rocks and would normally have thrown it back, it was so small, but they needed anything they could get at this point, so he smashed its head and slit it from its asshole to its gullet to see if it had eggs. It did, which was lucky, though they were very small and not many of them. He cut them out, left the fish and his pole, and walked toward the cabin to set the bottom lines, but then he could hear the wings coming down and turned and ran but wasn't fast enough. The eagle already had his fish in its talons and was lifting off with its huge brown wings before Roy could get there. He picked up a rock and chucked it at the eagle to make it drop the fish but he missed by too far and the eagle lumbered off across the inlet to a tree on the point and landed and sat there watching Roy while it ate the fish.

Roy considered the shotgun, but even maddened and feeling they were desperate for food and fearing what his father would say about losing the fish he didn't want to think about shooting a bald eagle.

He got an extra spool and hooks from the cabin to set the bottom lines.

Get something? his father called from the back.

Yeah, I got the eggs to set the lines, but it was only a small fish and when I turned away the eagle grabbed it.

Shit.

Yeah.

Well, go catch another one.

I'm planning on it.

He put big sinkers on the bottom lines and hurled them out by hand. He hoped the water was deep enough. He set two right out in front of the cabin and tied them to roots, then walked out to the point again and threw a line into the mouth where he'd been fishing and trailed it clear back to tie off to a tree. The eagle was still sitting high up, watching him.

Then Roy picked up his gear and walked farther down the shoreline, more than half a mile of slow going over the rocks and in some cases up into the woods to get to the next small inlet. Here when he cast over the mouth and trundled in, he got something bigger right away. It pulled sideways at the line heading out to sea, the reel singing, until Roy realized his drag was just set too loose and he tightened it up and then the fish still pulled but Roy had no trouble horsing it in. It jumped twice just as it was pulled in close to the beach, two twists into the air, the head ripping back and forth trying to free itself. It was an early pink salmon, very silvery and fresh. Roy walked backward with his rod tip high to pull it up smoothly and quickly onto the rocky beach. It flopped wildly and threw the hook, but by then it was too far inland and Roy ran over to scoop it quick by the gills and throw it farther up the beach, where it lay gasping and wild-eyed and he smashed its head three times with a rock until its body arched quivering and bloody and then lay flat. Its muscles still spasmed every few seconds but it was dead.

Roy covered it in a small cairn of rocks to keep it from the eagle and then he threw his line out again. Within a few hours he had six pinks and a Dolly. He strung them on a piece of nylon rope he had brought, tied up handles so that he could carry them, and hiked back slowly to the cabin, stopping periodically to rest.

Lookin' good, his father said when he saw him coming. Lookin' good.

I went to the next inlet. The fishing's a lot better over there.

I believe it, his father said and took the string of fish to look at them. Fresh pinks, he said. And the smoker's coming along, so why don't you go ahead and cut these into strips after you're done cleaning them.

By the time Roy was done cleaning and cutting into strips for smoking, it was getting late. He washed all the pieces well, took them inside in a bucket and made the brine with salt and some white sugar. They were supposed to use brown sugar for brine, but the bear had eaten or scattered all of that. Then he went around back to his father.

How's it looking? Roy asked.

It's pretty much together.

Roy couldn't see well, but it looked like it had four walls and a top and a gap below to put the wood chips in. Does it have racks? he asked.

I brought racks, his father said. And a pan for the bottom that has two levels to it, one for hot coals and one above that for the smoker chips. Without those things, I don't know how I would have done it exactly.

Are we gonna smoke them now?

We'll let 'em brine overnight and start early in the morning. It's just too much work keeping an eye on the chips and all, especially since we don't even know if the thing works. Why don't you cook up the pieces you left out and I'll finish up here.

So Roy cooked up the two large filets in a skillet with oil since they didn't have butter anymore, and by the time his father came in, he was tired and didn't say much and just ate the fish looking down at his plate. Roy didn't feel any closer to his father than he had on their occasional vacations, and he wondered if this would change at all.

Good fish, his father finally said. You can't beat salmon. And then they did the dishes together and went to bed.

Late that night, after Roy had fallen asleep and awakened again, cold, his father was talking to him.

Roy? he was saying. Can you hear me?

Yeah. I'm awake now.

I don't know how I got this way. I just feel so bad. I feel okay during the day, but it hits at night. And then I don't know what to do, his father said, and this last part made him whine again. I'm sorry, Roy. I'm really trying. I just don't know if I can hold on.

Roy was starting to feel now like he would cry, and he really didn't want this.

Roy?

Yeah, I'm here. I'm sorry, Dad. I hope you feel better.

His father let out an awful swallowed sound and said, Thanks. And then they just lay there like that listening to each other's rough breathing until finally it was morning again and Roy lay there remembering and smelling the stove, feeling the heat coming off it.

His father was already around back putting the fish in the smoker. Hey, son, he said. This is looking like it's gonna be pretty good. He wiggled his eyebrows up and down and smiled at Roy. Then he opened up the door and Roy looked in.

The strips of fish were all laid out in there, and Roy could see the pink meat already had a glaze on it from the brine, which was good.

Just have to get the pan now, his father said. I have the coals ready in the stove.

They went inside and he pulled out coals with tongs he had brought for that purpose and laid them in the pan, then set a small grate over them that fitted down into the pan and poured a large handful of alder chips on top. Gonna be tasty, he said.

They went back outside and he slid the pan in the small door at the bottom and checked all the seams once the smoke got going inside. It leaked some smoke here and there, but his father said it would be fine and really it looked pretty good to Roy. It looked like they might be eating some smoked salmon and have some jerky to put away.

Now we need some drying racks, his father said. And it wouldn't hurt to have a cache somehow to keep everything away from the bears.

A cache? Roy asked.

Yeah, to keep food away from bears and everything else.

Would it be a lot of work?

Yeah, I'm not saying we're building one right now, I'm just thinking. What we need to do now are the racks and the wood shed.

So they worked on the frame for the wood shed coming off the back wall of the cabin but a few large drops came down on them and as they looked up into the dark clouds the rain came down more so then they were running around front with the tools to avoid getting soaked as it dumped on them.

They built up the fire in the stove and tried to dry off some with a towel.

Not much dry wood left, his father said. Not much at all. We should have just stored a few pieces in here for now to slowly dry out. If this rain keeps up, we won't be happy.

They lit the paraffin lamp and got out the cards and sat on the floor playing gin rummy for the rest of the afternoon, waiting for the rain to stop. His father didn't seem very interested in the game and looked just as glum when he won as when he lost. The rain and wind beat on the roof and outside the window, and they couldn't see more than a hundred yards, the visibility was so poor.

After three hours or so, his father stood up. I can't just sit here anymore, he said. I think I'll work on my rain gear, then check the smoker. The truth is, we're going to have a lot of rain and we just have to get used to going out and working in it.

His rain gear had some long rips in it from the bear. He laid it flat on the floor and duct-taped both sides of each tear, then went out, Roy following in his own boots and gear.

Roy stopped in front of their cabin and looked out at the water in a pale U before him that seemed connected to the sky. There was no line at all between them, no horizon. It was impossible to tell where exactly the rain and mist touched down except very close in, at the water's edge. The trees on either side seemed hung in shreds. He walked down to the water, stepping carefully on the wet rounded stones, and heard the rain everywhere, an even sheet of sound erasing all others. It was the only smell, too. Even when it smelled of land or sea, even when Roy caught the scents of what he imagined were ferns and nettles and rotten wood, they seemed only a part of the way the rain smelled. And he was realizing that this was what it would be like, mostly. The clear days they'd had were the oddity. This dense rain, and the world enclosed by it, was what they would know. This would be their home.

Come back here, his father yelled, the yell muffled.

So he went back and helped on the wood shed. They nailed together the poles and then realized they should put the roof together first, then raise it, since they didn't have a ladder, so they brought the poles down again. His father worked grimly at the wood, his mouth and eyes tight. He kept telling Roy exactly what to do, and Roy felt he was more in the way and more work directing than he was worth, as if his father had him out here only so that both of them would have to stand in the shitty rain.

His father nailed together the shingles overlapping, and when he had finished the roof, they put up the poles again, Roy holding while his father reached up and nailed. When the roof was finally up, they stepped back and looked at it. It was wobbly-looking, most of all, the supports knobby and smooth and rain-slicked dark brown, the shingles above not all the same size and at slightly different angles and jutting out jaggedly at the edge, some with their bark still on and some not. It looked like the frontier, like the real thing, except not as sturdy. It looked like it might keep a little rain off, but when they stood under it, it wasn't great. It kept most the drips off their heads, and they were able to take their hoods off, but when the wind gusted they caught some rain, on their legs especially.

Well, maybe we can put some plastic over the wood, too, his father said.

That sounds good, Roy said. And it's okay if just the bottom of the pile gets wet, right?

No. His father looked up at the roof, his jaw tight and dark from five days of stubble. But this is as good as it's going to get for now. I should have made the shingles longer. Maybe when we take our little vacation and get our next load of supplies, I'll bring some lumber back.

When are we going?

Don't get too excited about it. It's not happening for another month or two at least, and that's if I get the radio working, although I suppose Tom'll just drop in and check if we don't call for too long. That's what he's supposed to do, anyway.

A month or two seemed impossibly long to Roy, a lifetime in a miserable place that was not home.

They checked the salmon before coming in, and it was ready. They left one tray to smoke harder into jerky, but the rest they brought inside. They put the rack on top of the stove and started eating. The outside had hardened and was sweet and salty but the pink meat inside was still moist and only delicately smoky. It wasn't as good as with brown sugar but it was still delicious. Roy ate it with his eyes closed.

Stop humming, his father said.

Huh?

You're humming when you eat. You always do that, and it drives me crazy. Just eat.

So Roy tried not to hum, though he hadn't even known he'd been doing this. He wished he could just take his pieces off somewhere else and eat them alone and not worry about it.

By the time they were full, they had finished at least a third. The rest his father left out to cool, then put in freezer bags just before they went to bed.

That night, his father spoke to him again. Roy repeated, Only a month or two and then I'm out of here and I'm not coming back, over and over in his head like a mantra while his father whined and wept and confessed. I cheated on your mother, he told Roy. It was in Ketchikan, when she was pregnant with your sister. I just felt something was ending for me, I think, all my chances, and Gloria was always staying late and coming into my office and looking at me like that, and I just couldn't help myself. God, I felt bad. I felt sick all the time. But I kept doing it. And the thing is, even after seeing all that that did, and all it destroyed, I don't know for sure that I'd act any differently if I had the chance again. The thing is, something about me is not right. I can't just do the right thing and be who I'm supposed to be. Something about me won't let me do that.

He didn't ask Roy any questions and Roy didn't say anything back. His father just talked and Roy had to listen and he hated to listen to this and he thought of his mother and how she and his father had fought in Ketchikan and he didn't know how to make sense of this new accounting of things. When they had told him they were getting divorced, they had told a different story, as if it were something neither of them could do anything about, and when Roy had asked if he could help, they had told him that he couldn't, it was just a kind of thing that happened to people.

The rain was constant outside, and their room small and dark. His father whispering to him and sniffling and making odd, frightening sounds in his despair was only a few feet away and there was nowhere else to go.

In the morning, they ate cold cereal and powdered milk and didn't start a fire in the stove because they needed to conserve wood. The rain continued on, the same as the day before. The windowsills turned dark as they soaked through, and there were a few drips in various places down the walls. His father stood looking at each of them with his flashlight and didn't say anything but just felt above them where the wall met the ceiling and then looked higher up into the ceiling, moving the beam of light slowly up each slat and along every timber.

Roy read a book, one in the *Executioner* series. What he read for especially was the woman the Executioner always got, and he tried to imagine having sex with her himself.

Okay, his father said. Time for the drying rack, and you can check the bottom lines, too.

Roy checked the lines first, relieved to get out of the cabin and away from his father. It was still raining fairly hard. He was dry in his rain gear but it was so damp and cold he felt wet, as if everything were soaking through. The lines out front had nothing, but the line at the point had a dead Dolly at the end of it that was already turning pale. Roy wondered if it would be any good still. He gutted it at arm's length, not wanting to get too close in case the guts were rotten and exploded or something, but it looked all right. It smelled a little more, but not too much more, and the meat looked okay. It was a male, with two long sacks of sperm instead of eggs, so he went back to the cabin for some eggs he had salted and tied those onto the hook with cheesecloth and put the line back in. Then he looked to the forest and thought it would be nice to jack off since he hadn't in so long, but he didn't feel the energy somehow and it was all wet and cold and he had a million layers on, so he just walked back to the cabin.

His father wasn't around, so Roy hiked back into the hemlocks and found his father finally up higher in the cedars.

Hi, he said.

Looking for poles for the racks, his father said. Try to find them about six feet long at least. Any fish?

One small Dolly that was already dead. The meat looked all right, though.

Yeah. It's fine. But we need more. Maybe you should just keep fishing while I build this. Although we really need wood, is what we need.

He stopped then and just stood in place looking down at the moss. Hell, I don't know. Do you feel like chopping some wood?

Sure, Roy said. And he went back for the ax. He had only chopped wood once before, for fun. He had a feeling this was going to be different.

He started with the leftover pieces from the shed project, stood them up and brought the ax down, but they just whumped and bounced against the ground and the blade jumped back and he nearly got whacked with it before he remembered that he needed a stump or something solid beneath.

He looked around for a while until his father came back and asked him what he was doing. Roy hung back resentful as his father set one of the pieces on end and put another piece on top and chopped and it fell in half in one swing. He looked at Roy and handed him the ax.

All right.

You're going to have to show some more initiative.

Okay, Roy said, but as his father was turning away he added, I'm already doing stuff.

His father looked at him. Don't pout, he said. This isn't a place for babies.

His father left then, back into the trees, and Roy took up the ax and chopped and hated his father. He hated this place, too, and listening to his father crying every night. What was he talking about, babies? He felt bad then, though, because he knew the crying at night was something else, something he was afraid to belittle.

When he had finished the leftover pieces, he went into the woods with the ax looking for dead wood. He found a few pieces, but they were too rotten. Should've known that, he said out loud to himself. When are you going to figure out how to do things right? So he went out to the point again and chopped down another tree and stripped it and sawed it into sections and dragged them back to the cabin.

His father was there working on the racks. Good job, his father said. It looks like you're getting the wood together.

Yeah.

You'll get the hang of all this. Me, too.

But his father cried again that night, and it seemed then to Roy that nothing at all was going to work. He tried to ignore what his father was blubbering to him and tried to have his own conversations in his head, but he couldn't block his father out.

There were two prostitutes in Fairbanks mainly that I went to see. One who had really soft skin and no pubic hair. She was just like a little girl, real small, and she would never look at me.

Roy stuck his fingers in his ears and tried to hum just loudly enough to block his father out and not be heard, but the confessions went on and he had to hear everything.

I kept seeing them, all of them, even when I knew that Rhoda knew.

Rhoda was Roy's stepmother, his father's second marriage and divorce, only recently ended.

I got crabs from one of these prostitutes, and I passed them on to Rhoda. You remember when we were supposed to go skiing that time in California, and we didn't?

This was rare and caught Roy by surprise. He wasn't usually asked questions.

Yeah, he answered. He remembered waking up and it was already midmorning, much too late and something wrong. And he didn't want to hear now that it was all because his father had been with a whore. His father had told him that he had caught the bugs from the bench in the locker room at the YMCA, and Roy had believed him, along with everything else.

That time she got unbelievably angry. She never would give me any room to explain. It was like I was just some kind of monster. Like I'd shafted her. What do you think? Do you think I'm a monster? The question came with the odd whining and gulping.

No, Dad.

Roy's dreams started repeating themselves. In one, he was in a cramped bathroom folding red towels while more red towels kept stacking up and coming in on him, pressing from every side. In another, he was on a bus that was trapped in sand and being swept down a hillside. In another, he was hung up on hooks and he had to choose between getting shot once, which would be quick but could kill him, or being dipped in a large vat of red ants, which wouldn't kill him but would take a very long time.

In the mornings, his father was always in a good mood, and Roy never understood this.

We're doing all right, his father said. We have some smoked fish put away, and some wood, and it's still early in the summer.

Then one day when it was raining hard and Roy came in from the outhouse, he found his father standing in the cabin with his pistol out. He was holding it in one hand, aimed toward the roof, and he was staring up into the darkness of the timbers, moving around like he was trying to get a bead on some big spider up there or something.

What are you doing?

Better just stay out of my way.

What?

Stay out of my way. Get in the other room or something.

What is it?

But his father wouldn't answer again; he just squinted up and sighted the pistol at something that seemed to be moving at the top of the ceiling.

Roy stepped back into the other room and watched his father from the doorway.

His father fired then, the blast deafening. Roy put his hands to his ears but they hurt and wouldn't stop roaring. His father fired again up into the roof, the .44 Magnum a huge pistol and ridiculous and spitting fire in the dim cabin, filling the air with sulfur.

What are you shooting at? Roy yelled but his father only fired again, and again, and again, and then he tossed the pistol down onto a pile of clothes by the door and walked outside into the rain, saying, It's so goddamn tight in here.

Roy went to the door and watched his father standing out there looking up into the rain and getting soaked without his rain gear or hat. His hair matted flat to his scalp and his red mouth open. His eyes closing and opening and closing. Steam coming from his breath and rising off his shirt. His arms limp at his sides as if there were nothing left to do but stand and let the sky come down.

Roy waited so long for his father that finally he sat down

against the stove and stared out through the doorway at the slice of gray air and water and his father soaked and making no sense. When his father started walking finally, Roy got up to see but his father kept walking on into the woods and didn't return until after dark.

There was no light in the cabin when his father returned, and no heat. Roy was in his sleeping bag against the stove and had put cans out for the various drips and streams that came from the new holes in the ceiling. His father came over and lifted him into the other room and told him over and over how sorry he was, but Roy pretended to be asleep and wouldn't listen and only hated and feared him.

When Roy woke in the morning, he was quiet. He grabbed some smoked salmon and crackers, walked out, and sat on the other end of the porch without a word or a look. He just stared down at his plate, though he knew his father was feeling bad about himself and wanted to talk.

His father stood up and leaned against the wall of the cabin. When Roy looked up, his father had his eyes closed and was feeling the sun.

Roy finished his breakfast and waited.

A nice day, his father finally said. Maybe we should go for a hike.

Roy considered.

Well, what do you think of that?

All right.

All right, then, let's go hunting for a buck. We could use something other than salmon, right?

Roy was slow to get his gear together, but finally they were on the trail, his father leading. Roy didn't want any kind of resolution. He wanted things to get bad enough that they would have to leave the island. He could make things terrible for his father, he knew, if he just didn't say anything or respond in any way.

They cleared the low forests and climbed higher and bushwhacked their way over to a rock outcropping from which they could scan two mountainsides and the shoreline and their cabin. Roy wondered whether many deer would come on this side, this close to their cabin, but now they were here, so it looked as if they were going to just try it.

What do you think of this? his father asked.

What do I think of what?

All this. The view. Being out here. Being with your dad.

It's nice.

His father looked out over the channel then and stared at the sun off the water. It was nowhere to look into, just glare. Roy moved around several times to different places to sit on the rock and in the brush, unable to keep still. He wasn't looking for deer. He wondered if his father was looking for deer.

His father put his rifle down and stood and walked too close to the edge of the small cliff and fell off. It looked almost like he stepped off. And then he bounced and sprang out and hit branches, ripping through them and tumbling, and then he was out of sight but Roy could hear him and the top of his own head was rising in hot wavering streaks as he panicked.

Roy grabbed his gun and stood but there was nothing to do. His father was already down through the trees and brush, already loud whumps and it was over and there was no sound

from down there. His blood was in his ears and he was afraid he
would fall over too, as if his father were pulling him, but then
he shouted to his father and set his gun down and ran back into
the brush to where they had come through. He tried to work his
way down fast but the brush was so thick and cutting at him,
and he was scared he would never find his father, that he would
just disappear in there and be dying.

He kept screaming as he went but there was no response.
He slid down through a patch of nettles, his hands on fire from
them, and then fell down through some hemlock and hit a flat
spot and got up and worked his way across to find his father.
He got to about where he thought he'd find him, but saw nothing. He looked up to try to see the cliff for reference, but it was
too thick in here and he couldn't see anything. He whined and
turned in a circle and then got hold of himself and stopped and
listened.

It was only wind and the leaves, but then he heard a moan close
by and parted the growth a few feet in front of him but there
was nothing. He pushed through farther, then backtracked and
checked all around. He couldn't hear the moaning anymore, and
he wondered whether he had only imagined it in the first place.
He started whining again and he couldn't help it and he just kept
looking. Then he had the idea to trample everything down so
he'd know where he'd already looked, so he stomped all around
in bigger and bigger circles, crushing the smaller stuff, and still
he couldn't find anything.

By now it had been at least half an hour, so he hiked back up
to try to find the base of the cliff. That was hard to find, too,
and when he found it he wasn't sure it was the right one, but he

searched below and he found, finally, a recently broken branch. He worked his way down from this to more branches and then a spot in the nettles and flowers and moss that had been crushed. A few feet farther on, he found his father.

His father wasn't moving or making any sound. He was curled on his side with an arm flung out behind, and the eye Roy could see was shut. He came up slowly and knelt down and leaned in close, not wanting to, and listened for breathing or anything, and he did think he heard something but he couldn't separate it from his own breath and told himself it might be just because he wanted to find something. But then he leaned in closer and put his ear to his father's mouth and did feel and hear breath and he said, Dad, and then he was shouting it and trying to make his father wake up. He wanted to shake him but he didn't know whether he should. So he just sat there and tried to talk his father awake.

You fell off the cliff, he said. You fell down here and you hurt yourself but you're all right. Now wake up.

His father's face was swollen and turning purplish already with red streaks where he'd been scraped. His hand was cut up and bloody.

Oh God, Roy said, and he wished he knew what to do or that there could at least be someone else around to help him. His father wasn't waking, and finally he couldn't think of what to do except grab his father under the armpits and start dragging him down the hill to the cabin. There was no trail, but they didn't have to go across anything else and there were no more cliffs that he could remember. So he pulled him down through the undergrowth, trying not to trip but tripping and falling backward occasionally anyway and trying not to drop his father or move him too much but dropping him anyway, dropping his head and seeing it bounce and loll around in the spongy moss, and still his father didn't wake or say anything to him but still he was breathing. And then the sun went down and it was darker but not completely dark when they cleared the last stand of hemlocks. He dragged his father over the grass, past the outhouse and down to the porch of the cabin, where he had to rest after each porch step before pulling his father up onto the next, and finally he had him inside the cabin.

He laid him in the main room on a blanket and put the other blankets and sleeping bags over him. He propped his head up on a pillow and he got wood for the fire. It was still fairly wet and it smoked too much but finally dried itself out in the stove after repeated lightings and then they had some warmth at least.

His father looked very pale. Roy put his hand next to his father's cheek to see the difference in their color. He was breathing, but only shallowly. Roy wanted to give his father some water but didn't know if he should. He wanted to put an ice pack on his head but there was no ice and he didn't know if that was the right idea anyway. He didn't know anything. He just sat back against the wall with his jacket over him and waited and watched for any changes as the light disappeared outside and the cabin grew smaller. The wind came up and the cabin creaked and let out a low howl occasionally and still his father lay there like a wax figure pale with his mouth open and red streaks on his face that didn't look real, as if he'd been painted. Even the hair didn't look right, and then the lamp went out and Roy was somehow too afraid to get up and find the paraffin in the dark so he only waited there seeing nothing, listening for hours until finally he fell asleep.

Waking in daylight he didn't know what had happened, couldn't make sense of his father lying in front of him like that, then he remembered. He went over to feel his father's face and his skin was still warm and he was breathing.

Wake up, Roy said. Come on. I'll fix pancakes. Cream-of-mushroom soup. Come on. Wake up.

Not a twitch from his father. Roy got the fire going again and the cabin slowly warmed. He stood in the doorway and looked out at the water, where there was no one, not a single boat. He came back in and shut the door, refilled the lamp and waited. Still his father hadn't moved. He wondered if a body could be dead and still breathing, and this thought was so creepy that he got up to fix breakfast.

Hotcakes coming right up, he called back over his shoulder as he mixed up the Krusteaz with water. He put some of the powdered milk in the mix as a special treat, got the pan hot and oiled and started making pancakes with an intense concentration on the bubbles as they formed, worrying constantly about whether they were cooking too much on the underside, afraid also that he might flip too early before they had browned. He took his time with each one and waited until he had a perfect stack before he turned around and saw his father lying there with his eyes open watching him.

Roy yelled and dropped the plate. His father's head moved slightly, the eyes on him. Dad, he said then, and he rushed over and his father said, in a whisper he could barely hear, Water.

Roy brought him water and helped him drink some of it, held the cup to his lips. His father threw up the water and then drank again.

Sorry, his father said, and then he closed his eyes and slept the rest of the day, Roy fearing all the time that he might fall back into a sleep that he wouldn't wake from. He wondered whether he should run out to the point with flares and try to signal someone, but he was afraid to leave his father for that long, and he didn't know, anyway, whether his father wanted him to set off the flares. He whispered it twice, Should I go set off the flares, Dad? But there was no response.

When his father woke again, it was near sunset and Roy had been on the verge of falling asleep but had opened his eyes for just a second and saw his father looking at him.

You're awake, he said. How are you doing?

His father didn't answer for a long time. Okay, he finally said. Some food. Water.

What kind of food?

His father considered for a while. Soup. Do we have?

You can't breathe, can you? Roy said. You can't say anything. Maybe I should go set off the flares, all right? I'll try and get some help.

No, his father said. No. Soup.

So Roy heated up the cream-of-mushroom he had planned for the pancakes. It was one of the last cans of anything because of the bear. He brought it to his father and fed him slowly with a spoon.

His father could eat only a few bites before he said, Enough for now.

What about the cuts and stuff? Roy asked. I didn't know what to do.

It's okay.

Roy brought him more water, lit the lamp and stoked the stove, and they waited together, not saying anything, until his father called for more soup and then more water and then rested and then fell asleep again.

In the morning, when Roy awoke, his father had pulled his arms from beneath the blankets to rest them on top. Only one was cut up, and it had scabbed over by now.

I should go light the flares, Roy said. You still can't get up. You might have something really wrong.

Listen, his father said. If we leave now, we won't come back. And I don't want to give this up yet. You have to give me another chance. I won't let anything stupid like that happen again. I promise.

I thought you were going to die, Roy said.

I know. I'm sorry. You don't have to worry about it anymore.

It looked like you just stepped off.

I got too close to the edge. It's all right.

So they waited. Roy fed him soup and water again, and then his father had to go to the bathroom.

I have to go, he said. And I can't get up by myself. Grab some TP and come help me up.

Roy grabbed the toilet paper and got behind his father to pull him up under his armpits. His father was able to help some with his legs, then with a hand on the table, and so they were able to stand and then make it to the door, where they rested.

It doesn't seem like you broke anything, Roy said.

No, it doesn't, his father said. I was really lucky.

They rested against the door for a few more minutes while his father looked out at the cove. Then they moved along the outside wall and out to the steps and took them one at a time, Roy going first, his father leaning on him.

This is gonna work, his father said. We'll be fine. I'm just a little sore and stiff, but it won't last.

They rested at the bottom of the steps.

The outhouse might actually be easier, his father said. Even though it's farther away.

I can try to carry you, Roy said.

I think I can walk if you help me.

So his father hung on him. They stepped slowly toward the outhouse, resting every ten or twenty feet, and then it started drizzling faintly but they decided to keep going and made it to the outhouse, where his father got help turning around and sitting and then Roy stepped outside to wait.

Roy standing there in the drizzle felt things he could not make sense of. His enormous fear had mostly lifted, but a part of him that he did not understand well wanted his father to have died in the fall so that there would have been a kind of relief and everything could be clear and he could simply return to his life. But he was afraid to think this, as if it were a kind of jinx, and the thought that he could have lost his father made his eyes well up suddenly so that when his father called out from inside that he was done, Roy was trying not to cry, trying to fight it down in his throat and eyes.

His father extended a hand when Roy opened the door. Help me up, he said. But he still had his pants down and Roy couldn't help looking at his penis hanging there and the hair on his thighs. Then he was embarrassed and tried to look away as if he hadn't looked.

His father didn't say anything. When he was standing, still holding on to Roy's hand, he pulled up his pants with the other, then turned to lean against the doorjamb so that he'd have both hands to button. Then they went on to the cabin, where his father lay back down, ate and drank a little bit, and slept the rest of the day.

Over the next week, his father strengthened. He became limber again, enough to walk himself to the outhouse and then walk around out front slowly and then finally walk out to the point and back. Soon after, he announced himself fully well.

Back from the grave, he said. Lungs never felt better. And I'm not gonna let anything like that happen again, I promise you.

Roy wanted to ask again whether his father had stepped off on purpose, because that was the way it had looked, but he didn't.

They hunted and shot deer, the first from the pass behind the cabin shooting down the other side. His father let Roy take the shot and he hit it in the neck. He had been aiming low behind the shoulder and so was way off, but he let it seem afterward that he had intended the neck.

They found it sprawled in the blueberries, its tongue hanging out and eyes still clear.

Good deal, his father said. This will be good meat. He unslung his rifle and got out his Buck knife. He slit up the stomach, pulled out the entrails, bled the neck, cut off the balls and everything else down there, and then slotted the hind legs and pushed the forelegs through to make a kind of backpack.

Normally I'd carry it, he said. But my back and side are still a bit sore, if you don't mind.

So while his father carried both rifles, Roy put the hooked hind legs over his shoulders, the deer's butt behind his head, and carried him that way up the side of the mountain and down the other side, the antlers banging his ankles.

They hung the buck and stripped off the hide, punching down between meat and hide with their fists. Then they cut most of the meat into strips and dried them on the rack or smoked them.

The rack's not going to be great, his father said. Not enough sun and too many flies. But we'll smoke most of it.

They stretched the hide just as it was getting dark, then salted it and turned in.

His father did not cry that night, nor had he since the fall. Roy listened and waited, tense and unable to sleep, but the crying simply never came, and after a few more nights, he got used to this and learned to sleep.

They set about stocking up for winter more seriously now. When his father was strong enough to work again, they dug a huge pit a hundred yards from the cabin, back in a small stand of hemlock. They dug with shovels until his father was shoulder deep and Roy in over his head. Then they widened it until it was over ten feet on every side, a huge square cut into the hillside, and after that they deepened it some more and used their home-made ladder to get in and out. When they hit a large stone, they dug around and beneath until it was free and then hauled it out by rope. They stopped when they hit solid rock and there was nowhere left to go.

The hole was to be their cache, but once the hole was dug, his father had second thoughts. I don't know, he said. I don't know how it doesn't mold, or how bugs don't get to it. And I don't know how to make it easy for us to get to stuff inside without it being easy for bears to get inside. And this whole place is going to be covered in snow, too.

Roy listened and looked down into the huge pit they had dug for a week. He didn't know, either. He had just assumed his father knew more about this.

They stood there some more until his father said, Well, let's think this thing out. We can put the food in plastic bags. It may mold, but it can't get wet or get bugs in it.

Are we supposed to build some kind of shed or something in there? Roy asked. Or do we just bury it all?

The pictures I've seen, they're made out of logs, whether they're in the ground or up in the air.

Okay, Roy said.

Let's sleep on it, his father said.

So they fished out on the point as the day drizzled and faded and then cooked salmon again for dinner and turned in.

Roy had trouble sleeping and lay awake for a long time. Hours later, he heard his father begin to cry.

In the morning, Roy remembered and stayed in his sleeping bag and did not get up until late. His father was already gone, and when Roy walked up to the pit, his father was standing down inside it with his arms folded, staring at the walls.

Let's think this thing out, his father said. We've dug a pit. We have a big pit here now. And we need to store our food in it. We need a low cabin-like thing, I think, and a door that we can get into but a bear can't. The door could be on the top or it could be on a side with an entrance that slants down to it. I'm thinking the door should be on top and nailed shut and buried. What do you think?

His father looked up at him then. Roy was thinking, you're not any better. Nothing has gotten better. You could decide just to bury yourself in there or something. But what he said was, How do we get to the food?

Good question, his father said. I've been thinking about this, and I think that a cache is what you save for late in the winter. You stock up in the cabin and just don't leave it. You keep your rifles ready and you shoot any bears that come by. And then when you finally run out, you still have something left. You come up here and dig and take it all and you're ready to go again. Or maybe you come up twice, but not more than that. So we don't have to have any easy access. And the reason the food keeps is that it's all frozen in addition to being smoked or dried and salted.

That sounds right, Roy said.

Voilà, his father said, raising his arms. I'm good for something, huh?

Maybe.

His father laughed. Maybe, huh? My boy's getting a sense of humor. Starting to feel at home out here, are you?

Roy smiled. A little bit, I guess.

All right.

They celebrated then by cutting down a bunch of trees and cutting them into posts for the walls of the cache. That took all day. By nightfall, they had the posts hauled to the edge of the pit.

We'll put them in tomorrow, his father said. Happen to have about a mile of twine on you?

No.

Well, we'll think of something. We don't have enough nails, either. But we'll think of something.

That night, Roy stayed awake again waiting for the crying, needing to know if it was every night, but then he woke in the morning and wondered whether it had not happened or he had simply not stayed awake long enough. It was hard to know. His father was hiding from him now, and Roy had to pretend he didn't know this.

They shoveled enough dirt back in to bury the posts side by side. They weren't attached in any other way, just buried next to one another.

I think they'll stay like that, his father said. Just the pressure of everything on the inside against everything on the outside.

What about when we take the food out, Roy asked, or when a bear digs down and tries to take it apart?

His father looked at him, considering. He looked at him more plainly than Roy was used to, so that Roy avoided his eyes and looked at the light beard his father had now and the hair longer on the sides and flattened against his skull from not being washed. He didn't look anything like a dentist anymore, or really even like his father. He looked like some other man who maybe didn't have much.

You're thinking, his father said. This is good. We can talk about what we're doing. I've been thinking about the same things, and it seems to me that we have to bury it deep enough and put enough stuff on top that a bear can't dig down, because if he does get down there, no way of putting the cache together will keep him out.

Roy nodded. He didn't know if it would work, but it made sense at least.

And when we take stuff out, finally, late in February maybe, the ground will be so frozen that nothing will move. It won't be able to cave in even if we take the wood away completely, which we may need to do for our stove.

Roy smiled. That sounds good.

All right.

They placed the rest of the posts, like the walls of a small fort town only a few feet high, and then sat back to look at it.

It needs a roof, Roy said.

And a door. We'll cut long poles that go clear across, and we'll figure out the door in the roof. Probably just a big hole with a second roof over it.

We don't have the food to go into it yet, Roy said.

Right you are. And we won't put it in until it snows. Until then, we have to keep it from caving.

We should have waited to dig it until a few months from now, huh?

Yeah. We dug it too early. But that's okay. We didn't know.

Over the next two days, in the rain, they cut the poles for a roof and a smaller second roof. They sawed the lengths and stripped off the branches with a hatchet, Roy watching this father with his grim unshaven face when he worked, the cold rain dripping off the end of his nose. He seemed as solid then as a figure carved from stone, and all his thoughts as immutable, and Roy could not reconcile this father with the other, the one who wept and despaired and had nothing about him that could last. Though Roy had memory, it seemed nonetheless that whatever father he was with at the time was the only father that could be, as if each in its time could burn away the others completely.

When they had finished cutting the poles for both roofs, they placed them all carefully and stood back to see. The sides were already washing in around the posts and caving the roof, rivulets of mud everywhere in the unceasing rain.

Some of the posts are soft, his father said. They're getting washed out. Oh well.

How can we stop it from caving in?

I don't know. We don't have enough tarp. Maybe I screwed up. Maybe it was too early. We should just be storing up now, I guess.

That night, Roy did not have to wait long to hear his father weep. It came within only a few minutes, and his father wasn't trying to hide it anymore.

Sorry, his father said. It's not the cache or anything like that. It's other things.

What is it?

Well, my head hurts all the time, but that's not it.

Your head hurts?

Yeah. It has for years. You didn't know that?

No.

Well.

Why does it hurt?

It's just sinuses, and I'm supposed to have them cleared out, but I haven't bothered. It doesn't always work anyway, and it's an awful operation. But that's not the problem. That's just what makes me feel weak and makes it easy to cry and keeps me tired. The bigger thing is that I just can't seem to be alone.

And his father started crying again. I know I'm not alone, he whimpered. I know you're here. But I'm still too alone. I can't explain it.

Roy waited for more, but his father only cried then and it went on for a long time, Roy not knowing how it was that he could be right here and still, for his father, it was as if he wasn't here at all.

The rain continued and the cache washed in further. Roy and his father stood at the edge looking down at the fallen posts and thinking and not saying anything until finally his father said, Well, let's pull all the wood out and we'll try it again when it first snows.

Roy didn't believe they'd still be here when it first snowed, but he nodded as his father climbed down in and then he took the pieces his father handed him and carried them back to the cabin. Roy knew that somehow this disappointment was worse for his father than the other disappointments had been. If Roy spoke now, he doubted he'd be heard. And he understood this about his father, that he was often gone into his own thoughts and couldn't be reached, and that none of this time spent alone thinking was good for him, that he always sank lower when he went in there.

They stacked the wood against a side wall, and when they

were done, they looked again at the pit, at the mud deepening and the walls caving, and both looked into the sky, into the grayness that had no depth or end, and then they went inside.

When the plane came a few days later, Roy was fishing several miles up the coast. He thought he heard it, then thought he must have made it up, but stopped and listened and heard it again. He pulled in his line, grabbed the two salmon he had caught, and started running. He was far enough off, though, and blocked by so many small points along the way, that he couldn't see it fly into the mouth of their cove. He ran over the rocky beach and, when he had to, up into the trees and down again, becoming more and more afraid that he would miss it. He assumed his father was there cutting wood, but what if he had hiked back over the ridge for some reason and no one was there? The pilot might not come back again for a long time, might just leave a note saying, Call me on the radio if you need anything. And there was another thing, too, that Roy didn't like to admit. Even if his father was there, what would he say? Was there a chance he would just say everything was fine and send the pilot away and not have him come back? It didn't seem impossible, and Roy needed to leave here, he needed to get away. Roy dropped the fish and his pole and ran faster.

He was only a few hundred yards from the final point when he heard the drone of it again and stopped to see it rush out of the mouth, tilt free of its own spray, and lift precariously over the channel. He stood there then, looking at where it had finally disappeared and breathing hard and feeling that something terrible had happened.

He left, he said out loud. I missed him.

He went back then for his pole and the salmon and walked on to the cabin.

His father was back at the woodpile. Tom came by, he said when Roy walked up.

I heard.

Oh. Well he was just here a minute but I ordered the supplies we need and he'll be back with them next week on his way to Juneau. Though not really on his way exactly, I suppose. And his father grinned then, pleased at how in the middle of nowhere they were.

Roy took his salmon down to the water and gutted them. He scaled them quickly and cut off their heads and fins and tails. He wanted out of here. He didn't care what his father thought about it; he was just going to go.

You want to leave? his father asked when he told him at dinner.

Roy didn't say it again but just ate. He felt terrible, as if he were killing his father.

We're not doing so bad, are we? his father asked.

Roy refused to cave in. He didn't say anything.

I don't understand, his father said. We're finally getting somewhere. We're getting ready for winter.

Why? Roy thought to himself. Just so we can survive winter? But he didn't say anything.

Look, his father said. You're gonna have to talk to me about this, otherwise you're just staying and that's that.

Okay, Roy said.

Why do you have to go?

I want my friends again, and my real life. I don't want to just try to survive winter.

Fair enough. But what about me? You told me you'd stay out here a year, and I made my plans. I quit my job and bought this place. What am I supposed to do if you just leave?

I don't know.

You haven't thought about that, have you?

No. Roy felt awful. I'm sorry, he said.

That's all right, his father said. If you need to go, then you need to go. I won't stop you.

Roy wanted to say right then that he'd stay, but he couldn't. He knew terrible things were going to happen to him out here if he stayed. He did the dishes and then they went to bed.

You know, his father said that night as they lay not sleeping, it's too out of control here. You're right. It takes a man to get through this. I shouldn't have brought a boy.

Roy couldn't believe his father was saying these things to him. He didn't sleep that night. He wanted to leave. He wanted to get out of here. But as the night went on, he knew that he'd be staying. He kept imagining his father out here alone, and he knew his father needed him. By the morning, Roy felt so bad he fixed pancakes and told his father, I've thought more about it and I don't think I really want to go.

Really? his father said, and he came up and put an arm around his boy's shoulders. Now we're talking, he said, beaming. We can lick this thing. We'll have fresh supplies and we'll put away enough fish and meat and I have a new idea for the roof of the cache. I was thinking . . .

And his father went on and on, excited, but Roy stopped

hearing him. He didn't believe anymore in exciting plans. He felt he had just put himself in a kind of prison, and it was too late to back out.

That day they began picking blueberries. They had been out here over a month, late July now, and though it was still a bit early for berry season, the berries would be fine for making jam. They picked into freezer bags, Roy remembering Ketchikan and his red coat with the hood and all the times they had hiked onto the hill behind the house to pick blueberries. They had churned homemade ice cream, soupy and rich, and stirred the berries in. He remembered the smoky smell of the air, too, and all the fall colors. It wasn't only the trees that turned in Alaska, it was everything, all the growth, and it began turning in early August. Still too early here, but it was coming soon. In more northern parts, in Fairbanks, where his father had lived, it would begin turning very soon, perhaps even now, and by September fifteenth, nearly all the tiny leaves on the blueberry bushes would have fallen and most of the leaves on the trees, also, the end of fall and beginning of the snows. Here it would be later, but not much later. One summer in Ketchikan, he remembered, it had snowed in August. He had ridden his tricycle out into it and tried to catch the flakes on his tongue.

Later in the day, they stood on the point and caught salmon every few casts. The schools were coming in finally, not just a few isolated salmon anymore. They could see them in thick beneath the clear water, dark shapes in rows undulating slowly and in time, another thing Roy remembered. They had pulled into small coves like this one in the cabin cruiser and Roy had stood on the bow with his father and looked at all of them gathered below him and he had come to believe that all waters were like this, that all waters were so populated. The Pixies bright in among them now, just as before, Roy dragging his across their noses until one rushed forward and took it, then flashed silver as Roy yanked to set the hook. He whooped like his father did whenever he caught one, and it seemed then not so bad that they would stay out here. Roy gutted his fish when he had caught five, then ran rope through the gills.

When we really get going, his father said, we'll be dragging twenty or thirty salmon a day back to the cabin. We'll be so busy we'll wish we had a second smoker.

The plane returned the next week with their supplies: more baggies, plywood, seeds, canned goods and staples, huge bags of brown sugar and salt, a new radio and batteries, Louis L'Amour Westerns for his father, a new sleeping bag and surprise tub of chocolate ice cream for Roy. The arrival of the plane made it seem they weren't really that far away, as if a town and other people like Tom were maybe just around the point. Roy felt relaxed and happy and safe and didn't realize until the plane started up again and was taxiing out that that feeling wasn't going to stay. As he watched it go, he realized he was starting over, that now it would again be a month or two, or maybe longer, and he remembered, too, that they had planned to get away for at least a week at the end of summer, which was now. That had been the plan, and somehow it had not happened.

But he didn't have much time to dwell on this. He and his father grew busier and busier in their preparations. They were up early and still working often past dusk. The mountains changing quickly then, turning purple and yellow and red, seeming to soften more in the late light, the air colder and cleaner and thinning each day, Roy and his father bundled now in their jackets and hats as they pulled in the salmon, as they cut more wood and stacked it behind the plywood walls. The time easy between them, busy and unthinking, working together to store up. Roy slept. If his father cried, he didn't know, and for a while, at least, he didn't care as much, perhaps because he knew now that he couldn't get away, that he had committed himself and would stay here with his father whether his father were sick or well.

They began the home schooling in the evenings, just two or three evenings that first week. Roy read *Moby Dick* and his father read Louis L'Amour. Roy wrote down answers to detailed and picky and seemingly insignificant questions about plot and theme and his father said, Now that was a real Western. After a week of this, they realized they just didn't have time for it with all the other preparations, so they put it off and went back to cutting wood and smoking fish and hunting full time.

They hunted anything now, anything they came across that they could smoke. They killed a cow moose several miles away in a marshy flat where a stream gathered before spilling into the ocean. She was alone and looking at them, chewing, her shaggy hide dark and dripping and they both fired and she went down immediately, as if she had been crushed by a great stone. His father carried the carcass back one haunch at a time while Roy guarded the rest, a shell in the chamber, looking all around him as it grew dark, watching for the red eyes of bears and whatever else his imagination could think of to fear.

They harvested salmon as his father had promised, in long

strings that they dragged back to the cabin, the open mouths still gasping, the bodies reddish late in the season and trembling on land. They caught as many as they had time to clean and cut up and smoke, the pink and red and white meat of chinook, sockeye, humpies, and chum.

They shot a mountain goat that had come down to the shoreline, Roy wondering at how red the blood looked at first against the white hair, and then how black. By this time it was cold enough that the animal steamed as they gutted it. The mountains the next morning had snow all along their tops, as if the spirit of the white animal had somehow fled into them, and within the week, the snow had lowered halfway down toward the cabin and sat still and windless and bright throughout the afternoon.

They set to work again on the cache. It had become rounded in all its corners and the earth around it had slumped. They dug it out shovelful by shovelful and sharpened its edges and deepened it again to the base rock and then Roy handed down the posts to his father, the posts lashed this time with twine and the corners nailed. Then they set the poles across the top and lashed them as well and nailed them along their edges with ten-inch nails deep into the posts and then they lashed together a small second roof and placed it over the uneven hole in the top and stood back and admired their work.

It looks right, Roy said.

It's ready for the goods.

The spare room in the cabin by this time was full with dried and smoked fish and meat carefully packaged in freezer bags then larger garbage bags. They began early one morning so that they'd be finished burying by dark and not have to keep watch over it during the night. His father placed all of the bags inside along with a large pile of canned goods that had been flown in, in case all the smoked fish and meat spoiled for some reason, and then he nailed down the second roof.

Hope it stays good, he said.

It better, Roy said, and his father grinned.

Let's bury it and forget about it.

So they threw in a deep layer of cold ash they had saved from the stove to mask the smell, and then a layer of rocks, then the dirt and they heaped it up high so that when it settled it would be level, and then they put more rocks on top of that and another layer of ash.

I don't know if any of this is right, his father said, but it seems like it should work.

They continued to catch the last of the salmon and also a few Dolly Varden and some small bottom fish. The original plan had been to go out in the inflatable for halibut, too, but his father had decided to save the boat and all of its gasoline for any kind of emergency that might come up. They shot another mountain goat. The smoker was going around the clock still, even as the first snows came down to the cabin, and the inside of the cabin seemed a smokehouse also with strips of salmon and Dolly Varden and sculpin and lingcod and deer and goat everywhere cooling and waiting to be bagged, the baggies and garbage bags that had already been filled piling up in the spare room.

They went to bed each night exhausted, and there was no time left awake to listen for his father, and so Roy managed on some nights even to forget that his father was not well. He began, even, to assume that his father was fine, in that he didn't think about his father one way or the other. He was simply living each day filled with activity and then sleeping and then rising again, and since he was working alongside his father, he assumed his father was feeling all the same things. If he had been asked how his father was feeling, he would have been annoyed at the question and considered the matter too far away to pay attention to.

Most of the snows were light and did not stick for long down close to the water or even for a ways up behind the cabin. They did not cover the cache consistently. Roy asked his father if the weather would stay like this, because it seemed like it might be the case. His father had to tip his head back to remember.

They didn't stick long, most of the snows in Ketchikan. But then I remember skiing around, and snowbanks, and shoveling snow and all the slush I had to drive through, so I guess the snow did stick and build up sometimes. Isn't that funny, though, that I can't really remember?

They went up to the cache several times a day and looked for bear tracks or any other tracks, but nothing ever came. The constant checking began to seem odd to both of them, as if they had developed some inexplicable fear of this one small piece of ground, so they decided to check less often and just trust that it would be all right, especially since it was growing colder and the days shorter. They came in earlier each evening from their work at the woodpile and the smoker and began reading again and sometimes played cards. They played two-handed pinochle, which technically could not be played, and his father rambled.

Remember what I told you about the world originally being a great field, and the earth flat?

Yeah, Roy said. How everything went to hell after you met Mom.

Whoa, his father said. That's not exactly what I said. But anyway, I've been thinking about that again, and it's got me thinking about what I'm missing and why I don't have religion but need it anyway.

What? Roy asked.

I'm screwed, basically. I need the world animated, and I need it to refer to me. I need to know that when a glacier shifts or a bear farts, it has something to do with me. But I also can't believe any of that crap, even though I need to.

What does that have to do with Mom?

I don't know. You're getting me sidetracked.

So they finished the hand and went to bed. But Roy kept thinking of his father's ramblings, and it seemed to him a strange father out here. It was his tone of voice more than anything, as if the creation of the world had amounted to the Big Screw. But Roy didn't think too much about it. He really wanted only to sleep.

The snow stuck lower and they quit fishing and smoking and chopping wood.

We have enough anyway, his father said. It's time now to settle in and relax. That should last about two weeks before I go insane.

What?

I'm just kidding, his father said. That was a joke.

They read by the light of the paraffin lamps and kept the stove stoked. Roy had as much trouble concentrating on his homework here as he had anywhere else, so he spent most of his long hours studying the wavering shadows on the plank walls and waiting for the next meal. It was the most delicious and anticipated food he had ever eaten, all the smoked fish and meat with rice and canned vegetables. His father read and sighed and sacked out for long naps.

They took hikes still, and brought their rifles, but as the snow built up thicker this became too difficult, so as Roy studied, his father began making snowshoes. He used fresh branches and strips of the moose hide they had salted and let dry. As it snowed and blew outside and occasionally rained, he bent over the shoes like the dentist he was, sewing them up carefully and inspecting them with prodding fingers. Red-eye, he finally said, his way of saying ready. They're finished. We're going into the snow, my son.

But it just rained, Roy reminded him.

Yeah, that's right. Okay, we'll wait until there's snow again, and then we go. But in the meantime, I have to go for a hike before I decay into some kind of marshmallow in here.

Me, too, Roy said, so they went for a hike along the water. It was overcast and drizzling, the waves indistinct, the waters shifting, surging. They walked along the steeper coast that they rarely hiked along, around the opposite point and on farther to the next in silence until his father said, I don't think I can live without women. I'm not saying it isn't great being out here with you, but I just miss women all the time. I can't stop thinking about them. I don't know what it is. I don't know how it is that something is so thoroughly missing when they're not around. It's like we have the ocean here and a mountain and trees, but actually the trees aren't here unless I'm fucking some woman.

Huh, Roy said.

Sorry, his father said. I'm just thinking out loud. I'm also thinking we can't leave our food for this long. If another bear comes, we're screwed.

So his father went back but Roy decided to hike on for a while, and though he thought he would try to think about what his father had said, he only looked at the water and at the smooth rocks beneath his boots and he didn't think anything.

When he returned, his father was listening to the new ham radio. There was a clicking sound over and over and then a voice gave the standard universal time and a storm report for the South Pacific, gale-force winds everywhere it seemed. Then another channel and warping sounds with a guy far in the background talking about his great ham equipment, which was all anyone ever talked about on ham radio, pretty much, and his father turned it off and began cooking some rice.

Tom should be here again soon, his father said.

Yeah?

Yeah. And I was thinking. I want us to stay here longer, but I know it's not fun to hear me talk about things like I talked about today, so if you want to go back to your mom and Tracy, you can. That would be okay.

We have to quit talking about that, Roy said. I already said I'm staying.

His father didn't turn and look at Roy during any of this, and Roy knew his allegiance was being tested, that it was being gauged, so he added, I don't want to go. I'm staying here until next summer.

Okay, his father said, and still he didn't turn around.

Tom came again and told them it was going to start snowing more. He was standing on one pontoon and they were standing on shore, about fifteen feet away, as if in a different world, unapproachable from the water. I won't always be able to fly in, Tom said, when the weather's bad, and I won't just be checking in on my way to other places anymore, so if you need anything, you need to call me on the radio.

Okay, Roy's father said. That's fine.

Is the radio working okay?

Yeah.

You have a VHF too, and you should be able to hail anyone passing through on that, and they can pass a message on to me. In case you have any more bears over for dinner. Tom grinned then. He was freshly shaven and showered and his clothes clean and he was starting to get cold out on the pontoon. Roy realized he had some kind of heater in the plane.

All right, Tom said. Enjoy.

He climbed up into the plane and started the engine and taxied around. They waved and then he roared away and was gone.

We're here now, his father said. That we are. And the two gone into the wilderness knew not the excesses of mankind and lived in purity.

You sound like the Bible, Dad.

We shall trot through snow like horses and know more winter than Jack Frost. The lichen and the high reaches shall cleanse our souls.

I don't even know what that sounds like.

It's poetry. Your father is one of the undiscovered minor geniuses.

Roy laughed, and then he realized it had been a while. Then he followed his father inside.

It did begin snowing a few days later, as Tom had predicted, and they tried out the snowshoes. Though the shoes felt unwieldy tied onto their boots, they actually worked well. Roy and his father rose high on the mountain with what seemed to Roy more ease than before, since the earth was no longer pitted and they didn't have to tear through the undergrowth or look carefully to see what would support them and what wouldn't. With the shoes, they sank no more than a few inches with each step, and everywhere the path was clear. It was cold, but they had many layers on and, as they climbed, they began shedding layers. It was clear and sunny. They could see past the near islands to other horizons beyond, farther than they had seen before.

This is what most people never see, his father said. Most never see this place in winter, and certainly not from their own mountain on a sunny day. What we are is lucky.

They climbed to the very top and stood on the rocks and it was still clear. They saw their entire island behind and no other sign of humanity on it, only white mountains and the darker trees spreading below.

His father spread his arms and yelped.

Roy wondered and heard the echoing.

I am so happy to be alive, his father said.

Since it was still early in the day, they continued partway down the other side and hiked on to the next ridge and up to the next peak. Another glorious view, and a different one.

Down there in that valley is where I killed the bear, his father said.

Wow. That's a long ways.

It was.

They walked around the top, taking in all the different views.

If you could have anything you wanted, his father said, what would it be?

I don't know, Roy said.

You're not giving the question any time to seep into your bones, me boy. What would it be? What's your dream?

Roy thought and couldn't come up with anything. It seemed to him he was just trying to get through this one dream of his father's. But finally he said, A big boat, that I could sail to Hawaii on, and then maybe around the world.

Ah, his father said. That is a good one.

What about you?

What about me. What about me. So many things. I think a good marriage and not to have broken up the two I had, and not to have been a dentist, and not to have the IRS after me, and after that, maybe a son like you and maybe a big boat.

He gave Roy a hug then, which took Roy completely by surprise. He felt embarrassed when his father finally let go of him. His father was going to cry, he knew.

But then luckily his father turned and headed back down the slope. They continued on without talking, and by the time they were descending to the cabin, the awful locked-in feeling had gone away and Roy said, Who's been eating my porridge? Who's been sleeping in my bed?

His father laughed. It would be time for the cache, all right.

When they had their shoes off and were inside with the stove going, his father said, You know, I've been thinking about what you said about already having said that you're staying, and you're right. I don't have to feel bad and apologetic after everything I say. I can just trust that you can handle a few things. After all, I'm never going to be perfect or without troubles, and I want to be able to talk with you and want you to know me, so I'm not going to keep apologizing like that.

I think that's good, Roy said.

I appreciate it, his father said.

Roy read from his history book then, thinking he never had weird talks like this with his mother and then missing her. She and his sister would be having dinner now, listening to the same classical music, whatever it was, that they always listened to, and his mom asking Tracy all about everything and Tracy getting to talk to her. But then his father seemed to be doing better, too, and this wasn't so bad, so he read on about the guillotine and tried to forget about home.

A few other things, too, his father said. I've been thinking about Rhoda and thinking that maybe things could still work with her. I'm having a more positive attitude. I think I could be more attentive like she wants, and make good on my promises and not lie to her. I think I could do those things now. I don't mean to make them sound like merit badges, like little tasks I can just check off, but I think I could do better now. I might call the operator on the shortwave.

Sounds good, Roy said. And he kept reading. *The people ran in terror of each other like a band of criminals caught, each wondering who would speak and betray the other, as if each had a knife at the other's back.* It seemed like he was getting very little actual information in this book. It was supposed to be a history book. Weren't there supposed to be facts?

They played cards again late in the evening, and his father won every hand.

My luck's a-changing, he said. I am a new man grown out of the ashes. My wings are of the eagle and I shall fly far above.

God, Roy said.

His father laughed. Okay, that was a bit much.

They continued to explore more of the island by snowshoe, only on clear days at first but then on overcast and even snowy days as well. They traveled farther and farther until one afternoon they lost all visibility and were still at least four or five hours' hike from the cabin.

Huh, his father said. He was standing only a few feet from Roy and still it was hard for Roy to see his father's jacket and hood and the scarf wrapped around his face. He seemed a shadow that could be there but might not be there. His father said something else, but Roy couldn't hear it clearly over the wind. He yelled to his father that he couldn't hear.

I said I think I screwed up, his father yelled.

Great, Roy said, but only loud enough for himself to hear.

His father came closer, leaning against him. We can do several things. Can you hear me?

Yeah.

We can hike back and try to find it and try to make it before dark, but we might not and we might get tired and cold and get stuck. Or we can use what's left of daylight and our energy and build a snow cave and hope it's better tomorrow. We won't have much to eat that way, but we might be safer.

The snow cave sounds fun, Roy yelled.

This isn't about fun, his father said.

I know, Roy yelled.

Oh. Sorry. And his father turned away then and Roy had to follow close not to lose him. They went to a stand of cedars, and up against a bank behind the trees where the snow was thick they began tunneling into the side of it. They were out of the wind already, and now Roy could hear his father's hard breathing.

What if it collapses? Roy asked.

Let's hope it doesn't. I've never dug one of these before, but I know people do use them from time to time.

They dug until they hit ground and then they continued enlarging from inside, but the angles were all wrong.

We'll never be able to sleep in here, his father said.

So they moved over a bit and dug a smaller entrance down lower and his father went in on his stomach to dig out from the inside until the roof collapsed on him and only his feet stuck out. Roy threw himself on the pile and dug wildly at it to unbury his father until his father finally backed out and stood up and said, Damnit.

They stood there like that, breathing hard, listening to the wind and feeling it get colder.

Got any ideas? his father asked.

You don't know how to make one?

That's why I'm asking.

Maybe we need deeper snow, Roy said. Maybe we can't dig a snow cave with what we have here.

His father thought about that for a while. You know, he finally said, you might be right. I guess we're hiking back to the cabin. As much as that's a stupid idea, I can't think of anything else. Can you?

No.

So they set off up the ridge, exposed again to the wind. Roy fought to keep up, to not lose his father. He knew that if he lost sight of him even for a minute, his father would never hear him yell and he'd be lost and never find his way back. Watching the dark shadow moving before him, it seemed as if this were what he had felt for a long time, that his father was something insubstantial before him and that if he were to look away for an instant or forget or not follow fast enough and will him to be there, he might vanish, as if it were only Roy's will that kept him there. Roy became more and more afraid, and tired, with a sense that he could not continue on, and he began to feel sorry for himself, telling himself, It's too much for me to have to do.

When his father stopped, finally, Roy bumped into his back.

We're over the ridge now. I think we go along this and have one more before the cabin. I wish I knew what time it was. It seems like it's still daylight, but it's impossible to tell how much of it is left.

They stood and rested a moment and then his father asked, Are you doing all right?

I'm tired, Roy said, and I'm starting to shiver.

His father unwrapped his scarf and Roy thought he was going to give it to him, but he only tied it around Roy's arm and then to his own. That's hypothermia, his father said. We have to keep moving. You can't give in to the tiredness and you can't sleep. We have to keep moving.

So they hiked on, and Roy's footsteps became softer and it seemed a longer time between them. He remembered riding in the back of his father's Suburban from Fairbanks to Anchorage, the sleeping bags piled in there and the road lolling him back and forth. His sister had been back there in a sleeping bag, too, and they had stopped at a log cabin that had giant hamburgers and pancakes bigger than any Roy had seen.

Roy was dimly aware of darkness and later of day and hitting hard and waking and then the rocking again and then, when he awoke, he was in their cabin in a sleeping bag in the dark and his father was behind him and he could tell they were both naked, could feel the hair from his father's chest and legs on the back of him. He was afraid to move but he got up and found a flashlight and shone it on his father, who lay curled on his side in the bag, the end of his nose dark, something wrong with the skin. Roy put on some dry clothes fast because it was so cold. He put more wood in the stove, got it going, and pushed the sleeping bag closer around his father, then found his own bag and got into it and rubbed his hands and feet together until he was warm enough and fell asleep again.

When he woke next it was light and it was warm from the stove and his father was sitting up in a chair watching him.

How do you feel? he asked.

I'm thirsty and really hungry, Roy said.

It's been two days, his father said.

What?

Two days. We didn't get back here until the next day, and then we slept through last night, too. I have food hot for you on the stove.

It was soup, split pea, and Roy could eat only a small bowl of it with a few crackers before he felt full, though he knew he was still hungry.

Your appetite will come back, his father said. Just wait a little while.

What happened to your face?

Just a little frostbite, I guess. It got a little burned. The end of my nose doesn't feel much.

Roy thought that over for a while, wondering whether his father's face would get completely better but afraid to ask, and finally he said, We came close to not making it, huh?

That's right, his father said. I cut it way too close. I almost got us both killed.

Roy didn't say anything more and neither did his father. They went through the day eating and stoking the stove and reading. They both went to bed early, and as Roy waited for sleep, he felt none of the elation he had always imagined people felt when they came close to death and narrowly escaped. He felt only very tired and a little sad, as if they had lost something out there.

In the morning, his father spent over an hour at the radio before he was finally able to place a telephone call to Rhoda, but what he got was only an answering machine.

Oh, he said into the mike. I was hoping I would get to talk with you. This is going to sound stupid into a machine, but I'm just thinking that maybe I've changed some out here and maybe

I could be better now. That's all. I wanted to talk with you. I'll try again some other time.

When he turned the radio off, Roy asked, If you talked with her and she wanted you to, would you leave here right away to go be with her?

His father shook his head. I don't know. I don't know what I'm doing. I'm just missing her.

They spent another day in the cabin reading and eating and staying warm and not talking much. Finally they played hearts with a dummy hand, which didn't work well.

I've been thinking about Rhoda, his father said. You may find some woman someday who isn't exactly nice to you but somehow reminds you of who you are. She just isn't fooled, you know?

Roy, of course, didn't know at all. He'd never even had a girl-friend except for Paige Cummings, maybe, whom he had liked for three years, and Charlotte, whom he had kissed once, but it seemed like he knew girls in porno magazines better than he knew any real girls.

His father tried the radio again that evening when they were done playing cards, as Roy was washing the dishes. He got through this time.

What are you thinking, Jim? Rhoda said. You've been away from everyone now for a few months and you think you can be different, but what's it going to be like when you're back in the same situations, with the same people?

Roy was getting embarrassed. There was no privacy to the radio. So he dried off his hands, put on his boots, his father stalling for time, saying, I, uh, waiting for Roy to get out of there.

And then Roy was out of the cabin for the first time in four days, sinking past his boots into the snow and heading for the shoreline. There was no ice or snow down close to the water. It wasn't cold enough there, Roy supposed, or else the salt melted everything away. He picked rocks out of the snow and hurled them at thin panes of ice farther up along the creek, cracking and shattering them like car windows. He didn't know how long he needed to stall out here, but he imagined it would be a while. He walked past the creek mouth and out to the low point, staying close along the edge, out of the deep snow, and wondered whether there were any fish in the cove now. He supposed there had to be, since there was nowhere else for them to go, but he had no idea how they survived. He wondered what he and his father were doing here in the winter. It seemed pretty dumb.

When his father had asked his mother whether Roy could come here, his mother had not answered or let Roy take the phone. She hung up and told him his father's request and asked him to think about it. Then she waited for several days and asked him at dinner whether he wanted to go. Roy remembered how she had looked then, with her hair pulled back and apron still on. It had felt like a kind of ceremony, attended with a greater seriousness than he was used to. Even his younger sister Tracy had been silent, watching them. He cherished this part of it, even now. He had felt he was deciding his future, even though he knew that she wanted him to say no and knew also that he would say no.

And that was the answer he gave that night.

Why? she asked.

I don't want to leave here and my friends.

She continued spooning her soup. She nodded slightly but that was it.

What do you think? Roy asked.

I think you're answering the way you think I want you to answer. I'd like you to think about it again, and if the answer again is no, that's fine and of course you know I want you here and Tracy and I will miss you if you go. I want you to make the best decision, though, and I don't think you've thought about it enough yet. Whatever you decide, know that it was the best you could have decided now, no matter what happens later.

She didn't look at him as she said this. She spoke as if she knew of events coming later, as if she could see the future, and the future Roy saw then was his father killing himself, alone in Fairbanks, and Roy having abandoned him.

Don't go, Tracy said. I don't want you to go. And then she ran back to her room and cried until their mother went to her.

Roy thought for the next several days. He saw himself helping his father, making him smile, the two of them hiking and fishing and wandering over glaciers in brilliant sunlight. He already missed his mother and sister and friends, but he felt there was an inevitability to all of this, that in fact there was no choice at all.

When his mother asked him again at dinner several nights later, he said yes, he would like to go.

His mother didn't answer. She put down her fork and then breathed deeply several times. He could see that her hand was trembling. His sister ran back to her room again and his mother had to follow. It was as if there had been some kind of death, he felt then. Certainly if he had known as much then as he knew now he would not have come. But he blamed his mother for this, not his father. She had arranged it. He had originally wanted to say no.

The clouds were high and thin and there were huge white circles around the moon. The air was white and seemed almost smoky even out over the channel. There was no wind and almost no sound, so Roy stepped hard into the rocks and snow to hear his boots. Then he was getting cold and hiked slowly back.

When he reentered, his father was sitting on the floor by the radio, though it wasn't on anymore and he was just staring down at the floor.

Well? Roy asked, then regretted it.

She's with a guy named Steve, his father said. They're moving in together.

I'm sorry.

That's all right. It's my fault anyway.

How is it your fault?

I cheated and lied and was selfish and blind and stupid and took her for granted and, let's see, there must be some other things, just general disappointment, I suppose, and now I'm going to get shafted and it's my fault. The big thing, though, I think, is that I wasn't there for her when she went through all the stuff with her parents. It just seemed like too much, I guess. And I suppose I left her alone to deal with all that. I mean, I thought she had her family to help, you know.

Rhoda had lost her parents to a murder-suicide ten months earlier. Roy had not heard much about it except that her mother used a shotgun on her husband and then a pistol on herself, and afterward Rhoda found out that her mother had cut her out of the will. Roy didn't really understand how this last part worked, but it was all part of something too awful to think about.

She felt I abandoned her then, his father said.

Maybe things will change, Roy said, just to be saying something.

That's what I'm hoping, his father said.

A big storm set in the next day. It sounded as if water were hitting the roof and walls in sheets, a great river rather than just windblown, it hit so heavily. They couldn't see anything through the windows except the rain and hail and occasionally snow hitting them from angles that kept shifting. They kept the stove going constantly and his father ran out for a few minutes to bring in more wood. He returned three times cold and swearing and piled the wood with the food in the extra room, then stood by the stove to dry off and get warm again.

Blowing like there's no tomorrow, his father said. As if it could wipe time clear off the calendar.

The whole cabin shook occasionally and the walls seemed to move.

It couldn't actually blow off the roof or something, could it? Roy said.

No, his father said. Your dad wouldn't buy a cabin with a detachable roof.

Good, Roy said.

His father tried the radio again, saying, I'll make it quick. I just have a few things to say to her. You won't have to go outside or anything, of course.

But he couldn't get any kind of signal in the storm and finally he gave up.

This is one of those things she's not going to believe, he said. I tried to call her but the storm kept me from doing it. But when the tally is made, I didn't get through to her, and the storm doesn't count.

Maybe it's not like that, Roy said.

What do you mean?

I don't know.

Listen, his father said. Man is only an appendage to woman. Woman is whole by herself and doesn't need man. But man needs her. So she gets to call the shots. That's why the rules don't make any sense, and why they keep changing. They're not being decided on by both sides.

I don't know if that's true, Roy said.

This is because you're growing up with your mother and sister, without me around. You're so used to women's rules you think they make sense. That will make it easy for you in some ways, but it also means maybe you won't see some things as clearly.

It's not like I got to choose.

See? That's one of them. I was trying to make a point, and you turned it around to make me feel bad, to make me feel like I haven't done my duty according to the rules and haven't been a good father.

Well, maybe you haven't. Roy was starting to cry now, and wishing he weren't.

See? his father said. You only know a woman's way to argue. Cry your fucking eyes out.

Jesus, Roy said.

Never mind, his father said. I have to get out of here. Even if it is a fucking hurricane. I'm going for a hike.

As he pulled on his gear, Roy was facing the wall trying to make himself stop crying, but it all seemed so enormously unfair and from out of nowhere that he couldn't stop. He was still crying after his father had gone, and then he started talking out loud. Fuck him, he said. Goddamn it, fuck you, Dad. Fuck you. And then he cried harder and made a weird squealing sound from trying to hold it back. Quit fucking crying, he said.

Finally he did stop, and he washed off his face and stoked the stove and got in his sleeping bag and read. When his father came back, it was several hours later. He stomped his boots out on the porch, then came inside and took off his gear and went to the stove and cooked dinner.

Roy listened to the kitchen sounds and to the howling outside and the rain thrown against the walls in gusts. It seemed to him they could just go on like this, not speaking, and it seemed even that this might be easier.

Here, his father said when he put the plates on the card table in the middle of the room. Roy got up and they ate without looking at one another or saying anything. Just chewing away at the Tuna Helper with sculpin in it and listening to the walls. Then his father said, You can do the dishes.

Okay.

And I'm not going to apologize, his father said. I do that too much.

Okay.

•   •   •

The storm continued for another five days, days of waiting and not talking much and feeling cooped up. Occasionally Roy or his father went for a short hike or brought in wood, but the rest of the time was just reading and eating and waiting and his father trying to reach Rhoda on the shortwave or the VHF but this never worked.

You'd think I could get through for just a few minutes, his father said. What good is all this shit if we can't use it in bad weather? Are we supposed to have emergencies just on good days?

Roy considered saying, Good thing we haven't needed it, as a way of getting talking again, but he was afraid this would be interpreted as some kind of comment about his father's need for Rhoda, so he kept quiet.

When his father did finally get through again, the storm had mostly died. Roy went out into light drizzle and ground so soaked it was like walking on sponges. The trees were dripping everywhere, big drops on the hood and shoulders of his rain gear. He wondered who Rhoda really was. He had spent a lot of time with her, of course, when she and his father had been married. But his memories were all a kid's memories, of how she threatened to stab their elbows with her fork if they left them on the table at dinner, for instance, and a peek of her once in the bathroom through the crack in the door. A few arguments between her and his father, but nothing distinct. They had divorced only one year ago, when he'd been twelve, but somehow everything was different now, all his perceptions. As if thirteen were a different life than twelve. He couldn't remember how he'd thought then, how his brain had worked, because back then he hadn't thought about his brain working, so he couldn't now make sense of anything from that time, as if he had someone else's memories. So Rhoda could have been anyone. All she meant to him now was this thing his father had to have, a craving as if for pornography, a need that made his father sick, though Roy knew it was wrong, incorrect, to think she actually made him sick. He knew it was his father doing it to himself.

Around the point, Roy sat on a large piece of driftwood that was soaked through and cold. He watched his breath fogging out and looked at the water and actually saw a small boat pass, about a mile away. An extremely rare event. A small cabin cruiser out fishing or camping, with extra jerry cans of gasoline tied along the bow rails. Roy stood up and waved but he was too far even to see if there was a response. He could see the dark patch inside where there was a person or several people but could not make out anything more distinct.

He wondered whether this thing his dad had with Rhoda would ever happen to him. Though he hoped not, he knew somehow ahead of time that it probably would. But by now he was just thinking to be doing something and wished he were back in the cabin where it was warm. It was just too cold out here. It was a miserable place.

When he returned, he was still too early, but he didn't go back outside. He figured he had stayed out long enough.

I know that, his father said. That's not what I'm saying. Roy's here now, by the way. He was outside.

Rhoda's voice came in unclear, warped by the radio. Jim, Roy's not the only one hearing this. Anyone with a ham radio is getting to hear everything.

You're right, his father said. But I don't care. This is too important.

What's important, Jim?

That we talk, that we work things out.

And how are things going to work out?

I want us to be together.

They listened to the static then for at least half a minute before Rhoda came back on.

I'm sorry I'm having to say this in front of Roy and everyone else, Jim, but we're never going to be together again. We've already tried that, many times. You have to listen to me, to what I've been saying. I've found someone else, Jim, and I'm going to marry him, I hope. And anyway, it doesn't matter about him. We still wouldn't be together. Sometimes things just end, and we have to let them end.

Roy pretended to be reading while his father sat bowed before the radio.

Fucking radio, his father said to Rhoda. If we could be together now, in person, face to face, this would be different. And then he turned the radio off.

Roy looked up. His father was hunched over with his forearms on his knees and his head down. He began rubbing his forehead. He just sat there like that for a long time. There was nothing Roy could think of to say, so he didn't say anything. But he wondered why they were here at all, when everything important to his father was somewhere else. It didn't make sense to Roy that his father had come out here. It was beginning to seem that maybe he just hadn't been able to think of any other way of living that might be better. So this was just a big fallback plan, and Roy, too, was part of a large despair that lived everywhere his father went.

There were no good times after this. His father sank into himself and Roy felt alone. His father read when the weather was miserable and went for hikes alone when it was only bad. They talked only to say things like, Maybe we should fix dinner soon, or Have you seen my gloves? Roy watched his father all the time and could discover no crack in the shell of his despair. His father had become impervious. And then Roy came in one day from a hike alone and found his father sitting at the radio set with his pistol in his hand. It was oddly quiet, with only a few small humming and chirping sounds from the radio.

Jim? Rhoda said over the radio. Don't do this to me, you asshole.

His father turned off the radio and stood. He stood looking at Roy in the doorway and then looked around the room as if he were embarrassed by some small thing and searching for something to say. But he didn't say anything. He walked over to Roy and handed him the pistol, then put on his coat and boots and went out.

Roy watched him go until he'd disappeared into the trees, then he looked at the pistol in his hand. The hammer was back and he could see the copper shell in there. He eased the hammer down with the pistol pointed away from him and then he pulled the hammer back again, raised the barrel to his head, and fired.

PART TWO

Jim in the trees heard the shot and didn't know what it was about. He wondered for a moment whether he had really heard it, but then he figured he had. Roy was making some kind of scene. He was going to shoot up their cabin because he needed to be taken care of now. Jim hiked on. He hoped Roy would hit the radio.

It was drizzling and the fog was in close. The trees had become ghosted and the entire island seemed uninhabitable. Jim hiked on, hearing his breathing the only rhythm, the only moving thing. He couldn't think about Rhoda. She had become a sense now, a part of him that he couldn't differentiate enough to think about. She was a longing and regret in him like a growth. And she was really doing it, really leaving him. Jim could feel himself on the edge of crying again, so he hiked on faster and counted his steps in rhythm, onetwothreefour in a group, fivesixseveneight, over and over. He hiked on until he stopped because he was tired and then he turned around and hiked back, but he didn't like the thought of arriving, of having to find the next thing to do to fill his time. The days were so long.

When he neared the cabin, he saw the door was still partway open, which pissed him off. It was like Roy to storm off on his own little hike and not close the door but just let them freeze.

And then he got to the door and looked down and saw his son. His son's body and not really his son because the head was missing. Torn and rough, red, with dark slicked hair along the edge and blood splattered everywhere. He stepped back because looking straight down he saw that he was stepping on a piece that had come free, a piece of his son's head. A piece of bone.

He stood there rocking and looking and breathing. He glanced around the rest of the room but there was nothing else to see, and then he had to sit down and he sat down in the doorway, a few feet from Roy, and as soon as he heard this name in his head, he started to shake and it seemed that he was crying but he wasn't crying or letting out any sound. What's happening here? he asked out loud.

He touched Roy's jacket then, and shook Roy's shoulder gently. Then he looked at the blood on his hand and back at the stump for a head that was all Roy had now and then from inside him he began to howl.

And howling did nothing but fill itself and he was like an actor in his own pain, not knowing who he was or what part now to play. He shook his hands oddly in the air and slapped them against his thighs. He pushed himself back farther away from Roy but this was phony, another act, and still he didn't know what to do. No one was watching. And though it couldn't be his son there, it kept being his son there.

Some of the inside was white. He kept waiting for it all to turn red, but it wouldn't. And soon there were small flies, gnats and no-see-ums, landing there inside his son's head and crawling and hopping around. He swished them away, but he didn't want to actually touch the head and they kept landing again. He leaned in close and blew on them and could smell the stink of blood and then he grabbed Roy's jacket and pulled him onto his lap, the stump with part of a face showing now, a jaw and cheek and one eye that had been hidden against the floor. He looked at this and kept looking and shook him there and looked when he could see and wasn't blinded by the heaving and all he could think was why? Because there was no sense to it at all. He was the one who'd been afraid he might do this. Roy had been fine, had always been fine.

No, he kept saying out loud, even though he knew this was a stupid thing to say. He kept trying to think because whenever he stopped thinking for a moment he was crying terribly. And yet even this he was aware of. It was as if he couldn't reenter the world to act unconsciously. As if every thought and feeling and word and everything he saw were artificial, even his mutilated son. As if even his son dead before him weren't real enough.

He put Roy back down on the floor and looked at all the blood on his hands and jacket and jeans, blood everywhere so he got up and went down to the water and waded in. He gasped from the cold and already his legs were numb. They were stumps, and then the terror ripped through him again from that word, stumps, and he was sobbing hideously. He walked around and around in the shallows and slipped and went under and came back up and walked out, shaking now from the cold also, and went back to Roy, who still lay there dead, who hadn't moved. He had just seen Roy alive. It hadn't been more than an hour ago, and Roy had been fine.

And then Jim felt an unaccountable rage. He went into the cabin looking for something and he went to the radio and picked it up and smashed it down onto the floor and then kicked it again and again and grabbed the lantern and hurled it against the wall where it shattered and then he grabbed the VHF and hurled that, too, and threw a bag of smoked salmon that lay open on the table, then kicked over the table, but then he stopped, standing in the middle of the room, because only a few more minutes had gone by, if even that, and all this destruction had not helped. He wasn't even interested in it. It had seemed like living but now it seemed like nothing.

Jim sat beside Roy again and watched him. He was still the same, still exactly the same. He picked up the .44 Magnum from where it had bounced a few feet away. He put the barrel to his own head but then put it down and laughed savagely. You can't even kill yourself, he said to himself out loud. You can only play at killing yourself. You get to be awake and thinking about this every minute for the next fifty years. That's what you get.

And then he cried, as much from self-pity as for Roy. He knew this and despised himself for it, but he stripped out of his wet clothing, put on his warmest clothes, and cried this time for hours and there was no break, no end to it, and he wondered only whether it would ever stop.

But it did stop, of course, in the evening and Roy still there on the floor and Jim didn't know what to do with him. He realized now that he would have to do something with him, that he couldn't just leave him there on the floor. So he went around back and found a shovel. It was past sunset already, getting dark, but he went off a hundred feet or so behind the cabin and started digging, then realized this was too close to the latrine and he didn't like that, so he went farther into the trees, toward the point, and then he started digging again, but there were roots, so he went back for the ax and chopped and dug his way through until he had a pit about four feet deep and longer than Roy's body, and then this idea, Roy's body, sent him crying again and when he finally stopped and returned to the cabin it was the middle of the night.

Roy was in the doorway, blocking it. He still hadn't moved. Jim knelt down to pick him up but what was left of his head lolled wet and cold against Jim's face and Jim threw up and dropped him and then walked around in circles outside saying Jesus.

He went back in and picked up Roy again and carried him this time fast out to the grave, and he tried to set Roy carefully into it but ended up dropping him and then howled and hit himself and jumped up and down at the edge of the grave because he had dropped his son.

And then it occurred to him that he couldn't do this, that he couldn't just bury Roy out here. His mother would want to see him. And the thought of having to tell her twisted him up again and he was off in the woods stumbling around again and feeling sorry for himself and by the time he got back it was already getting lighter, even through the trees.

I fucked up, he said. He was squatting beside the pit and

rocking. I really fucked up this time. And then he remembered Roy's mother again, Elizabeth. He would have to tell her. He would have to tell her and everyone else, but he wouldn't be able to tell them everything, he knew. He wouldn't tell about handing Roy the pistol. And then he was sobbing uncontrollably again, like some other force ripping through his body, and he wanted it to end but also didn't want it to end since it at least filled time, but after a while, after it was fully light out, the crying did stop abruptly and he was left there again by the pit looking down at Roy and wondering what to do. Roy's mother would have to see him. He couldn't just bury him out here. She would want to have a funeral and she'd have to know what had happened. He'd have to tell her. And Tracy.

Oh God, he said. He would have to tell Tracy that her big brother was dead. She would have to see him too. He wondered for a moment if there'd be some way of putting Roy's face back together a little, but then he saw right away that that was crazy.

He reached down into the pit and pulled Roy out, then hefted him up again and carried him back to the cabin. He was heavy and cold and stiff, bent up weirdly now from being in the pit, and he was covered with dirt. There was dirt all in the head part. He didn't want to look at it, but he kept glancing over and worrying. None of this would look good.

Jim laid his son back down in the cabin, in the main room, then sat against the far wall and watched him. He didn't know what to do. He knew he had to do something soon, but he had no idea what.

Okay, he finally said. I have to tell them. I have to let his mother know. And he went to the radio but then saw that he had destroyed it and remembered that he had destroyed the VHF as well. Goddamnit, he yelled at the top of his voice and kicked the set again. And then he started crying again, mid-yell. It could start any time, had a will of its own, and it didn't make him feel any better, as crying is supposed to. It was a terrible kind of crying that only hurt and made everything seem increasingly unbearable and though it filled time it seemed each time that it might not end. It was to be avoided, so when he could get his eyes clear enough to see he went out to the boat, which they had tied behind the cabin, and went back in for the pump and the outboard and life jackets, flares, oars, horn, bilge pump, spare gas can, everything, and carried it all out onto the beach and carried the boat out too and pumped it up there and mounted the engine and put all the stuff in. Then he went back for Roy.

Roy was still propped oddly against the wall, still stiff. The side that had his face was showing, but the skin was all yellow and bluish like a bloated fish and Jim threw up again and had to walk around outside, wishing he could just never go back into the cabin, saying, That's my son in there.

When he returned, he looked again at Roy and looked away and wondered how he'd carry him. He couldn't just dump him in the boat like that. He thought of garbage bags but then was weeping and shouting again, He's not fucking garbage. So when he calmed again he laid out a sleeping bag and rolled Roy onto it and zipped it up and drew the drawstring at the top. He picked Roy up over his shoulder and carried him out to the boat.

Okay, he said. This is going to work. We're going to find someone, and they're going to help us. He went back to the cabin for some food and water but when he got there he couldn't remember what he had come for, so he just closed the door and returned to the boat.

He had inflated the boat too far away from the water, so he unloaded Roy and the gas cans and then dragged the boat to the edge of the water, then reloaded the cans and Roy. When he finally pushed off, it was afternoon, not very smart, he realized now, but he pulled the starter cord and pushed the choke back in when it coughed to life and then he put it in gear and they were heading out. The water was very calm in their inlet and the sky gray, the air heavy and wet. He tried to get up on a plane, but they were too loaded down, so he throttled back to a slow five or six knots as they cleared the point, Jim shivering a bit in the wind and his son wrapped up in the sleeping bag.

They were exposed beyond the point to a cold breeze up the channel and small wind waves that splashed a little into the boat.

This isn't real good, Jim said to his son. We're not doing the smartest thing here. But he kept going and then began to wonder where he was going. I don't know, he said aloud. Maybe to wherever those houses are. But that's twenty miles or something. That's not close. We need a boat to find us.

And then he was thinking again of Roy's mother, of her face when she would hear about this and her face when she'd heard about all the other things, when he told her he was sleeping with Gloria, for instance. After they moved and tried to make things work and he had been what she'd wanted for a whole month, thirty days exactly of being considerate and affectionate and trying not to think of other women, she came to him in bed smiling and happy and he wanted only for her never to touch him again. He told her he'd just been acting the past month, that it wasn't him, and her face then and her face when they told their children they were getting divorced, and now this. This couldn't even be compared to the other things. This isn't just a thing, he said out loud, sobbing, and then he couldn't see to steer and they curved all over the channel and lurched and took on water until he could get himself under control again.

And Tracy. She would hate him. All her life. Along with her mother. Everyone. And they'd be right. And what would Rhoda say? She would know exactly whose fault this all was.

The boat steered badly and the current was pushing them sideways. Jim tried again to get on a plane, but the nose only pushed into the air and wouldn't come down, so he throttled back again. Everything was gray and cold and completely empty. There were no other boats, no houses, anywhere. By the time he was halfway across the channel to the next island, it was late in the afternoon and he was shivering uncontrollably and worrying about running out of gas and worrying what Roy would look like when he finally got there and whom he'd have to talk with first.

He stopped twice to pump out the water and continued on toward the shore, wanting finally only to make that and not worrying if they went farther today. He was so cold he was numb and had trouble thinking. He'd think, I wonder how far, and then his brain would stop for a while and then he'd wonder again how far to the shore and finally he realized this was hypothermia setting in, that if he didn't get to shore and get warm he would be in trouble. And he wondered why he hadn't brought more clothing and something to sleep in and some food. He was hungry.

When he made shore, it was close to sunset and Roy was soaked and they still hadn't seen anyone. Jim went for wood while Roy stayed with the boat and Jim wanted to make a fire and he piled up the sticks he had found but all the wood was wet and he didn't have any matches, so he cried. Then he went back to the boat and said Sorry to Roy as he dumped him out of the sleeping bag onto the beach and got into the wet bag himself and tried to get warm and woke again in darkness and was still cold but also somehow still alive. I got lucky, he thought, but then he thought of Roy and got out of the bag to go find him, frightened now that Roy had been picked at or even dragged away by something, but when he found him nearby he still seemed pretty much like how he'd been, though it was hard to tell for sure because he didn't have a flashlight and Roy only had half a head. That sounded funny and Jim laughed for a second, then started weeping again. Oh Roy, he said. What are we gonna do?

Jim slept again and in the morning Roy definitely had been picked at. The seagulls were still milling nearby and Jim went after them with rocks, chasing them so far along the beach that by the time he returned the others were back at Roy again, stealing away little pieces of him.

Jim put him back in the sleeping bag and tied it up again and reloaded the boat. This time, Jim said. This time we find someone.

Under way, he was hungry and cold and had trouble staying awake. He saw no cabins or boats of any kind, but he kept going into the waves and trying to look around and trying not to think but thinking anyway of what he was going to say. I don't know why he did it, he imagined saying to Elizabeth. I just came back from a hike one afternoon and there he was. There was no sign, no indication. I hadn't imagined he could do this kind of thing. But then he lost it again because there really hadn't been any sign and he really hadn't imagined Roy could do this. Roy had always been stable, and sure they had argued a little, but things hadn't been bad, and there was no reason to do this. Damn you, he said out loud. It doesn't make any fucking sense.

As he rounded another point, he saw a boat far away, heading into the next channel. He stopped the engine and fumbled with one of the flares, finally got it lit and then held it high over his head smoking orange and burning and stinking of sulfur, but the boat, something big, some kind of huge yacht with a hundred fucking passengers, one of whom must be looking this way, just passed on and disappeared behind another coastline.

So Jim continued along the island at a slow five knots maybe and against the current again and wondered how well he knew this area. He wondered if he could just keep going along this and other islands and run out of gas and never find anyone. It seemed possible. It wasn't exactly everyone living out here. But then late afternoon, after he'd poured in the spare gas and was sure he was just going to run out and have to drift around forever, he saw a cabin cruiser crossing on the other side, back toward the island he and Roy lived on, where they'd come from. They could have hailed it from there. Jim got out another flare and struck the end with the cap and nothing happened, so he struck again and looked up at the boat going fast and passing away from them now. He grabbed the last flare and struck it and it ignited and he held it high and the boat swerved slightly toward him and he was sure it must have seen him. But then it swerved back the other way, just avoiding a log or something in the water, and the flare went out and the boat was only a speck receding into the gray.

Jim yelled, over and over, growling at the shoreline and the water and air and sky and everything and hurled the burned-out torch and just sat there looking at the sleeping bag that held Roy and then at his hands on his knees. The boat was rocking and drifting and cold water was lapping onto his lower back and down his seat.

Jim continued on and, coming around a small point, happened to look over just in time to see a small cabin disappearing back into the trees. He turned the boat around and motored back and saw it was bigger, actually, than that, a home it looked like, a summer house, and he landed the boat on the small gravel beach before it and left Roy to go up and investigate.

It was hidden behind a stand of spruce and he'd been lucky to see it at all, though it wasn't far from shore. There was a path leading to it and when he got up close he saw it was a log cabin but big enough to be someone's house, with several rooms and storm boards on all the windows, locked up for the winter.

Hello, he said. Then he walked up onto the porch, which had debris all over it from the storm, and he knew no one would be around. Hey, he yelled, I happen to have my dead son with me. Maybe we could come in and chat and have dinner and spend the night, what do you say?

There was no answer. He went back to the boat and Roy and tried to think. It was late in the day and he hadn't seen anything else. He was on his reserve gasoline already. It wouldn't last long, and he was still shivering and starving and dizzy and they might have left something in their house for him to eat. And maybe a radio. They would certainly have some kind of blanket, and a fireplace and some wood. He had seen the chimney. And he had been lucky to warm up enough last night. He hadn't been sure he would in a wet sleeping bag, and it might not work out as well a second time, because he was much weaker now. He had to deliver Roy, he knew, but the truth was, the kid didn't look all that great anyway. Jim laughed grimly. You're a card, he said out loud. You're a hell of a father and you're a comic, too.

Wait right here, he said to Roy, and he went back up to the cabin again and this time continued around back. He was looking for a way in. The windows all had storm boards fitted and probably locked from inside. The front door had a big padlock and, as it turned out, so did the back door. He looked all around and there was nothing left open, no glass to break, even.

Okay, he said. It was quiet, only a few drips from the trees. And it was getting on toward sunset. He had no flashlight, no food. He continued farther and found the wood shed. The door was padlocked but looked weak enough, so he found a good-sized rock and threw it at the door and it made a crunching sound, then bounced back at him so he had to jump out of the way. Goddamnit, he said. He ran to the door and slammed himself against it, fell down and got up and did it again. He was breathing hard now. He kicked with his boot at the center of it and could feel it bend each time, but it wouldn't give, so he walked back down to the boat.

He saw the sleeping bag propped up there with Roy in it and realized he had forgotten about Roy for a few minutes. The thought that he could do that seemed terribly sad, but he didn't stop and indulge himself. He had work to do before dark. He loosened the engine from its mount and carried it stiffly up to the cabin, set it down on the porch. The thing weighed at least fifty pounds, all metal.

Jim went to the shed again for the rock and came back to the cabin. He had hoped to find an ax or a saw or something in the shed, but he decided now to just work on the cabin directly. He pounded at each door and storm board with the rock in his hand until he found one over the kitchen window that seemed to give a little more. It was because the window was bigger, he thought. So he carried the outboard around and then he grabbed the housing with both hands and rammed the prop end into the board and it only scraped a little on the prop and knocked him off balance so that he almost fell with the engine on top of him.

He was beyond swearing or yelling. He felt only a cold, murderous hatred and wanted to destroy this cabin. He picked up the outboard, this time by the lighter, skinnier shaft end, and could get the other, heavier end to lift only by turning like a shot-putter, so he turned a couple of circles like that and hurled the motor at the storm board and jumped back.

The crash was monstrously loud and the engine fell back onto the porch with a smashed housing.

Of course, Jim said. The housing was only plastic. He unlatched it and lifted it off twisted and crushed and now he had steel motor sticking out, the engine head, and he swung the motor around again and hurled it, screaming, and it bounced back again and almost got him but this time it had crushed part of the storm board. He picked it up and hurled it two more times and by then had destroyed his engine but also had shattered the storm board and the glass behind it and had a way in.

The cabin was dark inside and there was no electricity, no light to switch on. Fumbling around in the kitchen in the dark, he finally found matches and then a paraffin lamp that cast weird shadows everywhere as he hunted around from room to room. He found a wood stove in the kitchen and then another for heat in the living room. Beside this one there was still a stack of dry wood. There was a bedroom off this and it had been stripped, the mattress bare, without blankets. The whole place had been stripped, winterized. But he kept looking in every closet and shelf and drawer and under the bed and couch, and finally in a dresser drawer he found two sets of sheets and a blanket.

Okay, he said. Now, where's the food? You don't bring everything every time. You must leave something here. Some canned goods or something. Where is it?

He looked in the kitchen and found it surprisingly bare. He did find a few cans of soup in the cupboard, though, and then another cupboard with canned vegetables.

Not enough, he said. Not enough. I've got a growing boy with me, a strapping young lad. You must have a cellar. Your own little indoor cache in a fancy place like this. He stomped on the floor all around the kitchen and looked for latches and looked in the living room, pulling back the small piece of carpet, and looked in the bedroom, and then, giving up, on his way back into the kitchen followed by his own paraffin shadow like a nimble doppelgänger, he saw a latch in the passageway from living room to kitchen.

Open sesame, he said and lifted it and found the cellar, a hundred cans and jars and bottles and freeze-dried packets of Alpine Minestrone and vanilla ice cream and in a large bag even vacuum-sealed packets of smoked salmon. Okay, he said.

Roy was still in the bag. He lifted him over a shoulder and pushed him through the kitchen window, trying not to tear the bag on the bits of glass on the sill but tearing it some anyway. Then he climbed in himself.

Time to get to work, he said. We need to make this place home. He dragged Roy back to the bedroom, where he'd stay cold and out of the way. Then he started a fire in the kitchen stove and decided not to light the one in the living room, to conserve wood. He'd just sleep in here in the kitchen. And that would help Roy keep cooler, also.

He opened a can of ravioli and put the can right on the burner, then decided he wouldn't be such a slob and put it in a small pot. He heated canned milk in another pot and made himself some hot chocolate. A treat, he said. He ate there in the kitchen in the lamplight and was looking all around trying to find something to focus on, something to read. He kept thinking about Roy and Roy's mother and he didn't want to do this, so he looked all around the cabin for reading material and couldn't find any but finally found some family pictures in the bedroom and brought them back to the kitchen and stared at them while he ate.

This family was not good-looking. They had a parrot-faced daughter and a son with big ears and eyes too close together and a mouth that twisted up oddly. The parents were no lookers, either, the man stocky and a nerd and his wife trying to look surprised for the camera. They went for vacations everywhere, apparently. Camels and tropical fish and Big Ben. Jim disliked them and felt fine about eating their food. Fuck you, he said to the pictures as he slurped up their ravioli. But this lasted only so long and then he was sitting there at the table in lamplight with nothing to focus on. Time, he said.

He went back out to the boat, though it was dark now and very cold, and brought all of the gear up to the porch, then dragged the boat around back and left it and lifted his stuff through the window. Then he carried it all into the back room with Roy, who still was just there in the sleeping bag, not doing anything, not participating, just like a junior high kid. Fine, Jim said to Roy. Then he returned to the kitchen and made his bed on the floor.

That night he kept waking, paranoid that something awful had happened, and then he'd remember Roy and cry and then, because he was so exhausted, fall asleep again. He had no dreams and saw nothing. It was fear he woke to each time, his breath tight and blood pounding, and a sense that the sky was bearing down on him. And in the morning, when it had been light out for hours and he finally got up off the floor, the sense had not completely gone away.

He stoked the stove and wanted to boil water to cook Malt-O-Meal but no water came out of the tap. Okay, you fuckers, he said, you parrots, where's the water switch? He searched the kitchen and the cellar and then walked around the back of the cabin and searched for faucets but found nothing. He hiked up to the shed and still nothing so he searched the entire hill behind the house for two or three hours, foot by foot, and finally found a pipe buried partly in the dirt and then covered with bark. He went along it on his hands and knees feeling for fixtures until he found the faucet. He turned it and went back inside, found water and air sputtering out of the tap.

Okay, he said, give me a steady stream, and as if all things followed his spoken will, the tap stopped sputtering and emitted a solid stream of clear, cold water.

He made the Malt-O-Meal, put brown sugar in, and sat down to it but again needed something to look at and didn't have anything. So he went back and dragged Roy out, still in the sleeping bag, and tried to prop him up in the other chair in the kitchen, but he wouldn't bend right. The blue sleeping bag was terribly stained now, still wet and dark all around the top.

Okay, he said. If you're not going to sit right. He looked in the drawers until he found string and scissors and he wrapped Roy, then tied him to a rafter and a leg of the table and a hook that came out of the wall for hanging pots or something, and so Roy was standing there in his sleeping bag and Jim could sit down and eat.

Your father's becoming pretty weird, he told Roy. And it's not like you haven't had a part in that. And yet, the truth is, do you want to know the truth? Well, in some ways I feel better now. I don't know why that is.

Jim concentrated on his eating then and when he was through he did the dishes. Then he wiped his hands on his jeans and turned to Roy. Okay, big boy, he said, time to go back in the cooler. And he untied Roy and carried him back to the bedroom, then felt so lost all of a sudden he lay down on the bare wooden floor in the bedroom and just moaned for the rest of the day, no idea at all in his head as to what he was doing or why. The room was cold and dim and seemed to stretch on forever, and he a tiny speck lost in the middle of it.

At dinner, after dark, Jim ate alone. I don't feel like company, he said aloud. Then he went for a walk in the woods.

Jim, Jim, Jim, he spoke out loud, you have to do something. You can't just leave your son tied up in the sleeping bag and cooling in the bedroom. Roy needs a funeral. He needs to be buried. His mother and sister need to see him.

He hiked on some more, not bothering to duck much and getting scraped up a lot by small branches, one of his hands on fire from nettles. There was no moon or anything out, and he couldn't see a damned thing.

As he talked, he imagined he was in a great room, at a trial, and these words were being spoken to him. He was sitting at a heavy desk and listening and couldn't speak.

How was he tied up? someone was asking. Why did you tie up your son at the table? Did that make any sense at all? And what about the sleeping bag? Was that your idea, too? Have you been planning this for some time? Was that really what this whole trip was about? It could have been suicide, sure, but it could also have been murder.

This idea stopped him. He stood in place in the woods breathing hard and hearing nothing else and thinking that they could think that. How could he ever prove that he hadn't shot his son himself? And now he'd run away, too, and broken into someone else's place and was hiding out with the body. How could he possibly explain any of this?

Jim was scared now for himself, and turned around to hike back to the cabin, but he wasn't sure which way it was. He hiked for over an hour, it seemed, and much farther than he had come, he was sure, and still he couldn't see the cabin or anything familiar or really anything at all. He had just hiked out into the dark and not bothered to pay any attention to where he was going.

The ground was uneven and occasionally he fell through where the dead wood and undergrowth had built up and he was scraped from the sides and above. He had his arms out and head turned away and was walking sideways hoping just to find his way somehow and listening but hearing only himself and starting to feel very afraid of the woods, as if all he had done wrong had somehow gathered here and was out to get him. He knew that didn't make any sense and that scared him more, because it felt so real anyway. He seemed impossibly small and about to be broken.

He stopped periodically and tried to stand still and be quiet and listen. He was trying to hear what way to go, or because that didn't make any sense, maybe trying to hear what was after him. Up through the trees, he could see a few faint stars much later, after the sky had cleared some. He was cold and shivering and his heart still going, and the fear had sunk deeper into a sense that he was doomed, that he would never find his way back to safety or be able to run fast enough to escape. The forest was impossibly loud, even over his pulse. There were branches breaking, and twigs and every leaf moving in the breeze and things everywhere running through the undergrowth and larger crashings beyond that he couldn't be sure whether or not he had simply imagined. The air in the forest had bulk and weight and was part of the darkness, as if they were the same thing, and rushed toward him from every side.

I've been afraid like this all my life, he thought. This is who I am. But then he told himself to shut up. You're only thinking this stuff because you're lost out here, he said.

It was impossible that it was taking him this long to find the cabin. He'd never been lost in the forest in his life, and he had been in forests all the time, hunting and fishing. But once you take that first wrong step, he told himself, because he knew that after that it was possible to never find your way again, because you couldn't know where you were coming from and so wouldn't have any firm basis for any direction. And that seemed appropriate for more in his life, too, especially with women. Things had become so twisted early on that it had been impossible to know what was good, and now, with Roy dead, there was absolutely nothing left to go on. It wouldn't matter if he perished out in the forest tonight, if he just gave up and lay down and froze.

But he continued on anyway, until the sky lightened finally and then it was dawn and he had found the shore by going consistently downhill. It wasn't the shore in front of the cabin, and he didn't know in which direction to follow it, but it was a shore, and he went the way that seemed right, hiking along it and waiting for the cabin.

It was a sunny day, cold and bright, the first clear day they'd had in a long time. He was very hungry and tired and sore but grateful for the sun. He didn't find the cabin after several hours, so he turned and walked back the other way, but even this seemed all right. At what must have been about noon, the sun overhead, he passed the point where he'd started and continued on for another hour or so before he arrived at the beach in front of the cabin. He stopped and stood there and just looked at it for a while, then he went in.

Everything was where he had left it, and Roy still in the back room. Jim ate a can of soup straight out of the can, without heating it, and then he lay down on the floor wrapped in the blanket and slept.

When he woke, he was very cold and it was night. He found the lamp and then got a fire going in the stove. I'm going to be more careful now, he told himself as he was pushing more wood in. And I'm going to take care of things. I'm going to find someone on this island and let Roy's mother know and give Roy a decent burial. I'll go today.

He ate another can of soup and then some instant mashed potatoes and went back to sleep for a few hours and woke in the morning. Okay, he said as soon as he'd opened his eyes, I'm going.

He restoked the stove and fixed some breakfast. As he was eating, he realized he'd have to leave a note. If anyone came here and found this, found the broken cabin and Roy in the back room and saw he'd been living in here, they'd think the wrong things. And he'd have to close up the kitchen window, too, so nothing got in to eat his food or get at Roy.

Jim looked in drawers until he found a pen and an envelope that he could write on. I've gone for help, he wrote. My son killed himself and is in the back room. I didn't have any way of contacting anyone. I couldn't go farther in the boat. I'm hiking around the island now trying to find some help and I will be back. He reread it several times and couldn't think of anything better, so he signed it and then got some food together and packed the blanket in a garbage bag in case he had to sleep out there.

The window was a problem. He didn't have a hammer or nails or even good boards. So he carried the busted outboard to the shed and used it to bash in the shed door, the same as he'd done to the kitchen window. When he had broken through, he rested until his breath calmed and then he pulled away the pieces of splintered wood and went back for the lamp to search the shed.

All the tools were here: ax, shovel, saws, hammer, nails, even a sander and chain saw and chains and a ratchet and screwdrivers, wrenches, all just sitting in here rusting away. Jim chopped off a big piece of the door with the ax and then brought it over to the kitchen window to hammer it up. Before he did this, though, he went in to say good-bye to Roy and let him know what he was doing. I'm taking care of things now, he said, standing in the bedroom doorway. I'm sorry things have gone so badly so far, but I'm getting it together now. Then he brought out his bag of food and the blanket and the note and nailed up the board and nailed the note to it and started hiking.

It was already very late morning. He should have had an earlier start. But at least I'm going, he told himself. He hiked up the shoreline past where he had been the day before. He kept going, moving at a fast pace, keeping an eye out for boats or cabins or any sign of a trail that people might be using. The visibility was good enough he might be able to signal a boat. The air wasn't too cold, either, and the only clouds were thin and high up.

This coastline of banded rock and deadfall and dark sand seemed ancient to Jim, prehistoric. As he hiked along it quietly for hours, hearing only the sound of his boots and an occasional bird and the wind and small waves coming in, it seemed as if he might be the only man, come out to see what was in the world. He mused on this and walked more cat-like, hopping from stone to stone, and he longed for this simplicity, this innocence. He wanted not to have been who he was and not to find anyone. If he found someone, he would have to tell his story, which, he admitted to himself now, could only sound terrible.

He hiked on around point after point and so imagined he must be curving around the island, though he could not know for sure until the sun set slightly behind where it had before. It was a long island, apparently, and there was no way to know beforehand whether or where anyone might be living. It could be that his was the only cabin.

The late sunset was still red in the sky as the rocks at his feet became difficult to distinguish. The sky above the red was green and then faded into blue. He continued until it was no longer safe, until he nearly ran face first into a dark snag without having seen it at all, and then he stopped. He went up into the woods, wrapped himself in his blanket, and cut open a pack of smoked salmon for dinner. The salmon was tangy and good, a recipe with spices other than just salt and brown sugar. He sat chewing and looking at the pale light on the water and listened to the forest around him, which seemed more quiet than usual, no sound except light wind and an occasional settling, no movement of a living thing that he could detect.

Roy had not wanted to come here. Jim saw that now. Roy had come to save him; he had come because he was afraid his father might kill himself. But Roy had not been interested in this place,

or in homesteading. Jim had imagined that any boy would want
to homestead in Alaska with his father—though technically they
were not quite homesteading, of course, since he had bought the
land and it already had a cabin—but he hadn't really thought of
Roy or of what Roy might have wanted for even an instant. And
that had still been true after they'd landed. Jim had taken his son
for granted at every moment, and now his son was gone. That
was the odd thing.

If Roy were still alive, and Jim could take him somewhere now,
he would take him sailing around the world. That was something
Roy had actually wanted to do. He had said so himself. And it
was something Jim could have arranged just as easily as homesteading. He had the money for a boat, he knew how to sail, he
had the time. But for that to have been possible, he would have
had to listen to Roy. He would have had to notice him while he
was still alive. And that was what simply could not have happened. Jim had been thinking of Rhoda, and of other women.

Jim tried to sleep then, lay back on the moss in his blanket
and kept his food close to his belly. He didn't care if a bear did
come; he wasn't giving up his food.

But he couldn't sleep. He looked for stars, kept looking even
though there were none, kept his eyes open though there was
no light and nothing to see. He imagined what sailing through
the South Pacific might have been like. He had seen pictures of
Bora-Bora. Dark-green jungle and black rock, light-blue water
and white sand. It would have been warm always, and comfortable, and they could have snorkeled. They could even have
learned to scuba. Why spend any part of a life in a cold place? It
didn't make sense to him.

Jim didn't feel tired, couldn't imagine sleeping, so he rose again, put his blanket in his bag with the food, and hiked carefully back down to the shore.

The night was dark, without stars or moon. He couldn't see anything, though his eyes had had hours now to adjust. He put out one foot at a time and felt around with it before putting weight on. He moved slowly step by step this way along the shore until he came too close to the water's edge and slipped on seaweed and went down hard onto wet rock. He got back up fast and fell again, then groaned from the pain in his elbow and hip and found his bag and crawled up onto the dry rocks on hands and knees until he could stand safely. He continued on into the woods, his hurt leg trembling, and lay down with the blanket over him and rested and woke in the morning to find he had fallen asleep.

This second day he made good progress, though he was sore from the falls. His elbow ached as if he had bruised the bone and his leg felt badly attached, but this didn't matter to him much. He kept alert for boats and cabins and reassured himself as he walked that he would find someone. But then he wondered whether this might be Prince of Wales Island, the big one. It wasn't so far from where he had come from, it looked just like everything else around it, and it was almost more remote than Sukkwan just because it was so big. Long stretches of its shoreline were uninhabited. And he supposed there could be more problems with bears on the big island, too. There would be no way of knowing for sure whether this was a smaller island until he had circumnavigated it, but he was still going along this shore, with the sunset to his left.

At midday he rested and ate. He sat in the shade, though the sun shone only weakly through haze. He saw no boats. He had seen no boats at all at any point. It was remarkable to him how remote this place was. He had come into nowhere and had thought somehow that that would be a good thing; when he had originally looked on a chart, he had thought his cabin too close to Prince of Wales Island and the few towns along its southwestern coast, but now he wished he could remember those towns and the other small enclaves scattered on neighboring islands. Colonies, really, just two or three houses, with almost no roads. The kinds of places he had always romanticized. He had known a few families who lived in them, had visited their one-room cabins built by hand with homemade dressers and blankets hung to make a bedroom. Bear rugs on the floor and walls. What was the magic in those places? What was it about the frontier that made him feel nothing else was really living? It made no sense, because he didn't like to be uncomfortable and couldn't stand to be alone. Every moment of every day now he wanted to see someone. He wanted a woman, any woman. Landscape meant nothing to him if he had to see it alone.

He packed up and continued on. Within the next hour, the coastline fell back sharply to the right and he felt certain now that this was not the big island. When the sunset came, he could see pink in the clouds above to the east but the west was blocked by forest.

Still no one, he said. I might be spending the entire winter here.

It was getting colder again each night. He had been lucky to have this warm spell over the past week, but now the snow and rain would set in again, he knew. He had only his warm clothes and the one blanket with him. This had been enough so far, but he knew he needed to find someone soon or else get back to the cabin where he had left Roy before it became too cold.

That night he woke shivering several times and was never warm enough. He dreamed of hiking around and around in circles with something after him. In the morning, a dusting of snow on the trees, which the drizzle melted away by noon. He had a waterproof jacket but still felt soaked and cold. He ate his lunch sitting on a log at the water's edge and thinking. If no one else were on this island, he would have to stay here and wait. There would be almost no boat traffic now until the late spring, until May probably or even June, and the people whose cabin he was in would not come back until July or August. And he had wrecked the outboard and radios. So he could be here a long time. He wondered whether his food would hold out. It didn't seem that it would, and he had not brought his rifle or fishing gear with him. There was no way of going back, either, to all that food he and Roy had stored up. •

It was crazy how much food they had stored up. Enough to feed a small colony through the winter. But that was what the trip had become for him. Instead of relaxing and getting to know his son, he had worried only about survival. And when it had finally been time to stop putting food away, that was when he had become terrified; he'd had no idea how to pass the time, how to get through the winter. So he had started calling Rhoda on the radio. Within a month, he would have left, he was sure. He wouldn't have been able to stay. But Roy had believed they were staying.

Jim was crying again. Roy had wanted to go, and he hadn't let him. He had trapped him. But Jim made himself stop crying and got up. He continued on until dusk and by then realized he hadn't been looking for hours, had only been hiking along non-stop and not looking at all for boats or cabins. He didn't believe anyone else was here.

This night was so cold he couldn't sleep and instead tried to make some kind of shelter. It was black again, no light, so he could only feel around in the darkness for enough branches and ferns and such to make a pile that he could sleep in. He mounded it all up the length of his body and slid in carefully, trying not to disturb it. This was much warmer but he fell asleep thinking of all the bugs and things in his pile that must be working their way through his clothing right now.

The days continued like this and became indistinguishable. It was a monstrously long island. If he had been certain he could find his cabin, he would simply have hiked across the island and returned, because by now he knew no one else lived here, but he didn't know how wide the island was and he wasn't sure he'd recognize coastline on the other side even if it was coastline he had seen before. So he continued on, hiking the full length of the short days and then waiting through each night, waking more than sleeping.

He was thinking of Roy these nights, remembering him as a child, riding the toy green tractor in Ketchikan, wearing a chef's hat at three and standing up on a stool to reach the mixing bowl. He remembered Roy picking blueberries in his red jacket and knocking down icicles and finding the antlers Jim had thrown behind the fence. Jim had thrown them there because they were small, but Roy discovered them and treasured them as if they were artifacts of another people. They seemed mysterious and wonderful to him. Jim didn't know how these times became the last years with Roy, didn't understand any of the transformations, and remembering, Jim realized he was gone for years of Roy's life, even in Ketchikan when they all still lived together, because Jim was thinking then of women, scheming, beginning to cheat. He had fallen into his secret life with other women and not known anyone or anything else. After the divorce, he still didn't wake up, but continued after women. And so he could not say who Roy was in the end. He was missing too many of the years leading up to him.

Jim reflected on all of this more calmly now, as if he couldn't afford the expenditure of crying when he was trying just to stay warm and survive each of these nights. It was not a time for extravagance. He would have to conserve if he was to survive until spring.

During the day, he tried to cover ground but his hiking became slower and slower. He had run out of food nearly a week before and was surviving now on seaweed and mushrooms and small crabs he caught at low tide. He drank from the occasional streams he crossed but was thirsty sometimes for days on end.

The crabs were very good, actually, and he looked forward to them. They were only three or four inches wide, but he cleaned them as he would have a larger crab, grabbing all their flexing legs from behind, underneath the shell, and then smashing the face onto a sharp rock until the top of the shell flew off. Then he broke the crab in half and shook once to get rid of the guts. He rinsed in seawater and sucked out the tender clear meat. He did this throughout the day, eating four or five crabs at a time. The only hard part, really, was when he couldn't find enough fresh water for a few days and his lips became swollen and his throat sore. But sucking on the needles of the spruce trees in the mornings gave him some relief, and there was often rain. No snow, luckily. He was getting very lucky with the weather.

He daydreamed about the South Pacific, drinking water from large strange leaves, eating fruit that grew everywhere. Mangoes, guavas, coconuts, and wild fruits he had never seen. These new fruits he imagined to be purplish and very sweet. The sun would be out constantly, and he would bathe under waterfalls.

And then one evening he saw the edge of the sunset to the west and knew he had come around the southern tip of the island. He was on his way home now. He continued on to the point and sat in the trees watching the thin line of sunset devoured in watery gray clouds. Then he scraped up enough small stuff to make a mound, pushed his way in, and slept.

It was five more days before he reached the cabin. He arrived fairly early in the morning, had slept the night before less than a mile from it. Shit, he said. It's right here. He stood on the beach and looked at it for a while, through the trees.

As he walked up to it, up onto the porch, he could tell that no one had come. Everything was just as he had left it. The note had streaked and faded from the rain, but that was the only change. He went around back for the hammer. The deflated boat was still there, the broken door on the shed, no changes.

Jim pulled the nails from the boards he had placed over the kitchen window, starting to smell Roy even before the first board was fully removed. When he stepped inside, the stench was a thing with weight and heft. He threw up right there on the kitchen floor, threw up his few precious crabs and mushrooms and the fresh water he had sucked yesterday from dew. It seemed a terrible waste, even though he knew he would have better food and water now.

He cleaned himself up at the sink, rinsed out his mouth. The smell was overpowering. He could see well enough in the kitchen, but the back rooms would be dark, so he lit the paraffin lamp and walked back as if against a strong wind into the smell.

Roy was not as stiff as before. The sleeping bag was on the floor now and wet and had white fuzz growing even on the outside. Jim tried to grab the end of the bag but couldn't and stepped back again. I'm sorry, Roy, he said, weeping now for the first time in a while. And he knew he would have to bury him now. He had tried to find someone, had tried to find a way to show Roy to his mother and sister and give him a funeral, but now he would have to settle for burial on this island. There was no other choice. He couldn't live with this smell, couldn't let his son just rot here.

He had to go back outside first to breathe. He waited until he had stopped crying, too, then he went back inside quickly, grabbed the wet bag, and dragged it out to the window. When he hefted it through the window, the contents inside mushed together and some of Roy leaked out through the tears in the bag. Jim was making sounds, disgusted. He couldn't believe he was having to do this.

He grabbed a shovel and dragged Roy far into the trees. He didn't want to be close to the cabin, didn't want Roy's grave so near that these people might want to move it. So he went far enough into the trees that he didn't think Roy would be found, and then he stopped and began digging. The earth was hard for the first foot, then it was loose for another foot at most before he started hitting rock and root and sand; it was very hard to dig. He labored all day at the grave, stabbing and cutting roots, digging around rocks, smashing his way through with the tip of the shovel.

He had to rest often, and each time he would walk away from the pit and the awful smell of his son rotting. He would sit in the trees a few hundred feet away and think of how he would tell all of this. He wasn't sure the story could make any sense. Each thing had made the next thing necessary, but the things themselves did not look good. Though he couldn't admit it completely, part of him wished he would never be found. If no one ever returned to this cabin or noticed them missing from their own, then he would not have to try to tell anyone. He felt he could live now with what had happened if he didn't have to face anyone else. His son had killed himself and this was Jim's fault and now he was burying his son. He could believe this. But he didn't want anyone else to know.

He dug until late afternoon, near the end of the day, and then decided it would have to be good enough because he couldn't do this in darkness, so he dragged Roy and the sleeping bag into the pit, not wanting to try to empty him out of the bag, and then stood there wondering how he could have a kind of funeral in just a few minutes before heaping the dirt and getting back to the cabin.

I didn't mean to rush this, he told his son. I know this is your burial. It should be something special and your mother should be here, but I just can't do anything about all that. I just . . . and here he stopped and didn't know what to say. All he could think was I love you, you're my son, but this bent him so that he couldn't speak, so he wept and shoveled in the dirt and mounded it and packed it and walked back to the cabin in near darkness, not caring much anymore whether he lost his way.

The smell of Roy was still in the cabin that night and the next day and continued in traces for over a week. After that, Jim still thought he could smell it, but it had become faint enough to be indistinguishable from imagination. On cold days when it seemed to have gone, he walked around the rooms trying to remember it. Outside, too, during hikes through the forest he would sometimes smell it and stop and think of his son. He told himself that these had become the only times he would think of his son, as if only this one kind of memory were strong enough, but of course this was a lie. He was always thinking of Roy in one way or another. There was very little else to do. He had settled in for the winter, was waiting now.

It seemed to Jim that he hadn't understood Roy well. It seemed that Roy had been more dangerous than Jim had thought. As if all those years he had been ready to kill himself but waiting for the right time. This didn't seem quite accurate, but Jim followed it for a while. What if suicide had been in Roy's nature all along? What then? It would change responsibility, at the very least. And why was it that anyone ever killed himself? What had made Jim so sure that he himself could do it? It was difficult to understand now. It was hard to make the idea seem plausible. Jim didn't believe that he had ever really felt suicidal, even when he had decided to step off the cliff. Even then he had felt only self-pity, nothing more.

This thought made Jim pause. He hadn't thought about the cliff for a while. He wondered what Roy had thought of that, wondered whether Roy had known that he had done it on purpose. He had never really admitted to Roy that it had been on purpose. If he had, it would have been harder to make Roy stay. But Roy must have suspected something odd.

To get away from these thoughts, Jim tried to think of other things. He invented diversions. He tried to imagine who would find him, and how, and what they would say. The homely couple coming up the path with their children lagging behind. They would stop and watch him and consider him dangerous. They might run. They might arrive and leave before he'd even seen them, and he wouldn't know until the authorities arrived later. But he believed they would walk right up and be indignant. They were the owners and they were otherwise ignored by everyone, he was sure, so about this they would be fierce. They would come and drag him out and attack him with their parrot beaks and twisted eyes and peck and tear at him until they had stolen little pieces away. So then he was thinking of Roy on the beach and the seagulls and in this way he tortured himself each day and night under the guise of trying to fill his time and survive.

He still looked for boats occasionally, on good days. The rare ones he did see were too far away. He had no flares. It had occurred to him that he could try to light a giant forest fire on one end of the island and this would bring spotter planes at the least, but he didn't know how long they would take or whether he would end up dying in the fire. His own death seemed likely if he set a huge forest fire on an island. He would be in the water at the end, trying to find air. And he didn't like the idea of the firefighters shoveling at the dirt where Roy lay.

Then it occurred to him to set some other island on fire, if he could find a small one nearby that was uninhabited. He could row over there, get it going with the little bit of gasoline he had left, then row back or even just stay out on the water where they could see him.

Not a bad idea, he told himself. That could work.

But he didn't do it. Rowing in these channels wouldn't be easy, and he wasn't ready to face anyone yet. So he waited in his cabin and schemed and saw the flames everywhere and imagined himself rescued and tried to remember what Roy had looked like before he had blown off half his face. It was terrible that Roy had left Jim with that image. Jim couldn't remember the face before, the way his son had looked. It was as if his son had been born into the world mutilated.

At least no one else would have to see him that way. Enough time had passed now that no one else would have to see anything at all. This relieved him somewhat. He couldn't explain why the sight would have seemed such a personal embarrassment. But it would have. What he wanted now was to come up with some way of telling things that made it all seem sad but somehow unavoidable. Something along the lines that things had been hard, but he hadn't realized quite how hard for Roy because Roy hadn't said anything. If only Jim had known, they would have left immediately, but he'd had no way of knowing.

But then these thoughts disgusted Jim. He had no patience for his own mind.

· · ·

Mid-January and still no one had come. It was remarkable, really. It seemed the world had forgotten them, though they were probably less than ten miles from where they were supposed to be. Jim assumed that their cabin had been found by now with the blood on the floor and the smashed radios and the boat gone. The sheriff or someone must have searched the area after that, but he had not heard a single helicopter or plane, nor had he seen a boat for weeks, and never a boat close enough.

Jim's food was running low and he had lost weight trying to conserve. He had only one meal a day now, with a few light snacks at other times. He figured his food would last at this rate another month or two at most and then he'd be eating seaweed or starving.

He slept all through the night now and even sometimes part of the day. It was the easiest thing to do and didn't use food or even wood for the fire. He had cut several large pieces from the inflatable boat to lay on top of his blanket and sheets and he was wearing an extra sweater he had found as well as the clothes he had arrived in. He hadn't bathed in nearly three months. He had begun to smell almost clean again, as far as he could tell.

He tried not to think during this time. When it would start, he'd look at something, a board in the ceiling or even just the darkness, and try to lose himself in that and not let the thoughts get going, though he couldn't avoid them always. They were repetitive and insistent. Roy saying he wanted to go. He saw that scene over and over, couldn't get it out of his mind. Another repetitive one was about his neighbor in Ketchikan, Kathleen, the woman he had first wanted to cheat with. He kept seeing the gray afternoon when he'd stood out on their side porch chatting with her and asked her if she'd like to come inside, since Elizabeth wasn't home. The look of disgust on her face. She knew exactly what he meant. Elizabeth was in the hospital, pregnant with Tracy. Not the best timing, he saw now. He thought about food, too. Milkshakes, especially. That was what he most wanted. And barbecued ribs. He thought mostly about Roy, and he visited him when the weather was calm and he was feeling restless.

The mound had caved in with the rain; the grave was now a shallow depression grown over with mushroom and fern. At first he had torn out the mushrooms that grew there, considering them obscene, but as they kept growing back, he finally left them, gray-white bulbs and sharper, smaller cones like tepees. He wondered how long it would take for a nylon sleeping bag to decompose, and he imagined it must be a very long time.

You're still alive, he told Roy one day. I've been thinking about this. You don't get to experience anything anymore; your life stopped for you when you died. But things are going to keep happening to me because of this, and that makes you still alive, in a way. And because no one else knows, because your mother doesn't know, you aren't even completely dead yet. You'll die again when she hears, and then she'll keep you alive for a long time after that. And even after all of us die, someone's going to dig up that sleeping bag and find you again. Though I guess they might be digging you up earlier than that. They'll probably want to make sure it's you. They're not likely to take my word on anything after all this.

He liked talking out loud to Roy, so he made a habit of it. Unless the weather was terrible, he went out and chatted for a while each afternoon. He chatted about being rescued, and about the weather, and he confessed things from time to time. I was impatient, he told Roy. I know that. I should have relaxed a little. I just felt responsible. He talked with Roy about little things that were bothering him. The day I walked in on you, he said. When you were jacking off in the outhouse. I still feel bad about that. I don't think I handled it well. I should have said something, but I just didn't know what to say.

In the first part of March, Jim scrabbled around at the water's edge trying to catch crabs. They were still here, even in winter, but they seemed faster now. Each time he reached out, they retreated sideways into a crevice and disappeared. It took him a long time to realize that the crabs had not actually gotten faster but he had slowed. He hadn't eaten a regular meal in almost a week. He'd had mostly seaweed and water. And for several months before that, he'd been conserving. He saw now that this had been a mistake. He had made himself too weak. He went back to the cabin and tried to outthink the crabs.

The next day, he went after their babies. He overturned rocks and, sure enough, just as he had hoped, occasionally he found small colonies of baby crabs that were too small to get away from him. He picked them up by the handful and didn't see how he was going to be able to clean them in his usual way, so he just ate them whole and crunched them down, shells and guts and all.

I'll be shitting shell necklaces, he told them. It's going to be real pretty. He chewed well so that the pieces wouldn't come out too big.

At Roy's grave, he spent a long time talking about Roy's mother and how they had met and what had gone wrong. She was only my second serious girlfriend, really, he told Roy. My brother thinks that was a mistake, to settle down with only the second one, and I think he's probably right. The thing is, the first one had dumped me, and I think I was mostly scared when I went out with your mother. And there were things that were never right with her. Her parents, for instance. They didn't like me, thought I was too much a country boy, because they had money. Your grandfather, especially, I didn't get along with. The man was a bastard. Your mom didn't want to be critical of him, but he had been hitting his wife and doing other terrible stuff all along. So we couldn't talk about that. And then, generally, she wanted me to talk more, to entertain her more. She told me about a year into our marriage that she had just expected that eventually I'd have interesting things to say. That wasn't real nice to hear. I don't think she thought much about what she said sometimes. Anyway.

It was while Jim was out talking to Roy that he heard the boat go by close and slow down. He got to his feet and trotted as fast as he could toward the beach, but then he stopped. He could hear it out there, at low revs, probably checking out the cabin, but he couldn't decide whether to run the rest of the way and flag them down. That seemed like too much for this particular day. He didn't feel ready yet. So he hid in the trees and waited, unsure, and then he heard the engines rev up again and the boat was gone.

Jim went back to the grave. Oh God, he said. I can't believe I just did that. Something's wrong. I'm not ready yet to tell people about you.

He lay in bed that night under all of his covers wondering what was coming next. He couldn't stay out here and starve, yet that was what he had chosen just this afternoon. He couldn't hide Roy for-ever. Roy's mother and sister had to know. Jim felt so confused that he cried for the first time in weeks. I just don't know, he kept saying out loud to the ceiling.

The next day, he stayed in bed and didn't go to the grave. He didn't go hunting for crabs, either, or have any other kind of food. He kept wanting to get up, but it was cold out and he was preoccupied by daydreams that he kept extending, closing his eyes until finally it was night again and he was still in bed.

He was thinking about Lakeport, about high school, and how he had worked so many hours at Safeway. He had hated that, had known that it was all a waste, that his time there amounted to nothing since he'd eventually do some other kind of work. And killing mosquitoes in the spring. He remembered how they'd oil the ponds and spray insecticides to keep the mosqui-toes down. Big tanks of chemicals. He wondered now what had been in them. It couldn't have been good.

His sinus troubles had begun back then. Persistent infections and then the headaches. They were back now, the headaches. This was what had taken him closest to killing himself, just the pain in his head. It was impossible to get away from, impossible to sleep through. He'd been an insomniac most of the time for probably twenty years now. He should have gotten an operation, but he didn't like the idea of an operation. He'd worked on too many patients in his dentistry. He knew how brutal surgery was, and the terrible risks.

Another memory from even earlier was the boat they'd had on the lake, an old converted Navy cruiser from the 1920s. They replanked the hull and took it out on warm summer nights, sang out there on the water. That was what he wanted now, he realized, and what he hadn't had in decades: a community of people and a particular place and a sense that he belonged. What had happened to that?

The next day he rose and went looking for crabs. It was low tide and there was quite a lot to choose from. He found some kind of small rockfish hiding in one pool and finally killed it with a stick. It was spiny, but he cleaned it right there on the rocks with his pocketknife and ate it raw. Then he sat back in the rare bit of sunshine and smacked his lips. That was damn good, he said. Now that was a meal.

He finished off with a bit of seaweed and went back to the cabin for a drink of water, then went out to visit with Roy. Haven't been thinking about you as much, he told Roy. Been thinking about myself when I was your age. How I used to hunt ducks right in front of the house. Croppies and bluegill and catfish at night on the pier with a lantern. I've been thinking about all of that, too. It seems to me that one life is actually many lives, and that they add up to something surprisingly long. My life then was nothing like my life now. I was someone else. But what makes me sad, I guess, and the reason I bring all of this up, is that you won't be getting any other lives. You had two or three at most. Early childhood in Ketchikan, then living with your mother in California after the divorce. That would be two. Maybe being out here with me was the beginning of the third. But you know, you killed yourself, I didn't kill you, so that's what you get.

The rest of the afternoon, Jim poked around the shed, looking at all the rusting tools and odd projects. He was getting more active, mostly because it was a weirdly warm spell. Normally he wouldn't stay outside this long. But really, winter in Southeast was not that big a deal. He had been too freaked out with that cache and everything. It wasn't that hard to survive here.

And then Jim went through a time when he didn't seem to have any thoughts or memories at all. He stayed in bed and stared at the ceiling. When he went out, he stared at the trees or at the waves. The water was calm, no whitecaps. A surge more than waves at times, the water gray and opaque and thick-looking. He sat with Roy sometimes, but he was through talking. He was ready to get back to his life, to get back to other people.

But he stayed. A storm came through for over a week and he had nothing to eat. He didn't want to go outside. It seemed the cabin might collapse under the strain. Hail pelting the windows, rain, snow, outrageous winds, dark all the time. He hated this place. He wanted a hot tub.

When the storm finally ended, he was so desperate and starved he decided to set the fire. Everything was soaked, but he walked out into the trees with his spare gas can and a box of matches, resting several times along the way. He found a spot with a lot of deadfall and trees packed in close and he doused as much wood as he could with the gasoline, then struck a match to it and stepped back as it flared up. He started yelling, excited, as the flames devoured the deadfall and licked up the sides of the small trees. The heat was a beautiful thing. Truly warm for what seemed like the first time since summer, Jim stayed as close to it as possible, close enough that he could feel his face too hot and probably burning. The smoke obliterated the tops of the trees and the evening sky, and the sound of the fire overcame everything else. Jim danced around at the edges of it, telling it to consume everything. Grow, he yelled. Grow.

And it did grow, quickly. It took over the entire area where Roy was buried, burned all the way to the water's edge, and moved along the shoreline toward the cabin. Jim hoped it was spreading in other directions, too. The wind was coming this way, though, toward the cabin, so this was its main movement. He thought for a moment that he should have set it on the other side, so that the cabin would have been upwind, but then he didn't care. Let it all burn, he thought, and then let them come for me. I can't spend the rest of my life out here like this.

The fire grew over the next hour, through sunset, and reached the cabin just as it started to rain. Jim raged at the skies, threatened to punish the rain, but it kept coming. The fire burned part of the roof and one wall of the cabin, then drowned and smoked and finally only smelled. It was the middle of the night. He went into the bedroom, which had been spared and now smelled of smoke rather than of Roy, and he slept.

He woke to the roof collapsing in the kitchen under the weight of all the rain. The crash was monstrously loud, but he knew what it was and he didn't get up. He went back to sleep and woke again at midday wet and shivering. Though the section of roof above him was still good, the rain was blowing sideways into the room and drenching him.

You better find me, he said. You better find me now.

He hiked through the charred forest later that day to Roy's grave. The rain had ceased. He wasn't completely sure he was in the right place, but the depression was still there and the charred trunks in roughly the right places, so he sat down shivering in the wet black ash and visited for a while.

I don't know, he answered Roy. Could be they'll see it, could be they'll see it and not care. It's not burning anymore, after all. It's not a fire now.

He went to the unburned section of the forest and was stripping bark to eat when he heard the helicopter pass overhead and then come back and hover just offshore from the cabin. He walked out as fast as he could to meet it, but he was very slow and had to rest several times. It was still there, however, when he cleared the tree line and waved.

Hey, he yelled. You look beautiful. He kept waving. Come on, he yelled.

They weren't able to set down anywhere, he assumed, because they only hovered. It was a sheriff's helicopter, but it didn't have pontoons. He could see their faces, the two of them with their earphones and caps and glasses. He waved and rubbed his arms to make it clear he was freezing, and they waved in return. Their machine seemed a modern wonder to Jim. They stayed there hovering for probably five minutes before they came on over the loudspeaker.

We've radioed for a float plane, they told him. You'll be picked up in an hour or two. If you are James Edwin Fenn, please raise your right arm to confirm.

Jim raised his right arm. Then they rose and turned and flew off. Jim was excited. He was ready to have a normal life again.

An hour or two later, after he had gone back to the cabin, dug out the stove, and started a fire in it to warm himself, afraid now of hypothermia, a float plane came up the channel, banked, and landed hard in the small chop out from his beach. Jim waved and stood at the edge of his beach waiting. They taxied up until their pontoons hit the gravel and then they cut their engine and two men in uniform came down onto the pontoons while the pilot stayed inside.

Howdy, the lead man shouted.

Jim waved. I'm glad you're here, he said. I was over on Suk-kwan with my son.

We found that, the man said. Been looking for you and your son. Sheriff Coos.

They shook hands.

We've been worried about you. Had a missing persons out for both of you for almost two months now.

Well, I've been right here. Look, my son died. He killed him-self. So I went looking for help and I didn't find any. I ended up here and I had to survive the winter. I pretty much wrecked these people's place but I'll pay for it; I had to do what I did to survive. I buried my son out in the woods.

Whoa, Coos said. Slow down. Your son killed himself?

Yeah.

Okay, Coos said. Let Leroy here take your statement. He has to write all this down.

So Jim waited and then gave a slower, more complete version, though still not the whole story. They said they'd take a more complete statement when they got back to town. But for now, they took the basic story and then wanted to see where he'd bur-ied Roy.

The men were close behind him. Jim tried to walk faster but he couldn't. And then he got confused and was having trouble finding Roy. Hold on a second, he said. It's somewhere around here. It's hard to find now because of the fire. I came out here and talked to him earlier today, but I can't find it now.

They only stood close and didn't say anything. He knew this looked bad, that it looked like he was trying not to find Roy, and that panicked him and made it harder still. Every charred bit of forest was starting to look the same. I can't do this, he said. I'm sorry, but I just can't find him today.

He turned to face Coos. Jim knew he could be reasonable. I haven't seen anyone in so long, he said.

I'm sorry for your troubles, Coos said. And we'll get you home today. But you need to find your son.

So Jim kept looking until he was standing in one spot and looked down to see that he was in a small depression and saw his prints from earlier in the day and realized this was the grave. He started crying without meaning to and told them, This is it.

Jim backed away from the grave and sat down while the men inspected the depression and Leroy took pictures of it and then went back to the plane for a shovel.

I'm sorry, the sheriff said. But we can't leave the body here. You understand.

Sure, Jim said. He lay down on his side to watch them. The smell of smoke was so strong close to the ground that it was difficult to breathe, but he felt he was safer lying down here and had no intention of getting up. He would watch and then soon he'd see Roy buried decently. And then if they tried to charge him with anything, he'd get a good lawyer and get out of this. He hadn't done anything wrong. His son had killed himself, and though Jim had broken a lot of laws after that, it had all been necessary for survival. Jim felt an enormous pity for himself and hated the sheriff and Leroy, unreasonably he knew. They were just doing their jobs, and they hadn't even accused him of anything.

They were careful. And they took pictures. When they came to the sleeping bag finally, they took many pictures of that, from the first glimpse of it to fully uncovered, and then Leroy opened it and threw up.

Coos took over and got the bag open, and they took flash pictures of what was inside but didn't empty it out. They closed it up again and then Leroy went to the plane for a big clear plastic bag. They put the sleeping bag and Roy in this and duct-taped it shut.

I'm placing you under arrest, Coos told Jim. And then he read Jim his rights.

What? Jim asked, but they didn't answer. The two of them pulled him to his feet and Leroy held his arm as they walked back over ash and rock and beach to the water's edge.

They loaded Roy in the back and then put Jim in one of the aft seats. The pilot taxied, then gunned the engines and the plane lifted free. Jim was dizzy during the flight and fell asleep until they landed in water again.

When they got out, Jim was surprised to see that they were in Ketchikan. He had lived here with Elizabeth and Roy, and Tracy had been born here just before everything had fallen apart.

We've called the boy's mother, Coos said. And we're taking you to the hospital so they can take a look at you.

Thanks, Jim said.

No problem. But I have to tell you, if you've killed your son, and I think you did, I'll see you put in prison, and if you ever get out, I'll kill you myself.

Jesus, Jim said.

The doctor examined him quickly and said all he needed was lots of food, water, and rest. He looked at the end of Jim's nose and said he had lost a little piece to frostbite but there was nothing he could do about that. Then Jim was taken to the sheriff's office to give a longer statement. For the rest of the day, they made him give his statement over and over. They kept coming back to why his son would have wanted to kill himself.

I wanted to kill myself, and I came close to doing it. I was on the radio with Rhoda, and I intended to do it. Roy had been having to listen to a lot of that for a while. Not just on the radio, but when I would talk with him about it and when he'd have to hear me crying and such.

Jim shook his head. He was having trouble continuing, trouble breathing. His lungs were getting all gluey. So I was there with the pistol to my head and ready. I'd been like that for a while and hadn't been able to actually pull the trigger. I kept thinking, What if I'm wrong. But Roy walks in and sees this and the way he looked at me I didn't know what to do, so I turned off the radio and handed him the pistol and walked out. I didn't mean anything by that. I had no idea what he might do.

Tell us what happened then, Jim.

Well, I was out walking and I heard the shot, and even then I didn't figure out what had happened, so I kept walking around like a dumbass for a while longer and then I got back and found him.

What did you see when you found him?

Jesus. How much do you want? It was him lying there. He'd blown off his head. You know what that looks like.

No, I don't.

Don't you? Well, he only had half his face and parts of him were everywhere, and there was nothing I could do to put him back together.

What did you do after with the body?

I buried him. But then I realized he needed a burial with his mother and sister to see it, so I dug him up and then I guess I went looking for a boat or cabin or someone with a radio.

What happened to your own radios?

I broke them.

When?

Right after he killed himself. I don't know why I did it.

You broke the radios right after your son's death. Was this so no one would be able to contact you? Did you have something to hide?

Stop it, Jim said. Stop being idiots. I just broke them and then went looking and couldn't find anyone and had to break into that cabin to survive while I waited. It took you forever to find me, and that was only after I set half the island on fire. Otherwise I'd still be rotting out there.

Who was rotting?

Shut up, you fucker.

Mr. Fenn, let me remind you. We have you on many charges, not only murder. You need to cooperate with us and answer our questions.

I'm a dentist. This is outrageous. I didn't kill my son.

That may be.

This was only the first of many sessions. They had him tell the story over and over, all the details, trying to find pieces that didn't fit. Why Roy was in the sleeping bag. Where the pistol was, which was something Jim honestly could not answer. Where had he put it? He had no memory of putting it anywhere. The last he remembered it had been on the floor, but they hadn't found anything. So apparently he had done something else with it.

Breaking the radios was another thing they went back to again and again. And the time he'd stepped off the small cliff. And handing Roy the pistol. All of these things over and over until Jim could not be completely sure whether any of it had happened exactly as he remembered. It began to seem almost like someone else's history.

They kept him in jail for several days and didn't let him make any calls. No one except the doctor knew he was there until finally they sent in a lawyer. But this man wouldn't say much. He only paced back and forth in front of Jim's cell, then said, You want your own private lawyer, right? Is that what you're asking me right now?

Sure, Jim said.

Okay, the man said. I'll go call one and he'll be in today.

The man left then. Much later in the day, another man in a suit and tie came in.

Name's Norman, the man said. Be happy to have me. It

sounds like you're in trouble. But first I need to know whether you can afford me.

I need to get out of here, Jim said. On bail or something. That's all. I don't care what it costs me.

Okay, Norman said. I can work with that.

It was almost a week before they held the arraignment and Jim was able to leave. He wanted to fly to California to see Elizabeth and Tracy and Rhoda and try to explain, but the terms of his bail were that he couldn't leave Ketchikan, so he took a taxi downtown to a hotel, a crappy little place called the Royal Executive Suites. When Jim had lived here in Ketchikan eight years before, he had befriended the owner of this hotel, who at that time had been only a young guy fresh off the ferry. The man had been moving here, and though he was a Mormon and Jim was not, Jim had taken him fishing and let him stay at the house and helped him to find work. The man's name was Kirk, and he didn't have time for Jim now, but he did let Jim buy a room for twice what it was worth.

Jim stayed in his room with the heat on and made phone calls. He called Roy's mother, Elizabeth, but only got the answering machine. After the beep, he stood there with the receiver in his hand and had no idea what to say. He finally just said, Sorry, and hung up. Then he thought about calling Rhoda, but he didn't feel ready for that yet. He didn't feel ready to talk with anyone, really, so he gave up on the phone calls.

He spent the rest of the day sitting in a chair by the window, looking out at the water and not thinking anything coherent. He daydreamed that Roy had been shot and he had killed the men who had done it, picking them off one by one from around the cabin with the rifle, and then he carried Roy to the inflatable and sped over to the next island, where he found a fishing boat and got Roy aboard. They laid him on the deck with the red salmon and Jim pumped at his chest to keep him alive until a helicopter came and lifted him away. Jim tried to hold on to this last image of Roy spinning slowly above him on the stretcher, being lifted into safety. He felt his love for Roy hard in his chest and was overwhelmed by the grief of having saved his son.

But he couldn't hold the daydream forever, and soon he was just sitting in a chair by the window and it was another overcast day with the heater going. He looked down at his feet in socks on the clean beige carpet and looked at the cream walls and spackled ceiling and back down to the bad watercolor of a gillnetter pulling in its catch. He wanted to talk to his brother or Rhoda, but he also couldn't imagine calling. When he was too hungry to sit there any longer, he bundled himself up and prepared to face the good folk of Ketchikan.

Jim walked through the lobby without looking at anyone and crossed the street to a restaurant that served fish and chips. He sat himself in a corner booth and stared down at his own clenched hands. The waitress when she finally came over didn't seem to recognize him, though he had seen her here years before. He didn't seem to be famous yet for what had happened out in the islands, either. He had imagined the whole event might attract more attention.

Jim drummed his fingers on the red Formica and waited and sipped his water and wondered how it was he had ended up without friends. No one was flying up here to visit him or to help him wait this thing out. John Lampson in Williams and Tom Kalfsbeck in Lower Lake: he hadn't called them yet, so they couldn't know, but even if he did call, he was pretty sure they wouldn't come. And this was because of women, too. It was because of his obsession with Rhoda over these past years that he had lost touch with his friends in California and not made new ones in Fairbanks. He had done his work and bought things and talked on the phone and seen prostitutes and had dinner a few times with other dentists or orthodontists and their wives, but that was about it. It was no wonder to him now that he had fallen so low. He had cut himself off from everyone and had nursed what he thought was love but was only longing, a kind of sickness inside him that had nothing to do with Rhoda at all. And it had taken this to get him out of it, to get him to see it. His son had had to kill himself so that Jim could get his life back. And yet that wasn't going to work, either, because it wasn't just that his son had killed himself.

Jim held back his sobbing as well as he could for fear that someone might notice and he might seem like a guilty man, though they couldn't possibly know the crimes he had actually committed. None of the obvious ones like murder, but all of the more important ones.

The waitress set his food before him finally and he ate though it was tasteless to him and he could think only of Roy.

That evening, late, he went back out and walked along the waterfront. He walked past the downtown area where he had practiced and on to the old red-light district, preserved now as a kind of monument and converted to small tourist shops. The small wooden buildings hung precariously along the banks of the narrow river. He stood at the bridge and stared at them, trying to imagine life here before he'd been born. But this was what he'd never been able to do, send his life into another's.

In the morning, he heard knocking at his door and he opened it to Elizabeth and his daughter Tracy.

Whoa, he said. God, I didn't expect you.

Oh Jim, Elizabeth said, and she wrapped her arms around him for the first time in years. It felt unbelievably good. Then Jim bent down and hugged Tracy. She had been crying and looked exhausted. Jim didn't know what to say.

Come in, he said. They followed him in and sat down on the couch.

Tracy started crying. Elizabeth held her and kissed the top of her head, then looked at Jim and asked, What happened out there, Jim?

I don't know, Jim said. I honestly don't know.

Try a little harder? But then she started crying, and Tracy was crying, and they went away, Elizabeth promising they'd be back later in the day.

So Jim waited, in a chair facing the door to his hotel room, unable to believe they were here in town. He had been gone so long, and it was harder still to understand that they were all here in Ketchikan, all together, except Roy of course, and then his mind stopped again. It was all too much to take in. He felt very afraid, and yet had no idea what in particular was frightening him.

When Elizabeth and Tracy returned, it was past dinnertime, but they weren't hungry, so they sat in the room not talking and

Jim wanted this family and this life back, and he kept fantasizing that Roy might just walk in.

Did you kill him? Elizabeth asked, and then she was lost in loud, awful, ugly sobs that got Tracy going again, too. Jim wasn't crying; he was calculating, trying to figure a way to get them back, but he couldn't see how.

I'm sorry, he said. I was afraid all the time I was going to kill myself. He was taking care of me. Then he surprised me and ended up killing himself.

What happened, Jim?

I handed him the pistol as I walked out the door. I didn't mean for him to use it.

You handed him the pistol?

Jim could see this had been the wrong thing to tell her. I didn't mean anything by it, he said.

You handed him the pistol? And then Elizabeth was up and crossing the room and hitting him, hard, and he was looking at Tracy, who had this terrible frozen look on her face and was just watching, and then they were gone and he waited that night for them to return, and the next morning and still they hadn't, so he started walking around town, searching, and finally found their hotel but they had checked out. He searched until night and then realized he could call the airlines but he could only get a recording so he had to wait until morning, when he found out they had flown back to California, and with Roy's remains.

Jim called and kept calling Elizabeth, and finally one day she answered. He tried to explain himself, but she wouldn't listen.

I don't understand this, Jim, she said. I will never understand this. How my son became the boy who did that to himself. What you did to him to make him that way. And then she hung up and didn't answer for days and then changed her phone number with no new number listed and he couldn't leave Ketchikan or reach anyone he knew who would tell him her new number. Everyone, even his own brother and friends, was against him. The only person he didn't call was Rhoda. He couldn't call her, because in a way she had killed Roy, too.

Jim tried to discover how to spend his days. He would have to reenter his life at some point. He couldn't spend the next fifty years sitting here aching. But the truth was, he was scared now. He wasn't sure how he could prove he hadn't murdered his son.

Sometime after two a.m., Jim realized it had been almost a year since he'd been with a woman. So he bundled up and went looking for a prostitute.

The streets were wet, the fog down close. Sound carried oddly from the waterfront and from the road. Fishing bells, fog bells, seagulls, and the hiss of tires on asphalt. He walked downtown to his old office.

They had redone the front of the building. It looked more modern now and was a dark green. Gold lettering on the window with the dentists' names, two of them.

I could have stayed here, he said. If I had not cheated and broken everything up. If I had been able to stand my wife. If salmon had flown like birds through the streets.

He wasn't sure what to do with this office. He turned away from it, finally, crossed the street and headed down the other side toward the canneries.

The canneries were packed in summer with college students, but now, in the spring, they were deserted. He passed an old man sitting on a bench in front of a cannery and they ignored each other. He continued on past all of the canneries but couldn't find any prostitutes. He went to the old red-light district along the river just for the hell of it, knowing he wouldn't find any there, and he didn't. He stood at the wooden railing looking down into green-black water moving swiftly out to sea and he gave up.

But instead of walking back to the hotel, he walked in the opposite direction, away from town. Past the canneries, along the highway, he walked in fog and drizzle, the only walker on the road. It was a pleasure to walk, and a pleasure to be alone outside. He couldn't stay much longer in that hotel.

The forest on either side of the road loomed roughly out of the fog. It had been better out on the island, he saw now. He had still believed in his rescue then, and he had been able to go talk with Roy. Now Roy was fifteen hundred miles away.

A dark-green pickup came out of the fog quickly and swerved to avoid Jim. It stopped about a hundred feet past him and the two men looked back at him through the rear window. They looked for a long time; Jim stood in place and stared back at them until they moved on. He was scared, though, that they would come back with others. He had been stupid to stay here. It was too great a risk. Then he realized this was only paranoia, since no one could possibly know who he was.

Jim hurried back anyway, walking on the side of the road and hiding himself in bushes whenever he heard a car coming. It was a long way to town. He hadn't realized how far he had gone.

Curve after curve and the shoreline appearing twice through the fog, calm gray water lit by a shrouded moon.

He reached the canneries finally and stopped hiding from cars. He passed the old red-light district and the tourist area and then downtown and continued around the point to his hotel. It was nearly dark but he grabbed the few things he had: a change of clothes in a plastic bag, his razor and shampoo, his wallet, his boots. He threw everything in the bag, left a note to Kirk saying, Thanks for ripping me off, and walked out into the evening toward the ferry that could take him across to the airport.

The ferry terminal was over three miles away, past Jackson Street, at the end of town. He was tired when he got there, and hungry, and there was nowhere to eat. He looked at the schedule, then found out this wasn't the right terminal for the ferries that went across to the airport. This terminal was for the big Alaska Marine Highway ferries that went clear up to Haines and down to Washington.

He decided he didn't need to fly. He just needed to leave, and a ferry was leaving for Haines early in the morning. He would sleep on one of the benches.

On the ferry, he ordered a hotdog and a mini-pizza and some frozen yogurt. The constant vibration and sound of the engines beneath the floors were a comfort. It occurred to him that if his whole life had been spent under way, he might have been a lot happier. These ferries were heavy and solid and almost never rolled or pounded at all, but as he sat there eating, he did feel different, anyway. And then he got to thinking again about sailing away to the South Pacific. If he got through all of this okay, he might try that. He felt like telling this to someone, felt like talking about it with someone to find out how it sounded.

Jim looked around but everyone was sitting in groups. He chewed on through the rest of his food, then walked around the upper deck looking for someone standing alone at the railing, but this boat, at least on deck, seemed to be Noah's Ark, everyone in pairs.

Though he didn't drink, he went to the bar, because that seemed a likely place, even though it was morning. And he did find a woman sitting alone at one of the tables. Dark hair and an unhappy look, or perhaps just bored. She looked a few years younger than he was. She didn't look as if she were waiting for anyone.

Mind if I join you? he asked.

That's okay, I guess, she said, but this sounded so bad, so bored, he hesitated. She just watched him.

Okay, he said, and sat down.

It's not like you're doing me a favor, she said.

Jim got up and walked away. He stood on the stern and stared at the wake. He had wanted to tell that woman about Roy. He wanted just one person he could tell the whole story to, to work it out. Because when he left it alone, it just seemed more and more like he had killed Roy.

Jim couldn't think about this well. He stared at the wake. Though it trailed away and spread and dissipated, it remained exactly the same from his viewpoint. It would never catch up with the boat nor would it ever be lost. It seemed like this might mean something, but then Jim was only wondering what his life was now, and not knowing. One thing had happened after another, but it seemed to him random and odd that things had worked out the way they had.

Jim could smell the diesel exhaust back here. It made him nostalgic for the *Osprey*, his fishing boat. He had failed at that, finally, and had to sell the boat, but really it hadn't been a failure. He had spent all that time with his brother Gary pulling in albacore and then halibut; he had gotten to know the fishing fleet, all the Norwegians, even though he had not really talked to them. He had listened to them on the radio, their check-ins every morning and evening, their reports on the fishing, their evening entertainment. They had taken turns singing old songs and playing harmonica and even accordion. It had been an amazing time, really, though he and his brother had been outcasts. The *Tin Can*, they had called his boat, for the raw aluminum. They had older wooden boats, most of them. Some of them were fiberglass. He'd hear them mention him occasionally, but it was never an invitation to come on the radio and join in. He missed that life. He wished it had worked out. Roy could have worked on the boat in the summers.

One night, the Norwegians lost one of their boats. They came on in the morning, checking in, and no one knew where that one boat was. Most of it was in Norwegian, but there was enough said in English that Jim and Gary knew what was happening. They had slipped anchor themselves once when their sea parachute collapsed. The water was far too deep for bottom anchors, so the whole fleet put out sea parachutes off their bows and stayed anchored together that way, but the night their parachute collapsed, Jim and Gary awoke far from the fleet, no fishing boats around and right in the shipping lanes. So this was what must have happened to this Norwegian boat, they figured, and nothing was heard from it again.

In Haines, Jim called his brother Gary. Hey, he said, it's me, and then there was silence. He waited.

Well, Gary said. Some people are looking for you.

Looking for me?

You jumped bail, didn't you?

No.

Another pause. There might be a difference of opinion here, Gary said. And you might think about trying to make amends somehow, since I think the sheriff's opinion wins.

Why are we talking about this? Jim said. I called you to talk about other things. I wanted to talk to my brother. I've been thinking a lot about our time on the *Osprey*, thinking that it's too bad that didn't work out. I wish we were still doing it. And I was thinking it would have been nice if Roy could have worked on the boat in the summers.

Jim, where are you?

I'm in Haines.

Look, you have to turn yourself in. You can't run from them, and you're just going to make yourself look bad in front of a jury.

Are you listening to me? Jim asked. I wanted to talk about other things. Do you think about the *Osprey*, or about living out there?

Jim waited then. He could hear his brother breathing.

Yeah, I do, Gary finally said. I think about those times. And though it was hard then, I'm glad we did it. It was an adventure. I wouldn't do it again, though.

No?

No.

That's too bad, Jim said. You know, I've been a little lonely in all this since I've been back. I haven't had anyone to talk to. No one's come to visit me or help me.

No one can now, Gary said. They'd be an accessory or something. Harboring a fugitive. I don't know what they'd call it, but they'd call it something.

I don't have any chance of beating this, do I? Jim said. He paused, and Gary didn't say anything, and Jim realized finally that this was true. He was just waiting around for his own fall. He realized also that he needed not to tell his brother anything more. I need to go now, he said.

Okay, Gary said. I wish I could help you. I really do. I should have come to see you while you were still in Ketchikan.

That's all right.

Jim walked straight into town looking for his bank. They had to have a branch here. He found several other banks and got toward what appeared to be the end of the small town and started panicking, but then he saw it. He walked in with his checkbook and ID in his hand, waited in line, and then was ushered to a side desk because of the amount of his withdrawal, almost $115,000 in cash. He intended to clean out what was left of this savings account completely, though the sheriff had probably already frozen it. Coos knew about it because he'd already taken over $200,000 for bail and fees and a few thousand for living expenses in Ketchikan.

The financial officer assisting him didn't really want to assist him. This is a very large and unusual withdrawal, she said. Especially in cash. I have to let you know that we'll have to report this. We have to report any large deposit or withdrawal such as this.

That's okay, Jim said.

May I ask what the withdrawal is for?

To buy a house, Jim said.

We can have a cashier's check made out for that.

Nope, it has to be cash.

A cashier's check is cash.

Cash cash.

The woman frowned.

Look, Jim said, is it my money or is it not?

It is, of course, the woman said. I'm not sure we have that much cash on hand, though. In fact, I'm sure we don't.

How much do you have?

What?

I'll take whatever you have.

Jim left with $27,500 in cash. He knew he had been ripped off, that they had more cash than that, but it was enough. He didn't need to buy his own boat. He could find some fishing boat that had just finished the March opening and was waiting around. They'd need money.

Jim went to the bigger boats first. It was hard to find anyone around. He asked people, though, and got phone numbers and addresses of homes and bars. Then he found one guy cleaning up on one of the smaller gillnetters.

Howdy, Jim said, but the man only looked at him, then

went back to work. He was so much what one would expect he was laughable. A beard and battered old cap, a pathetic alcoholic.

I'd like a ride down the coast to Mexico. I'm paying fifteen thousand. Interested?

The man looked at him then. Just kill somebody? he asked.

Only my own life, Jim said.

Let me just go down to the sheriff and ask around, then we can talk about it.

Is this your boat?

No. But I know the captain.

Why don't we skip the sheriff's office and make it twenty thousand.

The man took off his cap and scratched his head. Will we be skipping the Coast Guard, too? And maybe offering a crew list in Mexico that might be a name short?

That would be the deal.

Well, let me talk to Chuck. There obviously ain't much else going on for us.

The man went inside the cabin house then and was gone a long time. Jim couldn't hear voices or anything. The boat was a piece of crap, rusted out and held together with wire. But it would get him down the coast. It was hell coming up the coast, but going down was easy enough.

The man returned with Chuck, who was in his sixties and seemed to be the captain and owner. He was a fiercely ugly man, liver spots on the bald top of his head fringed by a dark and greasy mane. He stared at Jim with such hatred that Jim knew immediately not to trust him, and yet what choice did he have?

He had nothing left. He needed to go and these were the only guys around.

What kind of trouble you in? Chuck asked.

Jim didn't answer but only waited. Finally Chuck said, All right. I suppose you'll be wanting to leave right away.

That's right.

We need to provision, get diesel, get some spare filters and such. The engine has a few problems. It's not going to be a fast or a glamorous ride. But the price is twenty-five.

I don't have twenty-five. I'm not trying to bargain or save up. I just don't have it.

All right, Chuck said. We'll need about three or four hours, and ten up front. And I want to see the other ten, too, just to see that you have it.

So Jim went aboard, handed over ten thousand and showed the other ten. And he stayed right there while they went out and provisioned. He wasn't going to let them slip out without him. Nine hours later, in the evening, they were on their way.

The wind was up and cold, the chop enough to put a little spray over the bow. It was clear out, though. Standing on the stern, Jim could see all the lights in Haines and a few scattered lights along the shoreline beyond and fishing boats out on the water rafted together, waiting. Beyond them, abandoned land and waters among the land, the boundary between them dark and changing. Boating in a strange place at night you could believe almost any-thing, he knew, any direction, any depth, so sure of innate fears you could distrust your compass and depth finder right up until you hit the rocks. He hoped Chuck and Ned were competent.

They motored through the rest of the night toward Juneau, slipping past darkened land barely perceptible against the darkened sky. He felt a stranger. He had lived in this land much of his life, but the land had not softened or become familiar in that time. It felt as hostile as when he had first entered it. He felt that if he were to let himself sleep, he would be destroyed. Chuck would be drunk at the wheel, currents would carry them, slip them sideways until the bottom rose to meet the hull and they would tip and fill with seawater and drown. It was just a fact that this was always waiting in close. They would be much safer far from land. He was thinking of this as a way of thinking about Roy. Roy had been hostile to him also. They had never known one another, never softened. He had not been wary enough of Roy. He had lost himself in his own problems and not seen Roy for the threat he was. He had let himself sleep.

The next day came slowly. A thin line of gray, or perhaps a blue less dark, and then the peaks outlined as if by their own emanation, and then a faster lightening above them until their edges curled in fire and suddenly everywhere was white and the orange sun ticked upward in thin, segmented lines between two peaks to grow heavy and yellow and merge into the world too hot to look at. All became blind. The water and mountains and air all the same brightness, glaring. Jim couldn't make out boats or waves or land, could not see a thing for nearly half an hour until the day filled out and land became land again, waves had distance, and he could see boats upon them everywhere. The surface still opaque, gray-white, a solid membrane. The boat wallowing slowly through at eight or nine knots, Haines in the distance now or gone, too far to see.

By eight o'clock, as Ned relieved Chuck and dug into an entire box of jelly doughnuts, they passed what Jim at first had thought was Juneau but was only Point Bridget State Park, he saw on the chart, connected to Juneau by a small highway.

If you know how to read a chart, you can take a turn at the helm, Ned said.

Fair enough, Jim said. I'll be next.

Soon after, Jim had his best chance of seeing Juneau down Favorite Channel. Then, a little later, down Saginaw Channel, but he really didn't see anything. They weren't very close and it didn't look like much. By noon Jim was at the wheel, exhausted, and they were around Couverden Island, heading west out Icy Strait.

He grinned when he hit Icy Strait because it was indeed suddenly a lot colder. It was a kind of joke. You could tell even from inside the pilot house, through the small cracks and vents.

The channel was huge—at least five miles across—but there was a lot of traffic. A few cabin cruisers and two sailboats but many other commercial salmon and halibut boats and some tugs with loads far behind them. Those were the ones he had to anticipate. He wasn't used to being so slow. He just couldn't get out of the way quickly in this thing. And he didn't turn on the VHF, because he didn't want attention.

They passed Pleasant Island around three o'clock, then Point Gustavus, and the wind howled down from Glacier Bay to the north, down through the Sitakaday Narrows.

As they passed the next small bay, Dundas Bay, a bit later, he saw a Coast Guard cruiser, one of the big ones, passing on the other side of the Inian Islands, and he felt panicked. If they came over to board him, to inspect for safety equipment and drugs, as they routinely did, he would be caught. He had no faith in Chuck or Ned to stand by him. He was afraid even to sleep, although he could hardly keep awake at this point. But the cutter passed far on the other side of the northernmost island and went into the next bay. Jim stayed as far out of the way as possible, ducking slightly into Taylor Bay as he passed. Brady Glacier looked enormous, a thing from another time, on a different scale that denied anything now, as if Jim could not possibly be Jim because the thought was too small, instantaneous as the glare. The glacier dwarfed mountains.

The wind tore down off the glacier in gusts that set the boat rocking, but this was good because it kept him alert.

And then he was out. He passed Cape Spencer by eight o'clock and was heading out to sea, free of the coast, free of the islands and southeast Alaska. On the chart, he was out of U.S. waters in less than an hour. He would cross them again because of the way the lines were drawn, but only briefly. Within another night and day, he'd be far enough offshore that no one would know to find him or care. He would be entering another life.

Again he thought of Roy. He couldn't seem not to. He would be thinking along and not expecting the shift, and then he'd see the pistol, handing it to Roy, or he'd come in after and find him there on the floor, or what was left of him. And then he was thinking of the sleeping bag and wondered what had happened to it. They had taken it away in the clear plastic bag with Roy's body, and they had not wanted to try to pour him out. It was too much to think of him that way, but then what could they have done? They must have done that at some point before they had buried him. But who? Who had poured him out? And what had

Elizabeth seen? What had his daughter Tracy seen? He might not see her again. He had lost her, too.

The Gulf of Alaska was very cold. The wind blew hard and the waves were large now and confused, wind waves and swells, breaking around him and soaking the foredeck, occasionally coming over the side. Chuck came up to relieve him at four. Get some sleep, he said.

How far out are we going? Jim asked. I'd like to be at least a hundred out all the way down.

We can do that, Chuck said. Though we're gonna have to stop for fuel somewhere. Oregon, probably.

Jim went below and sacked out in a tiny bunk that smelled terribly of Chuck's old sweat and alcohol. He was hungry, but he was too tired, so he tried just to sleep.

A boat under way is a noisy thing. He had known that. But this boat's walls creaked and popped in a way that couldn't be good. And her diesel was extremely uneven, dropping low in revs and then racing, not only because of the swells and cavitation. Jim lay curled up in fear and exhaustion and waited for it to pass, waited for sleep, but waiting and fearing like that he thought too much about everything. He thought about the IRS, the sheriff, the Coast Guard, his brother, Elizabeth, Tracy, Rhoda, Roy. He imagined a long conversation with Rhoda trying to convince her he hadn't killed Roy. He pointed out that Roy was thirteen, that he had a mind of his own, that he could do things that were his own choice.

His own choice? Rhoda asked.

It wasn't my doing, Jim said. It was never my idea that he kill himself.

Never your idea, Jim?

No, he'd tell Rhoda. But then he confessed one more detail. He told about the time shooting up into the ceiling.

And what was that about?

I don't know. I was just shooting.

Just shooting?

Shut up, Jim said aloud in the dark, but he could hardly hear himself, it was so damn loud. And then he worried about what course they were on. How would he know if the boat swung around, if Chuck decided to head back? And what about islands? It was an old, irrational fear of his when under way. He was always afraid of hitting islands that weren't on the chart, even in mid-ocean.

He couldn't keep his head still. That was why he wasn't sleeping. No matter how he wedged it in between a few shirts and the lee cloth, he couldn't get it not to rock when the boat rocked. He couldn't relax his neck. And the whiskers along his jaw scraped against the shirts every time his head moved. Roy hadn't gotten to the point where he'd had whiskers. He was starting to get peach fuzz. They talked about shaving one day, Roy worried about cutting himself, not realizing the blade head swiveled. Jim grinned. Then he was crying again and hating how weak he was. He saw himself in Mexico and maybe someday in the South Pacific, down there in all the nice weather with warm, beautiful blue water and the green mountains, and he saw that he would still be alone. Roy would never catch up to him. And he wondered what Roy's grave looked like. He realized he'd never get to see it now.

Jim looked across to the other side to see if Ned was awake, too, but apparently he wasn't.

Jim lay there against the lee cloth with his eyes closed and couldn't find anything. It was just windblown space inside him, a vacuum. He didn't care about anything, and it would have been better just to kill himself, but Roy had done that, and now he couldn't. Roy had killed himself instead, in a clear trade, and this was why Jim was responsible for killing Roy. It was not the way things were supposed to have been, but because Jim had been cowardly, because he hadn't had the courage just to kill himself before Roy returned, he had missed that moment, the one moment he had to make things right, and he forfeited that moment forever and handed over the pistol to Roy and asked that he fix things in the way that he could, even though it was not the right way.

And Roy had done it. Roy wasn't cowardly and didn't flinch, and he put the barrel up and pulled the trigger and blew off half his head. And Jim did not recognize what had happened when he heard the shot. He didn't know enough to recognize the sacrifice at the time it was made.

Jim still hadn't believed what had happened even after he saw Roy's body lying there in the doorway with his blood and brain and bone everywhere. He still had not believed or seen anything, even as the proof lay before him. And now here he was escaping, thinking he could run off and evade the law and his punishment and have his perfect life somewhere eating mangoes and coconuts like Robinson Crusoe, as if nothing had happened, as if his son had done nothing and he had played no part in it. But that was not the way things could be, he knew now, and he knew also what he had to do.

Jim got up out of his lee cloth and went into the pilot house.

Chuck was tilted back in his captain's chair, looking at a porno magazine. He raised his eyes from the page for a minute and said, What do you want?

We have to go back, Jim said. I can't run from this. I'm turning myself in.

Chuck looked at him steadily, and Jim had no idea what he was thinking. You're gonna turn yourself in, Chuck finally said.

Yeah.

And where does that leave us? We helped you get out of town, remember?

Jim wasn't sure what to do. Okay, you're right, he said. You'll get your full payment and I'll wait a few days until you're gone before I do anything.

Chuck went back to his porno. All right, he said. Go ahead and wake Ned up for the next watch before you sack out again.

Jim woke Ned, who complained that it was early. Jim lay down again and tried to sleep. He was practicing his confession as he drifted off. I, Jim Fenn, murdered my son, Roy Fenn, back in the fall, probably nine months ago. I killed him by shooting him in the head at close range with my pistol, a Ruger .44 Magnum, which was recovered, I think, by the sheriff. I was suicidal and had been talking on the radio with my ex-wife Rhoda, who said she didn't want to get back together with me and was planning to marry another man, and I couldn't stand it any more and I was too cowardly to kill myself so I killed my son.

That wasn't quite right. He went back to his motivations, because they would ask about those, he knew. He went over each incriminating detail, over and over, the pistol, the radios, using everything. He was so exhausted he couldn't keep it straight. His mind had stopped and his body felt tiny, as if he were an infant. He was a tiny golden infant shrunken inside himself with strings reaching out to each part of this larger body, pulling in. He was vanishing.

Jim woke with a rope around his neck yanking him from his bunk. He tried to scream but he couldn't. He was on the floor, hit a bulkhead, was struggling, then saw Ned with a wooden bat hitting him across the legs. He fell, was dragged along, got a glimpse of Chuck at the other end of the rope and knew he should have seen this coming. It should have been so obvious. Then he blacked out.

When he hit the water, it was so cold he woke and wanted them to find him and rescue him. Wanted Chuck and Ned to come get him. He struggled with the rope at his neck, freed it easily, but he was in his clothes, sinking, weighted down, and he didn't have a life jacket. He felt enormously sorry for himself. The open ocean was an awesome sight. Peaks forming everywhere, tossing and disappearing, hillsides rolling past. It was impossible to believe it was just water, impossible to believe, also, how far it extended beneath him. He struggled for what seemed forever and might have been ten minutes before he numbed and tired and began swallowing water. He thought of Roy, who had had no chance to feel this terror, whose death had been instant. He threw up water involuntarily and swallowed and breathed it in again like the end it was, cold and hard and unnecessary, and he knew then that Roy had loved him and that that should have been enough. He just hadn't understood anything in time.

KETCHIKAN

AT THIRTY, I rode the Alaskan ferry past the coastline of British Columbia, past white-ringed islands, forests extending beyond the horizon, gulls and bald eagles, porpoises, whales, all in close, rode past sunsets over the open ocean, lighthouses, small fishing villages, into Alaskan waters where mountains sloped steeply upward out of fjords, and on, finally, to the town of my childhood, strung narrowly along the waterfront, drenched perpetually in mist, the place of ghosts, I felt, the place where my dead father had first gone astray, the place where this father and his suicide and his cheating and his lies and my pity for him, also, might finally be put to rest: Ketchikan.

My first day and evening, I found a place to live where the houses were narrow and thin streets traversed but never descended directly. Long wooden stairways, their sea-grayed wood slick from mist and worn like stone, fell through skunk weed, fern, and salmonberry toward the docks and ocean below where fishing boats paused like apparitions, the small yellow floats in their netting the thousand eyes contained, rolled up, waiting. I stood before them that first night of my return, beyond sleep, and wondered at the spread of their nets, at the full transfiguration, the peacock eyes and fan sifting silently through half a mile of open ocean, drifting, seemingly, as grand and unplanned as jellyfish but more terrible, more calculating in their single purpose. This was overwrought, but it seemed in keeping with the indulgence of this trip, with the extravagance of an attempted return to childhood. The world had become, in brief moments, animated, and I its briefly unself-conscious observer.

I walked among the purse seiners and trawlers, gillnetters and great tugs, down floating planks iridescent with fish scales and waved to the two or three fishermen in their lighted cabins who heard or otherwise sensed me and looked up from their odd hours, their strange, solitary lives, to nod and look down again. Most had shotguns within reach, I remembered. Most did not feel strange and solitary at all, but hassled and trapped, limited, cheated. Fishermen, as a group, complain bitterly, despite appearances. All of which came back with a new familiarity, gifts from what felt like another life. Though I was an intruder, this was perhaps the closest I'd felt, in my few adult years, to belonging.

But I moved on, an intruder still, a tourist always, and wished I could find again the woman I had talked with just before I'd left who was working on a tug out of Seattle. She told of a seven-hundred-pound halibut, over nine feet head to tail and nearly as wide. This was during the time of waiting, when a group of tugs had to pause three days to wait out a storm farther north in their path. It was her crew's turn to fish, to pull up twelve hundred pounds of halibut to feed crews from all the tugs, and when they had pulled this great fish to the surface, they shot it six times through the head with a .45-caliber pistol before winching it from the waters onto the deck. Even shot through and drowning in the open air, its tiny brain pierced and huge, mythical lungs exploded, the halibut was too strong to approach. Smaller halibut were impaled on a long board with a spike at one end, then stripped immediately of their skin and cut into filets, but the crew left this one to lie alone on the whitewashed concrete deck and watched from a distance.

This woman, Kate, drew the lot to clean and filet. After waiting an hour, she began with a long knife to slice one side—the back, mottled dark green and brown—into thick steaks. The spine and thin bones radiating from it lay exposed before her and she went to the head to cut away the cheeks, where the meat is rich and stringy, a delicacy. One cheek had been shot through and could be recovered only in part, but the other came free in a single huge steak white as marble that lay folded over her hand as she went to the hose to wash it and drop it into a plastic bucket. As she walked, however, the halibut cheek convulsed and leaped in an arc four feet into the air, over a line and onto the deck, where it hit with more of a thud than a splat, though only a small remnant of the huge corpse before her. "Gods are born of less than that," she told me, leaning in close, laughing.

Cold dark deep and absolutely clear, element bearable to no mortal, to fish and to seals . . . I mumbled Elizabeth Bishop poems to the water, to the oil stains like rainbows in this artificial light and the red starfish rippling below. I had always imagined the poems set here, in Ketchikan, not on the Atlantic.

Out in the channel, the lights of a convocation, twenty to thirty boats all drawn together to wait for a storm to pass, for the time when they could leave the shallows and enter open ocean again. Their arrangement puzzled in a way that pleased, also: bright floodlights high up, small cabin lights, globes everywhere across their backs exposing the great nets, buffed aluminum, floats orange and red, all intermingled and reflected on waters calm as mirrors and no horizon visible, no clear seam for the surface, for water and air, reflection and light. And the only sound that of small bells, seeming to come from much farther away, the bells high up on the lines of trawlers, the bells that signaled fish. No voices.

I walked to the end of the docks, studied for a long time a small rowboat. A rare quiet night, no fishermen visible at this far end, no one to see me, and this rowboat tied only by two frayed ropes, bow and stern. It was old wood, green paint blistered and cracked, patchy pale white showing underneath, and the name on its stern the *Lady J,* in black lettering, also cracked. I stepped into it, still not deciding to take it out but dreaming already of rendezvous with ocean liners, of guests in tails and sequins, voices near as infants, intimate, faces thin and sharp as beaks. A warm, strong breeze carrying all but the water, no ripple but its hold strong on everything else, making distance impossible. I rowed unnoticed beneath masts and sonar, bells and spotlights, rowed, I fancied, with the seamless propulsion of jellyfish in the one element, rowed past jagged rocks onto a sea nostalgic and opaque, swelling slowly, as if considering spilling over until the rim of the world lifted inevitably, slipped, and I was in a rowboat, wet from mist and shivering, hearing the slap of oars, the creaking of the locks. I sang because the high moment had passed and that was what was left, sang a song by Memphis Slim, crooning the lament of a fool in love back to the docks, seemingly loud and a little dizzy and, by all apparent signs, invisible. Small sucking noises from the boats in their slips as I returned, trapped water beneath tri-hulls and the rub of bumpers against wood.

My father loved something about Alaska. Though frustrated himself, he had many friends who lived the kinds of lives he imagined. One was a man named Healy who lived a hundred miles off the Parks Highway at a point between Anchorage and Fairbanks where the highway cross-sected nothing. No other human habitation as far as any horizon, so that on a cool summer evening, when the ranges far off, their snow gone violet near midnight, seemed to float up out of the tundra as if out of oceans and the ground everywhere lost its solidity, its particularity, in my father Healy vanished, became him, and he knew freedom.

Then the night would grow colder, the light would almost fade, and my father would go inside, see the cabinets Healy had built, even the walls of his small cabin, and the blankets hung between the bed for himself and his wife and the bed for their two small children. Over a couch, Healy had draped the hides of black bears, brown bears, mountain goats, deer, caribou, and my father would touch these with one hand but keep the other in his pocket. At this point, he would have lost words, too broken any longer to praise. I touched these hides, also, forgotten by my father but watching him, feeling a child's portion of regret, desire, longing, my father's longing. If only a life could be bent into the shape of another's, momentum diminished. After a long drive home very late, during which I slept, my father would rise again early to drill out the tiny infected nerves of teeth, fill cavities, make molds, instruct and squint and see his whole life reduced to something cramped and small.

On my break from rinsing out tubs, I talked of breeds and life spans with an old man who had stopped to watch, of place and home while the man waited for the time he could return. Trouble there, he hinted, but I didn't ask questions. There were oil stains on the man's vest and hands, his thick nails yellow-brown. His baseball cap was of the Alaska State Bird—the Mosquito—and his eyes were marbled red.

Though we hadn't been introduced, I knew who this man was; I had been in Ketchikan three weeks now and looking for a way to meet him, because his wife was the receptionist my father had slept with, a kind of turning point, I thought, in all our lives. Her name was Gloria Sills, though she had married him and taken his name, and his Bill Douglas. I was planning to invite them both to dinner, to talk with her and maybe tell her who I was.

"Timber, I worked in originally," Bill was saying. "Not a good business anymore." He was the kind of coherent drunk who told everything to anyone. Bill hadn't officially told me even his name, but he'd told me he was looking for a job, that he'd been doing odd jobs since he retired but the garage he'd picked up work at for the last eight years had closed down. Amway hadn't brought in the diamond rings as promised. Instead, because of overinvestment in products he couldn't sell and time lost from other work, he'd had to sell his house and lived now with his wife in a trailer. He had no Cadillac, nor even a pickup truck. He did have an old Chevy Monza, rusted out, that needed a few parts. His wife had become more bitter than he had thought possible.

"She's a wonder, all right," he said, chuckling. "I didn't know she had it in her."

I smiled with him. Absurdity is all that makes grief bearable.

"So how many you let out each year?" Bill asked. And he pointed to the nearest pool of fingerlings.

"Fifty to sixty thousand," I told him, "and we take in most years about two hundred and fifty, maybe three hundred. But I just got on here. This is my first season." The returning salmon were in concrete pools closer to the river, where they came up the shallows, their dark backs exposed above pebbles and ripples, the small humpies and reds mixed in with the great kings over three times their size. Leaving snake tracks in the water, they slipped through a narrow chute to leap over four low concrete walls against the current—simulated waterfalls—until they had so packed the slim borders of the final pool that many fell back out and had to leap again. They were solid and earnest, single-minded, pure muscle decaying yet elegant in its movement.

"Bill Douglas is the name," Bill said. He put out his hand and we shook.

"Roy Fenn. My dad, Jim Fenn, used to live in town here. He was a dentist. Did you know him at all?"

"When was this?"

"Until '72, I think."

"Sounds familiar, maybe," Bill said. "He might have been down in the county building on Third Street, with Doc Iverson and some other dentist. Sound right?"

"That was him. My grandfather caught a big halibut once—

two hundred and fifty or sixty pounds. There was a picture of the three of us on the front page of the paper, three generations standing next to one very large fish."

Bill chuckled.

"Does that sound familiar at all?" I asked.

"Could be," Bill said, wiping the corners of his mouth with his handkerchief. "Could be."

"Well," I said. I was unsatisfied. I felt displaced by the fact that no one really remembered us in this small town.

"Mind if I take a closer look?" Bill asked.

"No, go ahead."

We walked over to the nearest pool and watched king salmon fingerlings leap into the two-foot stream of a hose. Even at two and three inches, they looked exactly as they would full-grown, perfect miniature replicas, and I couldn't help but see these great fish leaping forty, fifty feet in the air at a speed that defied normal gravity. Their falls were not suspended but vanished in a wink. In pairs and threes or singly, tiny slivers of light. When I had come late and turned the flashlight on their silvery-blue sides and eyes, even then they were leaping.

Bill dipped his hand in and the fingerlings caved one side of their ring to avoid him. "Hard to believe those are kings," he said.

His hand removed, the circle re-formed. "I came here when I was twenty-two. That was in 1946. I arrived on the ferry in a red Ford pickup. Even the hubcaps were painted red." Bill shook his head. "I was pretty interesting then. I wore cowboy boots."

"Maybe that's what I need," I said. "Cowboy boots and red hubcaps, and then I'll be all set."

Bill wiped his hand on his jeans. "They came with some other things, too, unfortunately. You'd have to be a drunk and have no money and marry a woman you met here, mostly because you were scared."

"Scared?" I asked.

"Yep." Bill zipped his jacket and walked around the pool, bent to look at the pump and hose, then the leaping. "Ever find any of these on the wrong side?"

"'Fraid not," I said, and smiled, though I had already been asked that question a few times now. I wanted more about his wife, too. "Would you like to come for dinner sometime, you and your wife?" I asked him.

"What's that?"

"Sorry. That sounded kind of sudden, I guess. I need to get back to work here, but I was thinking I'd invite you and your wife over for dinner, if you'd like."

"That's a nice offer," Bill said. "I'll give you my phone number, and you can talk to the wife."

My father was an insomniac. He once told me about an experiment in which thousands of mosquitoes in a large tank were exposed to flashes of bright light at odd hours. For many of the mosquitoes, one bad night knocked them off-kilter for the rest of their short lives. Perhaps they seemed less focused in the way they buzzed along the tank's glass walls afterward, wobbled a little or hung at odd angles, and certainly they no longer slept normally, though who ever thought of mosquitoes sleeping? My father told this story as if it explained him. One bad night, or perhaps he was claiming to be a visionary. Or perhaps he simply felt a bit odd. The only real solution, of course, was that he thought this little tale funny, as he did all the other little tales. Everything my father had left me vanished. I glanced at the remains and they shifted the light until opacity became translucence and I could see only a diffusion of the unparticular ground beyond, the clutter that promised but gave nothing.

I sometimes walked up the hill to visit the house I had lived in as a child. Up on a slope set between two mountains, the small house that once had been bordered on two sides by forest was now dwarfed by a dozen two- and three-story dark wooden houses with stained glass and gazebos. The view of the channel and ranges beyond was blocked by lower-cost developments. The house had not been painted in the twenty-five years since I had left, nor the fence repaired. The green my father and mother and I had applied had decayed to show pink beneath and, beneath that, white and, finally, bare wood. The roof showed tar paper, the metal screen door and mailbox at the street both stood at angles, though each distinct, the pavement of the driveway had become its own map of small islands, and the fence hung bare where it hung at all. The current residents remembered my family and invited me in, but there were no memories here, only the foreign stains of smoke, pets, food, and children, cans and clothing strewn everywhere across the floor. The cherry tree in back, which I remembered as very tall, since I had climbed, hidden in, and fallen from it, stood maybe ten or twelve feet, narrow and unimpressive. The tall fence came to my waist. Memories are infinitely richer than their origins, I discovered; to travel back can only estrange one even from memory itself. And because memory is often all that a life or a self is built on, returning home can take away exactly that.

On the phone with Gloria, I didn't use my last name. I wondered whether she knew, but there were no indications either way. The conversation was cordial and short and told me nothing, really, except that she sounded like she was from Boston, not the loud Bostonian dialect but the classier kind, upper-crust, not that this meant anything in particular. I wondered for the hundredth time why I was doing all this, why I was here in Ketchikan. After the initial return and rush of belonging, I had felt only out of place. The divorce and my father's suicide seemed to exist in another world.

I looked all around my house that night, feeling a little crazy, I think, studied the wood and even the cracks in the linoleum. Part of the mountainside had been dug away to accommodate. Rock had been blasted. The wood was old and had perhaps never been fully dry, but I was convinced it would remain forever. The stains on the walls, too, the fierce green linoleum, the teapot with its inward formations of minerals white, red, and other, as well as the windows that warped what was looked at— all of these would resist wearing away, would remain for as long as the house could be called a house, and longer.

Late night, I wandered. At the gates of the hatchery, I spun the lock, slipped inside. I took hundreds of fingerlings by net, dumped handfuls in my pockets, walked along cliffs above the roadway, bare rock cut in grooves, and held out the fish one by one in an open palm. The miniature salmon leaped each of their own accord, a tail flash into the night, glint of silver, sixty feet of twisting, and an inaudible slap to the pavement below. Waiting, then. For water, for some new rule, new possibility, that could make pavement not pavement, air not air, a fall not a fall.

I made each fish do this, waited patiently for each to send itself, all the time muttering obscenities: "Walk the plank, matey. Time to sleep with the fish."

I watched the last one vanish, listened for the tiny slap, heard nothing. The mist was orange from streetlight. The air cold. I took off my coat, my shirt, folded them and placed them on a stump. I removed my shoes, pants, underwear, watch, and put my shoes back on. I double-knotted them. I would run through the forest until I was exhausted and could sleep; perhaps even as I ripped through ferns and over the rotting logs invisible now beneath the false second rain-forest floor I would have some kind of vision. So I set off running. But before long, I only felt tired and stopped and turned around and walked slowly back. I had no faith in that kind of thing anymore, I realized. It had worked in high school, a few times even in college, but it seemed ineffectual now. So I put my clothes back on, descended past rubble and wire, concrete, brush, and stood over the wide-flung fingerlings to twist each delicately under my heel.

At work the next day, my boss, a young biologist whose eyes were not quite in alignment, so that I could never be sure whether or not I had been seen, asked me to write a letter to the *Ketchikan Daily News* and to post flyers asking for information leading to arrest. I suggested a reward of dinner for two at the Fisherman's Grotto, but my boss didn't think that was funny.

"I don't think you understand," he said, scratching at one of his sideburns. "If this asshole keeps this up, and we don't catch him, you and me are out a job."

"Okay," I said. "I'm your man. I'm the one. I'll have the letter and flyers ready by the end of the day."

So I wrote a short press release, included the fact that the theft had probably occurred at night, asked for vigilance, suggested the ever-expanding threat crimes like this posed to us all, and delivered the release to the newspaper. I made flyers with a close-up photo of fingerlings schooling, a shot with rings like a peacock's fan, difficult to recognize but startling in its way. Under this, I printed, in bold letters, missing, and beneath this the details of the crime and numbers to call. I wrote that they had been netted at night and taken away for unknown purposes. I asked, "Is your neighborhood known to you?"

Bill and Gloria arrived in the Monza and I swung my rickety door wide. I had made everything inside as cozy as possible, despite the fact that Gloria was the woman my father had cheated with. I had baked sweet potatoes and lit candles, tuned the radio to the softer of the two available stations, beer-battered fresh halibut. I was determined to have a good time and to make Bill and Gloria have a good time, too.

Gloria was taller than Bill. Younger, also—early fifties, perhaps. Her hair was still mostly blond. "Hello," she said. "It's nice to meet you."

I muttered something inane, then moved on to what I really wanted to know. "You're not from here originally, are you? You're from the East Coast, right, somewhere in New England?"

"Boston," she said.

"Boston," I repeated. "Well," I said, "I have food. And would you like something to drink?"

"Howdy," Bill said, and shook my hand. He was more awkward around his wife.

"A beer?" I asked.

"Sure."

I could not believe this was the receptionist my father had slept with. I had always imagined her with a wide smile in red lipstick, a brassy, obnoxious voice, and no brain. This was a child's conception, of course, built from the feel of my mother's attacks on my father more than their content, but still it had persisted. Even the conversation over the phone had somehow dispelled nothing. I was embarrassed.

"It's getting colder out there," Bill said from the couch. "It'll be an early one this year, looks like."

"Yeah," I said. "I heard them talking about that on the radio. That and the decline in tourism this year seem to be about all I've heard about."

"That's true, you know," Gloria said. "And agencies everywhere are suffering. At the library we've had to trim our hours and staff and reduce or even eliminate many of our services. You can't call us with reference questions anymore, for instance. And there will be more cuts next year."

"You work at the library?" I asked, a doubly pointless question since I already knew the answer from trying to track her down when I first arrived in Ketchikan.

"Yes," she said.

"In Lake County, California, where my grandmother still lives," I said, to cover myself, "they don't even have a public library now. Not a single branch in the whole county. They've all closed down. And a few of the elementary schools, too."

I joined Gloria and Bill in the tiny living/dining room off the kitchen. The table was along one wall of this room, the couch along the other. I sat in a chair with its back touching the table.

"I don't know," Bill said. "It doesn't seem to me we need to give everyone a handout. I know that view will be unpopular with my wife, but I just have to say, if someone's going to make it in this country, they're going to make it, that's all."

Gloria scooted closer to her husband on the couch and took his hand in hers. "I'd prefer not to talk about Amway tonight, honey, if we could. I want to hear what Roy's up to."

"Oh," I said. It was hard to hear her voice. "That's fine. I haven't been doing much of anything." I didn't know what to do about Bill's conversational minefield. And I knew I would have to say something stupid now to try to smooth things over. "My uncle used to sell Amway," I said.

"It's not such a bad organization, really," Bill said.

"Yeah," I said. "I used to listen to the tapes when I'd go goose hunting with him up to Modoc. My uncle and this friend of his named Big Al. They kept the windows up and shouted a lot— my uncle was from Nebraska—and every once in a while, Big Al would turn to me and hold out his finger and . . . you know, I probably shouldn't continue with this. I'm sorry."

"No, no," Gloria said.

"I think it should wait till another time," I said.

"That's all right," Bill said.

I looked down at the linoleum. "Well," I said, "why don't we go to the table. I'll bring over the halibut and sweet potatoes."

"Sweet potatoes?" Gloria asked. "That sounds lovely."

"Yeah," I said. "I got them at the store."

I hated sounding like an idiot. But I was shaking now for some reason, and I couldn't think well. I took the tray of halibut out of the oven, where I'd been keeping it warm, used tongs to transfer the pieces onto a plate, and served up the sweet potatoes. I'd put miniature marshmallows on them, not because I thought that was a classy touch, because it isn't, but because I had felt so warm and happy earlier, a rare and simple feeling I was trying to prolong, and this was how my mother had fixed them when I was a child. Now they looked a bit odd.

"Sorry about the marshmallows," I said as I brought over the plates. "I was suffering from nostalgia earlier today."

"I like marshmallows," Bill said.

"Our own oven has seen them as recently as last week," Gloria said. "Though we did pull the blinds to be sure no one else saw."

I laughed. "That's pretty good," I said, but I felt sick. None of this was working out right. Gloria was not disturbed at all. I was the only one. Then this thought made me wonder whether I had been looking for some kind of revenge. "So what brought you out to Alaska, Gloria?" I asked.

The radio was playing Miles Davis, a rare moment in Ketchikan. Nothing was solid or reliable. I felt that maybe I was somewhere else.

"This halibut is delicious, Roy," Gloria said.

"Yeah, it's really great," said Bill.

"Thank you," I said.

"To answer your question, I came out to work in one of the

canneries for a summer after my sophomore year of college, and I met Bill through a friend who came out with me."

"Wow," I said. "So you came out for a summer, and here you still are."

"Yes," Gloria said.

I let her pause for a moment to eat. I picked a few marshmallows off my sweet potatoes, saving them for last. As I glanced up, Gloria was looking right at me. She knew who I was; I was sure of it.

"I wanted to be an ichthyologist when I was a little kid," I said, just to be saying something. "And now here I am cleaning out the strainers at a hatchery, not studying anything. I even have a college degree, but not a useful one for anything I want to do." I raised up my fists in a boxer's stance. "I coulda been a contender," I bellowed. I have always entertained when I haven't known what else to do. Gloria laughed. Bill laughed, too, though he looked confused.

"It's never too late," Gloria said.

"Can you pass the halibut, Gloria?" asked Bill.

I saw fingerlings falling end over end through the air, their eyes rings of blue-inlaid silver, huge, unblinking. "Jesus," I said.

"What?" Gloria asked. "What's wrong?"

"Sorry. I thought I saw something outside the window. Did you know these windows are real glass and they warp everything?"

"Really?" Gloria asked. She and Bill both got up to see.

"It's dark out," Bill said. "How can you see anything?"

"Go outside," I said. "I'll walk around the living room, and you can watch me."

"All right," Bill said. "But no funny business."

Gloria laughed.

"You got it," I said.

So the door banged shut and I stepped out across the floor as if for the first time. I couldn't remember how I usually walked. My steps felt too small, and the linoleum made crackling sounds, I realized. The lighting in here was too bright. No decoration of any kind on the walls. I waved my arms a little for effect and puffed my cheeks out; I swung my head back and forth toward the ceiling; I wondered what all this meant. I wondered how soon I could end the dinner and not appear rude.

Bill and Gloria were laughing when they came in.

"No funny business indeed," said Gloria.

"That was quite a show," Bill said. "Like seeing myself in one of those funny mirrors, except it wasn't me."

"Bill," Gloria said, "you're waxing poetical."

"I'm not waxing anything," Bill said. "And I don't do windows, either."

I laughed. "Especially not these windows," I said.

I sat back down and motioned for Bill and Gloria to do the same. I endured the small talk. I finished my halibut, sweet potatoes, bread, and even the marshmallows. I had a beer, then another beer. I talked about the fishing boats my father had owned, which was a mistake.

"Was your father a commercial fisherman?" Gloria asked.

"Sort of," I told her. "He had a lot of jobs." It struck me that Gloria was a very attractive person, that my father might have found in her first a kind of friend. Perhaps he had never felt this with my mother. Perhaps he had even been, to some degree, lonely.

This was not the kind of thinking I wanted to take very far. My pity for my father up to this point had been limited to a man who had inflicted avoidable pain on everyone around him but who must have suffered some himself. I didn't care to enlarge on this.

"But anyway, my mother's working as an elementary school counselor now on Kauai," I told Gloria and Bill. This was as much to escape my own thoughts as to escape the conversation. We talked about pineapples and sugarcane, about running around in bare skin all year and even the rain being warm. Then I added that I had run around naked at night right here in Ketchikan, which I of course shouldn't have shared.

"Here?" Bill asked.

"What were you thinking?" Gloria wanted to know.

I spread my hands in the air, having no idea what to say.

"We probably shouldn't touch this one, Gloria," Bill said.

"Well," I said, "maybe it's getting late anyway."

So I had them out the door, coats and all, but Gloria walked back as Bill was warming up the Monza.

"Back again," I said.

"You know, Roy, I appreciate you having us over. Bill drinks a little more than he should, but I appreciate you having us over." She put her hand on my arm, a simple enough gesture, but one that made me wonder nonetheless what my father had felt under her touch.

"That's fine," I said. "It looks like the car's warmed up now." I should have talked with her then, told her who I was, asked about my father and perhaps learned something real, but I didn't have the courage. I couldn't even look at her.

"Good-bye," Gloria said.

• • •

Two a.m., standing knee-deep in the channel off Ketchikan, ashamed of myself. The water gnawing at the rocks. Loons hidden away somewhere at the edge of the trees calling. The dusk that never seemed true darkness thickening in the mist. All the stupid images of loneliness, a mockery.

I am wearing a coat, I thought to myself, trying to keep the tone light. My mother would be proud. And then I was crying again, and then I was disgusted again, and then I took a step deeper into the channel, my shoes sliding over the stones. My thighs were very cold now. The rest was numb. I'm standing here in the water, I told myself in an attempt to banish the feeling that perhaps the tragedies I had imagined for years, the divorce and suicide that I had let shape my life so permanently, had been something else altogether, or at least not as I had imagined. And what, then, of what I had become?

The mist in gauzy layers like summer cloth, which could only be deception. Salmon beneath me right now, beautiful silver salmon, their dark bodies slipping invisibly on all sides, running for the creek mouths, considering me what? Jellyfish, too, floating, and starfish orange and red. The rockfish my father called crappies and slammed against the side of the boat until their bodies flew off the jigs and sometimes only their heads remained. Red snapper swollen and discolored, eyes popping, exploded swim bladders protruding from their mouths like secondary, translucent tongues. Brought from a world where weight and air were known differently, a world held in place, as it turned out, by nothing at all.

THE HIGHER BLUE

IN THE VERY end—always a surprising time—my father fixated on zabaglione. This is all hearsay, you understand, but I like to think that when my father purchased his first copper pot, when he stood in his dental smock in a tiny kitchenware store in the only mall of a nearly abandoned Alaskan town and vaulted startlingly into his new life, I was at his elbow selecting a whisk.

My father's house had no furniture. It was brand new, and everything was still bare, no address even. A faint hill near the top of a ridge, paper birch spaced regular as candles, darkness at 4:00 p.m., March 15, 1980, aurora borealis in pleasing shades of green unnoticed, a boy and his father in parkas, a flashlight, copper bowl, whisk, last-minute sugar, and though the mind refuses it, a sense of home. All of this carries the boy and his father, the father and his boy, into the kitchen, where the air is not quite right for zabaglione, too dry perhaps, so the father closes tight the windows and doors, leaves water in the sink, isolates the kitchen from the rest of the house while the boy shoves dish towels in all the cracks for a tight seal.

"I need an apron," the father says. But there is no apron, he knows. This is a new house. Until the boy arrived, there was no one. If curtains existed, he would take one down from the window above the sink and use that.

"Okay," the father says, tying his winter parka around his middle. "This'll have to do. Let's put everything out on the counter."

Three new cookbooks, three eggs, plastic yolk separator, tablespoon, five-pound bag of sugar, measuring cup, marsala wine, two bowls, two sherry glasses, two spoons, whisk, and a copper pot. I like to think the boy is helpful, that the items are neatly arranged. The father doesn't have a double boiler, but he does have a metal gravy bowl, and this, filled with water, he places on the burner. "Hmm," he says when he turns on the gas and the self-starter clicks away but there's no flame.

" 'Pure zabaione would be overly rich to eat by itself,' " the boy reads aloud to his father. "But that's what we're making, right?"

"Where'd you read that?" the father asks and takes the book from his boy. He reads, his opaque brow etched. The window is dark, and the only sound is the clicking. The boy hasn't had dinner yet and senses himself about to complain. The more he thinks about this, the more hollow his stomach.

"This isn't the one I read before," the father says. "Or at least not all of it. The author—Giuliano Bugialli—ha, what a name— keeps talking about a wooden spoon, and I don't even have a wooden spoon. 'Just at the moment before boiling,' the guy says here, 'zabaione'—and he's spelling it different, too—'zabaione should be thick enough to stick to the wooden spoon. That is the moment it is ready.'" The father returns the book to his boy. In a faked Italian accent, one arm waving in the air, he repeats, "'That is the moment it is ready.'" The boy grins.

The father opens another recipe book. "Here we go," he says, "Simple—'whip vigorously with a wire whisk until the custard foams up.'"

"Let's use that one," the boy says, agreeable to the last.

"Okay," his father says, fulfilling dreams.

The stove is clicking away but still no flame. The father moves his metal gravy bowl to the counter and lifts off the top of the stove to get a closer look. "Brand new," he says, and tries another burner. Still only clicking and a faint hiss. "Why don't you crack the eggs and separate the yolks while I'm fixing the stove," he says.

"Okay," the boy says, agreeable to the bitter end. But when he looks at the recipe, he sees that it calls for six egg yolks. They have only three eggs. The other recipe called for only three eggs. The boy grapples with his fear of annihilation. Does he dare point out another flaw? Won't it start to look like his own fault? The boy cracks the three eggs and separates the whites into one bowl, the yolks into another.

The father closes the oven door. "No clue in there," he says. "I don't know how the hell this thing works." He grins at his boy.

"We could try using a match," the boy suggests.

"A match!" the father yells triumphantly. "That's my boy." And lo and behold, one of the kitchen drawers by the sink does, in fact, contain a box of matches. The boy is emboldened; perhaps this is a flaw in his own character. But forgetting the consequences for a moment, he points out to his father the thing about the six eggs.

"Six?" the father asks. Annihilation comes rushing in. The boy backs up against the sink as his father reads extensively in all three books. The boy isn't hungry anymore. He's lost his appetite and he's a little dizzy. If his father is intent on killing himself, the boy doesn't want a part in it anymore. He opens the cabinet beneath the sink and crawls in.

"Oh, hell," the father says. "We're just gonna have to try it with three." The boy hears the metal gravy bowl placed on the burner, the water sloshing a little, the thin sides ringing—a kind of water gong, almost, a low shimmer. Then the scrape of a match, an explosion, the air sucked from the boy's lungs, and the boy imagines one tiny glimpse of a burning parka, of a father whirling fiery through the air.

The boy survives, of course, because he's thousands of miles away. The father isn't so lucky. Red lights, the trees quiet. But I should start closer to the truth.

The bachelor, prefiguring my existence, was living on his own, measuring out his life by soup can and frozen waffle carton. Were it not for the persistence of habit and a metal gravy bowl never washed but used over and over, kept warm on the stove, life as I know it might never have begun.

Hunched and dim-sighted, bent over tomes of anatomy, periodontics, endodontics, and the other dental sciences, clenching a jaw that was understood but underused, locked in realms of fluorescence and linoleum, dreaming only of sunny wilderness, of rod and gun and the clomping of trail-worn boots, this creature inspired pity in a woman who herself had no domestic talents but had the sense, at least, to eat out occasionally.

"I bought him one dinner at a Chinese restaurant, served him one cup of coffee and a bowl of mint-chip ice cream at my apartment, and he was mine," my mother told me.

The creature began to walk upright, lose his pallor, see occasionally the light of day, sample rich foods from many lands, and dream of things softer and more varied than his own leathery boots. The creature was given a name. He was called Honey.

"The first two years were good. Then he took me for granted. I gave him a life, and he was so pleased, he started giving it to others. To a receptionist named Gloria, to be exact."

The thing called Honey, which had learned to walk, see, sample, and dream, walked farther, saw more, sampled extravagantly, then dreamed about it, over and over. The thing was told to stop walking, but the thing kept walking. The thing became inflated and soared over the city, lighter than air.

"I gave him a can opener the day I divorced him," my mother said. "He didn't know what it was for. I told him he'd find out soon enough."

The thing popped, landed like minestrone, a fall more terrible than the face-plant of Icarus. Out of the goop grew a hand that could turn, and turn, and turn, and turn, and turn.

In later years, I tried to know the father. I called him Dad, brought groceries to his house, and, despite my native inhibitions, learned to cook spaghetti. In hopes of drawing some response, I even asked pointed questions about his life.

"When did you first realize you had made a mistake?" I asked.

"What mistake?"

I might have given up if not for the fact that he was the only father in the world, the narrow remnant of all those suitors and potential suitors. I worked with what I had.

And what I had was this: a sulky thing, easily wounded, that sat at a card table in a dental smock and made promises: "Let me help you there with the noodles. Your mother never understood me; there's more to what happened than she thinks. I could make the salad. Would you like me to make the salad?"

The father had receding gray-blue eyes and various minor aches and pains. When he was cheating on the current girlfriend, there was always diarrhea in the mornings. Spring and fall, he had allergies. When he thought about money, about all the shaky, hasty investments over the years, a thin trail of intense pain rose from behind his right eye and spiraled across his forehead.

Occasionally, jarred for a moment, the father would realize I had a separate existence and fire off a few questions of his own.

"How's that girl you're seeing, what's her name?"

"We broke up in August, Dad. It's November now."

"Huh." But he rallied quickly. "Do you remember the tractor?"

"What?" I asked.

"The green tractor, you know. I used to give you rides on it when you were little. Do you remember anything like that?"

"No. I don't think I do."

Then there was the trip to the mall. The father was very nervous about this. A present was needed for current girlfriend's birthday.

"I don't know," he said, which communicated several things:

no gift meant no girlfriend, no girlfriend meant landing once
again like minestrone, landing once again like that meant a lifetime of guilt, shame, and general self-hatred in the one responsible, which would, of course, be me.

"I'd love to do it," I said.

Once in the domain of hair spray and Lycra, I buoyed a cow-
ering thing with remembrances of hunting trips past. I spoke the
well-known tales of the buck at close range who had leaped over
my bullet and vanished in the brush. I spoke of the wild boar
who had sneaked up from behind when I was armed only with
binoculars, who chased me along razor-backed ridges till I nearly
fell (the small stones twisting out over the edge), whom I escaped
only by stretching across the top branches of the only tree, an
oak barely ten feet high. Neither the buck nor the boar had ever
existed, of course. I had fired that shot into blank air. The pig,
also, had been born alchemically of boredom, pride, fancy, and
innate terror.

"You've had some amazing experiences, all right," the father said as he gazed at the behind of a junior higher, causing a
moment's doubt in me: a liar, after all, would be the thing most
likely to know another liar.

But the father was buoyed, in any case. "Let's go hunt down a
necklace, maybe," he said, "or some other kind of ornament."

For the rest of the afternoon, we ran our trigger fingers over
every piece of gold and silver the mall could provide. The bowed
legs of the father became nimble, and his tongue was loosened.

"Did I ever tell you I wanted to be a painter?" the father
asked.

"You?"

"Sure. I was a kind of Brueghel with less patience."

I thought about that for a while. Then I asked, "What else?"

"What do you mean, what else?"

"What else should I know about you? I know very little, you know."

"Well, son, let me tell you everything."

The father never told me anything, of course, but looking back, I can see that I felt closest to the father on that very afternoon. Perhaps it was only gestures—the way the father hitched up his jeans, his sideways grin at the spiel of a salesman, the gratitude and love I thought I saw in certain small movements of the eyes—but even if these indices were only imagined, they did seem to provide what I had wanted for a very long time.

Looking back, I can see also that the father reached a kind of high point that afternoon in the mall. I could say, even, that the father soared once more over the city. Well pleased with a choker in three colors of gold, not suspecting the inevitable plummet to come, as if the downward spiral of his life had been arrested for a moment, the father climbed a display case in the corner of Oshman's, and, as I distracted the salespeople by smacking a squash ball again and again against the far wall in a two-player match for one, he strapped himself into the harness of a hang glider strung from the ceiling. He wore a yellow fluorescent windbreaker and sporty strapless helmet, gave me the thumbs-up, and soared.

My mother, of course, had predicted the entire series of inevitable plummets in the father's postmarital life.

"Some things never learn," she said. "If your father were a lemming, he would climb back up the cliff just to go over again."

Perhaps we never were generous enough to the father. A father, after all, is a lot for a thing to be. That sounds bitter, I suppose, but I don't mean it to be bitter; there were times when the father showed me most clearly what I would become, and that, certainly, is a kind of gift, if not always a blessing.

Currently the father is a small slab of granite planted near my mother's cottage, in a field of wild grass and ice plant by the sea. Mother likes to have him near and claims their conversations have improved.

"I don't have to be angry anymore," she says. "I can feel sorry for him now and do the old-woman-rich-with-memories-and-longing routine. Though occasionally I give it a rest."

The small slab of granite suits my own needs fairly well, also. I bring flowers and sit with him, just like the old times, except that now I don't have to fix spaghetti. I listen to the self-shredding waves, squeak a finger of ice plant between my own, gaze into the higher blue, and sometimes, when among the upper currents I catch the hint of a hopeful, insistent flapping, I almost imagine the father has come finally to life.

ACKNOWLEDGMENTS

JOHN L'HEUREUX HELPED me most in shaping these stories, and also in shaping my life. Michelle Carter helped enormously, also. The truth is, I received more generous help from great writers than any young writer could hope for. Grace Paley and Adrienne Rich sponsored me for an early writing grant (run by Laura Selznick) when I was an undergrad at Stanford. In grad school at Cornell, Stephanie Vaughn and Robert Morgan tried to help me see how the stories might become a book. Mike Curtis at *The Atlantic* published my first story, "Ichthyology," and Kim Witherspoon gave me early encouragement. When I returned to Stanford as a Wallace Stegner Fellow, Toby Wolff, who had long been my favorite writer, encouraged me also.

I've been lucky, in other words. I'm grateful to Gail Winston and many others at HarperCollins, grateful also to the folks at the Association of Writers and Writing Programs and at UMass Press, for first putting this book into print. It's especially nice that it's a prize in Grace Paley's name, since she was such a great teacher and inspiration. I still think of all she taught us, including that "Everyone, real or invented, deserves the open destiny of life."

I owe a debt, also, to a lot of writers I don't know whose works inspired these stories. Marilynne Robinson and Elizabeth Bishop, most of all, but also Annie Proulx and Cormac McCarthy and others.

I want to thank David Forrer for his tireless work and constant good humor, Stewart O'Nan, Robert Olen Butler, and Noy Holland for their generous endorsements, and also thank the National Endowment for the Arts for a Creative Writing Fellowship in 2008. University of San Francisco, where I currently teach, has also been tremendously supportive.

Finally, I need to thank my family, because it was an uncomfortable topic I was writing about—my father's suicide—and there's exposure in these stories. They're fictional, but based on a lot that's true. My stepmother, Nettie Rose, was especially generous in helping me talk through everything for several years. She had faced a lot of other deaths in her life and seemed fearless to me then.

P.S.

Insights,
Interviews
& More...

About the author

About the book

Read on

A Conversation
with David Vann

What's your earliest memory?

Trying to tie my shoes in Ketchikan,
Alaska. An early sign that things come
undone easily.

Who are your favorite writers?

I'm a sucker for landscape description,
so I love Elizabeth Bishop's poems,
Marilynne Robinson's *Housekeeping*,
Annie Proulx's *The Shipping News*, and
Cormac McCarthy's *Blood Meridian*.

Why did you write this book?

After my father killed himself, my sister felt a drop on her cheek on a cloudless day and knew that it was his way of saying good-bye to her. My mother saw him vividly in a dream, again saying good-bye. But nothing happened for me. Just a void. So this book is my attempt to reach him again, to bring him back to life.

Why did you write about his suicide as fiction instead of nonfiction?

My father killed himself when I was thirteen, and for three years afterward, I told everyone he had died of cancer, because the way he killed himself felt too shameful. And I also didn't quite believe his death. I lay awake at night and could see him running through the snow in Alaska, trying to come back to me. Everything about his death was mythical from the start, and Alaska is that way for me, also. As a kid in the rain forest of Ketchikan, I ran from imaginary wolves and bears, but we had real ones, too. I had this class once with Grace Paley in which she told us that every line in fiction has to be true. It has to be a distillation of experience, more true to a person's life than any moment he or she has actually lived. So this book is as true an account as I could write of my father's suicide and my own bereavement, and that was possible only through fiction.

66 Everything about his death was mythical from the start, and Alaska is that way for me, also. 99

My Father's Guns

First published in *Men's Journal*, July/
August 2009, reprinted in *Esquire UK*,
November 2009

My FATHER gave me my first gun at age
seven. It was a Sheridan Blue Streak pellet
rifle, powerful enough to kill squirrels if
I hit them in the right spot, behind the
shoulder. The giving of the gun was a
ritual, my father's pride and pleasure
as he showed me how to pump the gun,
how to pull back the bolt. He even read
a poem from Sturm, Ruger & Co. about
a father and son, using it to teach me
safety: never point a gun at anyone, never
leave a gun loaded but always assume a
gun is loaded, always keep the barrel
pointed down. This was very soon after
he and my mother had divorced, and we
had only the weekends now. Roaming
his ninety-acre ranch near Lakeport,
California, one of those weekends,
I didn't realize the rifle was pumped
and loaded, and it fired as I walked.
Luckily the barrel was pointed at the
ground. But my father turned around,
the disappointment clear on his face,
and my shame was nearly unbearable.

The next year, when I was eight, he
gave me a twenty-gauge shotgun, for
hunting dove and quail. That gun felt
inevitable, as if it were a given that
couldn't be turned away from. As if we
were put here to hunt and kill, and the
only true form of a day was to head off
with a gun and a dog, hike into the hills
for ten or twelve hours, and return with

meat and stories. That shotgun became an extension of my body, carried everywhere, the solid heft of it, cold metal, a sense of purpose and belonging. I gazed at it in the evenings, daydreamed of it during the week at school, looked forward to when I'd head out again.

When I was nine my father gave me a .30-30 Winchester lever-action carbine, the rifle used in all the Westerns, and he actually went down on one knee when he presented it to me, holding it in both hands, as if it were a ceremonial sword. "This is the rifle I learned on," he said. "This is what we pass down through the family. The rifle I hunted with when I was a boy, the rifle I shot my first buck with, the rifle you'll shoot your first buck with. It's a good gun, an honest gun, with only a peep sight, no scope. You won't be shooting long range, and you'll need to hit the buck behind the shoulder."

He moved back to Alaska then, where I had been born and spent my early childhood, and when I visited, a tourist now, we flew into a remote lake with a float plane, camped on a glacier, and slept with our rifles loaded, a shell in the chamber, beside our sleeping bags. "If a bear comes," he told me, "the bullet from a .30-30 will only bounce off his skull, or bury in his chest and not do anything. You'll have to hit him in the eye or in the mouth if he roars." There was no moon. We were the only humans for a couple hundred miles, and I lay awake imagining the bear attacking my father in the middle of the night while I tried to sight in on an eye in the darkness. This felt like the nature of ►

our relationship: I saw him only during vacations now, and he would give me tasks that seemed impossible, including making up for lost time. We were supposed to cram half a year into a week.

Age seven, with his father and a buck his dad bagged on California's White Ranch

I shot my first buck at eleven. A rainy weekend in September 1978, on the White Ranch, my family's 640-acre hunting spread in northern California. A two-hour drive away from civilization, it was the entire side of a mountain, with high ridges, enormous glades, pine groves and springs, ponds and switchbacks, an old burned area, and even a "bear wallow." Our entire male family history was stored in that place. As our Jeep pickups crawled along the fire roads, my father and uncle and grandfather would tell me the stories of past hunts. Places of triumph and shame, places where all who had come before were remembered.

My father flew down from Alaska every fall for this hunt. He was in his late thirties then, a dentist like his father, in years of despair leading toward his suicide. Grim-mouthed, hair receding, thin and strong, impatient. But he hadn't always been like this. He'd hunted here since he was a boy, and he was known then for being lighthearted, a joker. Whenever he came back here, he could see each year recorded in the place, wonder at who he had become.

At eleven, though, I could think only of who I would become. Shooting my first buck was an initiation. California law said I wasn't allowed to kill one until I was twelve, but family law said I was ready now.

I imagined sneaking up through pine trees or brush to make my first kill, but the weekend was rainy, so we hunted directly from the pickup. It felt unfair, even at eleven. The deer would be standing under the trees in the rain, flushed out from the brush. I stood in the back of the pickup with my father, holding on for the ruts and bumps. And when I saw the buck, hidden mostly by a stand of half a dozen thin trunks, I immediately felt pounding at my temples. "Buck fever," we called it. Heart going like a hammer, no breath. The moment of killing something large, another mammal, something that can feel individual, that moment is not like any other. You could call it many things—brutal, wrong, irresistible, natural, unnatural—but what it felt like to me was straight out of Faulkner, the rush of blood and belonging, of love for my father. This was the largest moment of my life so far, the moment of being tested.

I saw two points on one side of the buck's horns, making it ▶

legal to shoot. I levered a shell in the chamber and raised my rifle, but my father put his hand on my shoulder.

"You have time," he told me. "Rest an elbow."

So I knelt down in the bed, rested my left elbow on the side of the pickup, much more stable, and looked through the peep sight, lined it up with the deer's neck. I couldn't shoot the deer behind the shoulder, because its body was hidden by the trees. I had only the neck, long and slim. And the sight was wavering back and forth.

I exhaled and slowly squeezed. The rifle fired and the neck and head whipped down. I didn't even notice the hard kick or the explosion. I could smell sulfur, and I was leaping over the side of the pickup and running toward the buck. My father let out a whoop that was only for killing bucks, and it was for me this time, and then my uncle did it, and my grandfather, and I was yelping myself as I ran over ferns and fallen wood and rock. I charged through the stand and then I saw it.

Its eyes were still open, large brown eyes. A hole in its neck, red blood against soft white and brown hide. I wanted to be excited still, I wanted to feel proud, I wanted to belong, but seeing the deer lying there dead before me in the ferns seemed only terribly sad. This was the other side of Faulkner, conscience against the pull of blood. My father was there the next moment, his arm around me, praising me, and so I had to hide what I felt, and I told the tale of how I had aimed for the neck, beginning the story, the first of what would become dozens of tellings. And I slit the deer with my Buck knife, a gift from my father, slit the length of its stomach, but not deep, not puncturing innards. It seemed a monstrous task. I had both hands up to my elbows in the blood and entrails—not the overpowering foul bile of a deer that's been gut shot but foul nonetheless—ripping out the heart and liver, which I would have to eat to finish the kill, though luckily they could be fried up with a few onions first, not eaten raw. I pulled out everything, scraped out blood, and cut off testicles, then my father helped me drag it to the truck. He was grinning, impossibly happy and proud, all his despair gone, all his impatience. This was his moment even more than mine.

The next day, in the lower glades—wide expanses of dry yellow grass on an open hillside, fringed by sugar pines—I saw another buck. It was in short brush off to the side, a three-pointer this time, bigger. I aimed for the neck again, but hit it in the spine, in the middle of its back. It fell down instantly. Its head was still up, looking around at us, but it couldn't move the rest of its body. So my father told me to walk up from behind and finish it off execution-style, one shot to the head from five feet away.

I remember that scene clearly in all its detail. The big buck and its beautiful horns, its gray-brown hide, the late-afternoon light casting long shadows. After all the rain, the air was clear and cool, distances compressed, even in close, as if through a viewfinder. I remember staring at the back of his head, the gray hide between his antlers, the individual hairs, white-tipped.

"Be careful not to hit the horns," my father said.

I walked up very close behind that deer, leaned forward with my rifle raised, the barrel only a few feet from the back of his head, and he was waiting for it, terrified but unable to move. I could smell him. He'd turn his head around far enough to see me with a big brown eye, then turn away again to look at my father. I sighted in and pulled the trigger.

The next year I began missing deer, closing my eyes when I shot. We were on an outcropping of rocks over the big burn, an area consumed by fire years before, with only shorter growth now. A buck leapt out from a draw and bounded across the hillside opposite us. My father hunted with a .300 Magnum, a gun he'd bought for bears in Alaska. It was an outrageous caliber, sounded like artillery, and would tear the entire shoulder off a deer.

My dad was an excellent shot, but this deer was far away and moving fast and erratically, dodging bushes and rocks. I was firing, too, but only pointing the gun in the general direction, closing my eyes, and pulling the trigger. I opened my eyes in time to see one of my bullets lift a puff of dirt about fifty feet from the buck, and my father saw this, too. He paused, looked over at me, then fired again.

That was the last time we hunted, and we never talked about what had happened.

I turned thirteen that fall, after the hunt, and I saw very little ▶

of my father. At Christmas, he was having troubles I didn't understand, was crying himself to sleep at night. He wrote a strange letter to me about regret and the worthlessness of making money. At the beginning of March, he asked whether I would come live with him in Fairbanks, Alaska, for the next school year, eighth grade. I wanted to spend time with him, but I was afraid of his despair. I was afraid, also, of the kids I knew in Alaska, who were already doing drugs at thirteen. I wanted badly to say yes, but I could feel a terrible momentum to what my life would become in Alaska. So I said no.

Two weeks later, my father called my stepmother in California, where she'd moved after their divorce. He was alone in Fairbanks in his new house, with no furniture, the ides of March, cold, sitting at a folding card table in the kitchen at the end of a day. He had broken up this second marriage the same way he had the first, by cheating with other women. And now my stepmother was moving on. She'd found another man and was thinking of marrying him. My father had other problems I would learn about later, including the IRS going after him for tax dodges in South American countries, failed investments in gold and a hardware store, unbearable sinus headaches that painkillers couldn't reach, in addition to all the guilt and despair and loneliness, and he told my stepmother, "I love you but I'm not going to live without you." She was at work in an office and couldn't hear well. She had to duck behind the door with the phone and ask him to repeat what he had said. So he had to say again, "I love you but I'm not going to live without you." Then he put his .44 Magnum handgun to his head, a caliber bought, like the .300 Magnum, for grizzlies, capable of bringing a bear down at close range, and he pulled the trigger. She heard the dripping sounds as pieces of his head came off the ceiling and landed on the card table.

After my father's suicide, I inherited all his guns. Everything except the pistol. My uncle wanted to get rid of that, sold it right away. But I was given my father's .300 Magnum rifle, and though I had stopped hunting, I began using that rifle.

I learned to break it down into several parts that I could fit into my jacket. Late at night, when my mother and sister were sleeping, I rode my bike through our suburban neighborhood into the hills.

I'd ditch my bike, find a spot hidden in trees, and reassemble the rifle. I sat in the braced sitting position, elbows on my knees, that my father had taught me, calmed my breath, and eased slowly back on the trigger. The recoil was so powerful it literally knocked me flat. But nothing was more beautiful to me than the blue-white explosion of a streetlight seen through crosshairs. The sound of ▸

The author in Alaska at age nine, with the .30-30 his father passed down to him.

My Father's Guns *(continued)*

it—the pop that was almost a roar, then silence, then glass rain—came only after each fragment and shard had sailed off or twisted glittering in the air like mist.

I also sighted in on people. A man with the curtains open in his living room, the crosshairs on his chest, a shell in the chamber, the scope powerful enough I could see him swirl the drink in his hand. I had done this with my father. When he spotted poachers—hunters trespassing on our land—he would have me look at them through the scope.

No one would have guessed I was sighting in on neighbors and shooting out the streetlights. I was a straight-A student, in student government, sports, band, etc., but I came to live a double life for the year after his suicide.

I don't think I'll ever entirely understand that year. I told everyone my father died of cancer, and I didn't see a therapist. I didn't have a real conversation with anyone. Instead, I shot things, the guns a terrible substitute. A year of the most basic brutality, a year I'm lucky to have escaped without hurting anyone.

I was an insomniac—and would be for the next fifteen years—and as I lay wide awake in bed every night, I couldn't help thinking over and over that the .44 Magnum had a hair trigger. I had fired it once, at maybe eleven or twelve years old, and though I had used both hands, it flew back so hard it nearly hit me in the face. But the scariest part was that it fired with only the slightest pressure on the trigger. It was difficult to put your finger on the trigger and not have it fire. So what I kept wondering was whether my father had really decided to kill himself. What if he was just thinking about it, just testing it, or what if he had one moment of deciding but it was only a brief moment and, with the hair trigger, that was enough. I wanted to hold that pistol in my own hands, feel the possibility, feel the heft of it and know what it felt like pressed against my head. And I'm glad now I didn't have that opportunity.

I finally sold my father's guns when I was in graduate school. I needed the money, but I also just didn't want them in my life anymore. What I really wanted was for them never to have existed. But once I sold them, I was surprised by this terrible feeling that I had sold off a part of my father, because I have so little of him left. He vanished with his suicide. We sold our land, also, that hunting ranch, for peanuts, stupidly, and it was mostly the land that held our family's history and that connected all of us every year, scattered now.

I still love my father, even twenty-nine years after his suicide. The feeling hasn't diminished at all, hasn't faded over time, but I have nothing left to attach it to. If I could hold his .300 Magnum now, would he come back to me, some closer memory, some echo of hiking with him through live oak and manzanita, watching him raise that rifle high over his head as we pushed through brush? If I remember that rifle, really focus on it, I can remember the sunlight on my father's light-brown curly hair, receding, his lopsided grin as he looked down at me. But more than that, I can almost remember how the moment felt, what it was like to be there with him, to hunt with him, what it was like to belong. My father was what attached me to the world. ∽

Have you Read?
More by David Vann

***Caribou Island* by David Vann**

> Available from Harper Perennial
> January 2011

*Fault lines in the snow. A thin
dusting, faint ridges raised up
where the ice has cracked. No other
footsteps, no tracks of any kind. Irene
the only figure on a broad pan of
white.*

A SMALL ISLAND in a glacier-fed lake on
the Kenai Peninsula of Alaska, Caribou
is the setting for David Vann's new novel,
which explores the true story of the
death of his stepmother's parents by
murder/suicide and the true story of his
grandmother finding her own mother
hanging from the rafters. These two
family tragedies collide in unforgettable
fiction.

Irene and Gary are in their mid-fifties,
setting out to build a cabin on the island.
They'll build it by hand, without plans
or advice, in good weather and in terrible
storms, in sickness and in health, and
they'll punish each other along the way.
Irene, driven by the abandonment of
her mother's suicide, will not see her
husband clearly, and Gary, driven by
thirty years of regret, will not see what's
coming. Their daughter, Rhoda, will try
to save them, but her life is falling apart:
Her fiancé is cheating on her with a
younger woman. Their son Mark is
too busy fishing and smoking pot to

notice anything going on. As winter comes and Rhoda begins to fear what her mother is capable of, her father will push too far. Vann returns to his native Alaskan landscape to explore marriage, suicide, murder, infidelity, nostalgia, and the idea of Alaska itself.

A Mile Down: The True Story of a Disastrous Career at Sea by David Vann

National Bestseller
#4 Washington Post list
#7 Los Angeles Times list

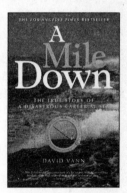

"Damn exciting."　　　—Stewart O'Nan

"Pure adrenaline."—Melanie Thernstrom

"As if one of the heroes of *The Perfect Storm* had lived to write his memoirs."
　　　　　　　—Julie Hilden

"At once memoir, confession, travel book, and thriller, David Vann's *A Mile Down* is so vivid and intense you will dread to see it end. . . . The book is a testimony of passion and courage in deadly storms and scarier calms, of a man wrestling with his ghosts and gifts in the very shadow of paradise."　　—Robert Morgan

A Mile Down: The True Story of a Disastrous Career at Sea is a harrowing—and heartbreaking—true story of one ordinary man's misadventures at sea. David Vann builds a ninety-foot charter yacht in Turkey, the ship of his dreams. But the war in Kosovo destroys his upcoming charter season, the Turkish builder takes advantage of him, and ▶

Have You Read? *(continued)*

the boat begins falling apart as soon as it's launched. Vann faces an unrelenting crush of disasters, bad luck, and ill will, yet remains in good spirits and picks himself up repeatedly to carry on. A storm near Casablanca tears his rudder off, a German freighter captain endangers the crew to go for a salvage claim, and finally a freak storm in the Caribbean sinks the boat a mile down. As the author's debts escalate and his troubles multiply, he begins to wonder if he is merely repeating his father's dreams and failures at sea. *A Mile Down* is an unforgettable true story of struggle and redemption by a writer at the top of his form. ∽

Don't miss the next book by your favorite author. Sign up now for AuthorTracker by visiting www.AuthorTracker.com.